SAINT JUNIPER'S FOLLY

FOR EVERY QUEER KID WHO FEELS TRAPPED IN A LIFE
THAT FEELS TOO SMALL AND CRUEL FOR THEIR BIG HEART.
IT ONLY GETS BETTER FROM HERE ON OUT.

Published by Peachtree Teen
An imprint of PEACHTREE PUBLISHING COMPANY INC.
1700 Chattahoochee Avenue
Atlanta, Georgia 30318-2112
PeachtreeBooks.com

Text © 2023 by Alex Crespo
Jacket illustration © 2023 by Bri Neumann

Edited by Ashley Hearn
Design by Lily Steele
Composition by Amnet Contentsource Private Limited

Printed and bound in March 2023 at Lake Book Manufacturing,
Melrose Park, IL, USA.
10 9 8 7 6 5 4 3 2 1
First Edition
ISBN: 978-1-68263-577-3

Cataloging-in-Publication Data is available from the Library of Congress.

SAINT JUNIPER'S FOLLY

ALEX CRESPO

PEACHTREE
Teen

CHAPTER 1
JAIME

NOTHING GOOD EVER HAPPENED in Saint Juniper, Vermont.

Okay, that might have been a little dramatic. Nothing good ever happened to *me* in Saint Juniper, and if I'd had to bet on it, nothing ever would. Maybe I didn't have the authority to make a sweeping statement about a place I barely remembered, but hey, lack of common sense had never stopped me before.

For years, Saint Juniper had only existed inside my head as a sort of a fever dream—a tourist trap nestled neatly between the Adirondacks and the Green Mountains, seemingly staged for the sole purpose of producing exceptionally charming postcards. Everything about it felt suffocating, except for the vast forest and craggy peaks that formed a massive valley on the north side of town.

I didn't remember much of anything else, but I didn't think it mattered. As far as I was concerned, the odds I'd ever go back to my hometown were near zero. But when the summer before my senior year came barreling into my life, the universe and the Vermont Department for Children and Families had other plans for me. One flight and two bus rides later, I was unceremoniously dumped back into a past I had spent the better part of eight years trying to forget.

I'd set my expectations comfortably low, but I did have *one* goal when I came back to Saint Juniper: I wanted a fresh start. This was my last shot to get things right before I turned eighteen. I didn't want to mess things up with my newly assigned legal guardian before I had the chance to unpack the single trash bag full of belongings I'd salvaged from my cross-country foster-care extravaganza of a childhood.

But the second I stepped onto Saint Juniper soil, I realized I was screwed.

It was like if a picture book about Colonial America and *Children of the Corn* had a baby. There was one elementary school, one high school, and one grocery store, all within walking distance of the town center, with its little brick sidewalks and candy-striped awnings. Every neighborhood was lined with white picket fences and two-hundred-year-old oak trees that probably had more laws protecting them than I had protecting me. I was eighty percent convinced that the adults in Saint Juniper had been beamed in by aliens or planted by the government, because I refused to believe that anyone would live here of their own free will.

And then there was the gossip. I'd lived in enough small towns to know that my entire existence would become a public spectacle. But Saint Juniper wasn't like other small towns. It was worse. I thought I'd be able to enjoy a few days of anonymity, but when I ventured out to Main Street for the first time after my move, I realized that everyone had already gotten the memo about me. The cashier at the corner store held the twenty-dollar bill I gave him up to the light, and the woman bagging my groceries leveled a scowl at me that said she already knew my entire life story.

Anywhere else, dirty looks could have been about anything from the way I dressed to the color of my skin. It had never been a cakewalk, and I'd learned to shrug it off as best as I could. But in Saint Juniper, it was impossible not to wonder if the woman with the salt-and-pepper hair bagging my groceries remembered me from when I was a kid, or if the clerk at town hall had known my mom before I came into the picture. Every sidelong heavy-with-judgment glance carried the extra weight of possible recognition, or worse, pity.

After only two weeks in town, my nerves had practically rubbed themselves raw. I felt trapped, and I found myself—not for the first, the tenth, or even the hundredth time in my life— daydreaming about running away. But I wasn't thinking about some far-off city where nobody knew my name or my face or the people who had given both of them to me. I was thinking about the valley. Because in the back of my mind, there was a persistent drumbeat telling me I would be safe in the woods. That something was out there to meet me on the other side.

I got the final push I needed when I stopped by Maple City Diner one night. The waitress knew which takeout order was mine before I could give her my name, and two women at the counter fell silent the second they noticed me.

"Oh, you look *just* like Samantha," one of them said. It felt like all the oxygen was sucked out of the room as she turned to her friend. "Doesn't he look just like her?"

The other woman nodded. "Totally. You have her eyes. Shame about the way things ended up. We all thought Sammie was going to do such amazing things. And then, well—"

The door shut behind me before she could finish, my order still sitting on the counter. I walked out of the restaurant and down the street, not caring where I was going. I didn't want to be seen. I wanted to disappear. So even when the sun set beyond the pines, when the sidewalk gave way to grass and the grass gave way to the forest floor, I kept walking.

I couldn't help but wonder if my biggest mistake was wanting too much—from Saint Juniper, from my ridiculous pipe dream of a fresh start. I wanted so badly to have a future that didn't look exactly like what everyone else expected it to be. I didn't want to be another foster kid who fell off the map, who never got to be happy. But maybe I was better off alone, out of sight and out of mind. After all, who would really care if a person like me walked into Saint Juniper's Folly and never came back?

CHAPTER 2
TAYLOR

EVEN AFTER RINSING MY hands with rose water, the smell of cinnamon oil clung to my skin so strongly I almost got up to open a window. I wrinkled my nose, making a mental note to use rosemary oil next time, and forced myself to breathe through it. I only had a little time left, and I sure as hell wasn't going to waste it.

In through the nose, out through the mouth. After weeks of trial and error, I thought I had finally found the right setup. The yarrow and bay leaves had spent hours charging in the light of a full moon, and I had swapped fresh thyme for dried in the wax-sealed jars spread in front of my crossed legs.

Another breath in, another out. I let thoughts meander through my head uninterrupted, and just when one of my legs started to fall asleep, I felt the unmistakable buzz in my chest that could only mean one thing: for the first time in months,

I was tapping into my sixth sense. *This is it.* I let my eyelids flutter closed. *You just have to reach out and—*

Half a second later, a knock at my bedroom door made me jump so hard it practically gave me whiplash.

"Hija, do I smell smoke?"

My eyes flew open and instantly landed on the culprits: the white pillar candles that surrounded my makeshift altar. *Shit. Shitshitshit.* "Uh, no?"

I was leaning in to blow them out, careful not to let my ringlets get caught in the flames, when I remembered that blowing out candles disrespected the intention you set for your spellwork. In a panic, I licked my finger and tried to snuff the wicks as quickly as I could. Instead, I ended up with a burned thumb and a mouthful of truly foul curse words that tumbled out before I could stop them.

"What's wrong?" Elias said from behind the door. "Forget it, I'm coming in—"

"No!" I squeaked, cradling my throbbing fingers against my chest as I shoved the altar under the bed with my foot. "I'm changing, I'll be down in a sec."

Elias didn't respond right away, but hearing the floorboards creak as he rocked back from the door let my heart rate lower to a nonlethal tempo.

"Fine," he replied, "but if you don't get your ass downstairs in two minutes, we're going to lose customers."

I knew I'd cut it way too close for comfort as I listened to his footsteps retreat down the hallway. Elias wasn't stupid, and if I wasn't more careful, I was definitely going to get caught red-handed.

Not a lot scared me in life, but pissing my dad off was up there in the top five natural disasters I'd like to avoid at all costs. Elias had always made it very clear he didn't think parents were supposed to be friends with their kids. Parents were supposed to be firm, strong, and unwavering. I was pretty sure it was more of an old-fashioned parenting thing than machismo, though I guess you could never rule that out completely with a traditional Boricua dad.

I rushed to get ready, which was a real feat even on the best day, given my room's layout. Maps and movie tickets and hand-scrawled quotes covered the walls, while my floor space was taken up by houseplants and an amalgamation of vintage furniture salvaged from secondhand stores across New England. It was a great space to hide things, but terrible for getting ready in a hurry.

I quickly swapped the grungy tee I slept in for a flowy white linen shirt, checking myself out in the full-length mirror to make sure it wasn't too wrinkled. After arranging my curls into the world's messiest topknot, I snagged my apron off its hook and rushed down the stairs. There were plenty of drawbacks that came with living in the apartment above our family shop, but the nonexistent commute made it hard to complain.

I was still wrestling with the tie on my apron by the time I made it onto the shop floor. I always thought it looked prettiest in the mornings, clear light filtering through the latticed windows and bouncing off the dark hardwood floors. The walls were painted black, though you couldn't see much of them behind the books, crystals, and relics that lined the shelves from floor to ceiling. The only exception was the spot over the fireplace, where a taxidermied owl spread its wings wide above the mantle.

The group of customers Elias had mentioned was clustered around our assortment of potions at the back of the shop, and Elias was nowhere to be seen. If I had to bet money on it, I'd have guessed he was in the storeroom going over the books. Customer service wasn't exactly his number one priority. After all, a guy who hated witchcraft owning an occult shop wasn't the greatest combination.

The whole situation was still ridiculous to me, even after four months of him running the place. Avalon Apothecary was the reason my family had moved from Boston to Wolf's Head, Vermont, when I was thirteen. It was my mom's passion, not just as a business owner, but as a true-blue ancestral witch. And yeah, to a lot of people that was like saying my mom was the queen of the damned or something equally outlandish. But I was the latest and greatest in a long line of witches. I grew up smack-dab in the middle of magic, so much so that my parents once had to sit me down and explain that it only existed for other kids in the pages of storybooks. Until that point, I thought everybody's mom could help spirits pass to the other side, just like I thought everybody washed their hair on a specific day of the week or had a dozen mismatched containers of homemade salsa in their fridge.

Elias revered magic when I was a kid, cherishing it with as much care and admiration as he loved every other thing about my mom and our little family of three. He had grown up in Puerto Rico surrounded by Santería and Brujería, so when he'd moved to Boston for college and met my mom, none of her practice seemed out of the ordinary to him. Running the apothecary wasn't just her dream, it was his too.

But Elias's attitude toward magic inexplicably soured when we moved to Vermont, and his resentment had only grown after my mom suddenly passed away in the spring. He decided to keep the shop open until we managed to sell off our remaining inventory, but after that, I was pretty sure he'd shut the place down and never want to hear a peep about spellwork again. In the meantime, Elias made one thing perfectly clear: I was forbidden (yes, that was really the word he used) from practicing magic on my own.

Personally, I thought he was full of crap. But even though we didn't see eye to eye, helping him run the shop felt like the only way to keep my mom's memory alive. It hurt and healed in equal parts that every time I looked at our antique cash register, all I could see was her perched on a stool behind the counter, bronze hair piled into an impossibly messy bun, gray eyes bright as she talked to customers about divination even if they didn't believe a word she was saying.

I was pretty sure that wasn't how the interaction between me and the gaggle of teenagers at the back of the store would go, but I kept my head held high as I made my way to the rack of potions.

"Can I help you with anything?" I asked.

They all jumped apart like I'd doused them with a hose. It probably would've struck me as a bit funnier if it didn't happen so often. It was painfully obvious that they were from Saint Juniper—the postcard-perfect next town over that was stuffy as hell. Most people from there saw Wolf's Head as Saint Juniper's earthier, grungier younger sibling. By extension, our shop was just a tacky little tourist pit stop. They would come in for a laugh, then get embarrassed when I actually expected them to buy something.

One of the girls held up a glass jar sealed with red wax, similar to the ones I'd been working with upstairs. "How much for this one?"

"The love potions are forty-five a pop," I said coolly, and her face pinched.

"My god, why?" muttered one of the boys at the back of the group. Another kid jammed an elbow into his ribs, and the girl holding the potion had the decency to glower at him too.

"Well," I replied with a smile, "you're paying for quality."

The girl nodded and chewed her lip while the boys shuffled behind her. After she finally announced she would take it, the group whispered among themselves the entire time I rang them up at the register.

Okay, I'll admit the quality comment was bullshit. The love potions we sold were fake and always had been. Forcing someone to fall for you without their consent was beyond creepy, and no self-respecting modern witch would make the real thing for just anyone. Plus, that kind of stuff was never really the focus in our house.

There were some witches that were all about potions and alchemy, while others had grimoires full of info on every crystal you could imagine. But my mom had always been drawn to herbalism and spiritualism, and by extension, so had I. Our brand of witchcraft was all about drawing energy from nature to connect with spirits, living or dead.

Under Elias's judgmental eye I couldn't do much, but I still managed to practice in my own way. I remembered how to purify spaces with smoke cleansing and minor spells, mimicking how my mom used to do things and hoping for the best. I worked on tapping into my sixth sense, tuning in to the energy around me, like I'd been trying to do that morning. But I couldn't improve much without proper direction, and without access to my mom's catalogue of spells and vast breadth of knowledge stored in our family grimoire. Her things were packed in a box somewhere, and any chance I had to advance my magic was packed away with them.

After the girl paid for her love potion, the rest of the day dragged on for what felt like forever. A handful of other customers wandered into the store, and Elias checked in with me a few times before closing. In my downtime, I wandered the shop floor, tucking a bay leaf into my apron here and a sprig of lavender there. I liked to think it didn't count as shoplifting if it was from your own business. Elias was desperate to be rid of the stuff anyway, so figured I might as well take it off his hands.

Later that evening, when the store had been swept and locked up for the night, I returned to my room and emptied my pockets to take stock of my spoils. As I carefully hid my new stash between my box spring and my mattress, I wondered for the millionth time if things really had to be like this between me and Elias. I didn't want to feel like a criminal in my own house, but I also knew there were some things he would never budge on no matter how hard I pushed.

With my dad, the big, bold questions in life always got answered with some variation of "ya, se acabó la discusión" or "I don't want to hear that from you again." My mom was a bit different when she was still around, but not by much. "Why aren't there other kids at school who look like me?" and "Why can birds fly but I can't?" were usually answered the same way. She would sweep a ring-heavied hand across my curls, a perfect mix between the color of her hair and the texture of my father's, and say, "Sweetie, that's just the way things are sometimes."

That was the answer I got right after we moved, when I asked my mom why my dad suddenly seemed so wary of magic. It was the answer I got in the years after that, when she got sick but never went to the hospital. And it was the answer I gave myself when the principal pulled me out of class in the spring to tell me that my mom was gone. That's just the way things were sometimes.

It took me too long to realize the questions my parents didn't want to answer were the ones that held the most power. Questions like why they insisted I stay away from Saint Juniper's Folly—the massive, yawning valley on the south side of town. When I asked, they didn't say people slipped and fell and went missing. Instead, they brushed it off or changed the subject every single time.

After my mom passed, I started to understand why. There was something about the valley that wasn't quite right. I had always felt it tugging at the edges of my mind, thrumming with a magnetic sort of energy that I couldn't identify. And then I found the note.

The weather had turned in May, and I'd been cleaning out our coat closet when I found my mom's favorite jacket crumpled on the floor. My chest ached just looking at it, but the ache shifted to a painful sort of pinch when I saw it was caked with mud. I couldn't imagine she would've gone on a hike after being chronically exhausted for years. When I shook off some of the larger chunks of debris, a piece of paper had fallen out of one of the pockets.

Still kneeling by my bed, I felt around my hiding spot until my fingers connected with the well-worn note. Pulling it out, I turned it over in my hands like I had a hundred times. When I unfolded it and flattened it out, I saw *four miles south, three miles west* scrawled in handwriting I knew as well as my own. A crude drawing at the bottom was crowded with shorthand for different species of trees, the kind only a dedicated herbalist would think to note. It took me a while to figure out that the lines formed a map, and along with the mud on the jacket, there was no doubt in my mind that one of the last things my mom had done was go into the valley. A week after I found it, Elias moved all my mom's clothes into storage.

I didn't ask him about what I'd found, because by that point I'd learned it would save us both a lot of heartache if I stopped asking questions I'd never get proper answers to. It was the same reason I deferred my acceptance to my dream college so I could keep running the shop without asking my dad if he wanted the help in the first place. It was the same reason I didn't beg him to let me practice magic, and just resigned to doing it in secret.

But once I stopped asking, "Dad" became "Elias" and Elias became a stranger. He'd lost his wife and I'd lost my mom, but it felt more like we were mourning the loss of two completely different people the more time passed. I didn't understand it, but

I knew I had to find out what had happened to her, even if it hurt, even if I had to do it all by myself.

I was still shifting my bed back into place when a sound outside cut through my thoughts. The blue glow of the moon caught me across my face as I moved to my window and peered down at the alley, trying to place whether the noise was a human voice or just some of the local wildlife causing a racket.

From where our apartment sat at the northernmost point of town, I could see all of Wolf's Head stretched out in front of me like a constellation. I used to sit at my window for hours and trace our maze of one-way streets down to the dark expanse of the valley. Tonight, the forest and its indigo gloom seemed more like a living, breathing thing than it ever had before, and it didn't seem happy.

The sound picked up again, much louder than before, and I could instantly tell it was a person calling out in the night. My heart jumped into my throat as I tried to muscle my heavy, stubborn window open. It only budged a little, but just as I was beginning to make out the words, the screaming stopped.

I took an unsteady step back from the window. Any other day, I would have found Elias and asked if he'd heard it too, or maybe even gone down to check things out for myself. But something about that voice didn't feel random. It was like I was meant to hear it, and I would've bet money it was because my attempt to connect with my sixth sense that morning had actually worked.

The only thing that had been on my mind was finding out the truth, and something out in the enigmatic darkness of Saint Juniper's Folly was telling me I might finally get what I wanted.

CHAPTER 3
THEO

IT WAS THE KIND of damp, humdrum morning that begged to be seen only from under a blanket, but when I hit the road, Saint Juniper was coming alive regardless. The early light was faint and thin, wrapping my neighborhood in a blueish glow that left most of the houses in soft shadow. It had been slate-gray skies and torrential downpours all week, but the town wore gloomy weather well.

As I drove down Main Street, wrought-iron streetlamps were still casting warm light on familiar, rain-slicked streets, framed by an untamed landscape of moss green and ash gray. Up on the eaves of the three-story shops of the historic district, seagulls and crows fought for coveted spots to hunch together and watch the day unfold. At the café tables and benches on the sidewalks below, people did the same.

It only took fifteen minutes for me to get to work, but the short drive usually put me in a good mood. The heaviness of whatever was on my mind would lift as I drove beyond the town limits, crossing the covered bridge into the forest that marked where Saint Juniper ended and Wolf's Head—the small town to the north—had yet to begin. But that morning, the drive wasn't enough to make me forget the pamphlet weighing my backpack down in the passenger seat.

By the time I parked my beat-up Subaru in the library's cramped back lot, it had started drizzling in earnest. I jogged to the door and ducked inside before I could get too wet, shaking stray raindrops out of my hair as the bell on the door chimed to announce my arrival.

The smell of old wood and even older books hit me, as did the freezing AC. The library was small but well-preserved like the handful of other public spaces shared between Saint Juniper and Wolf's Head, funded almost entirely by the tourists who flocked to Saint Juniper each autumn. The clean, bright space was all dark wood and natural light, with huge windows that got as close to bringing the beauty of the forest indoors as you could get.

The library had been a true safe haven for the past three summers I'd volunteered there, and it was pretty much the only thing that made me sad I wouldn't be in Saint Juniper the following year. Well, that and my supervisor, Carla, who was making a beeline to intercept me at the front desk before I even had the chance to sit down.

"Theo, something terrible has happened," she sighed. A pair of tortoiseshell reading glasses were tangled at the top of her nest of unruly gray hair, and another pair balanced precariously at the end of her nose. I thought about pointing it out but decided to keep my comments to myself. "I made a list of holds I needed to pull this morning, and it seems to have run away from me in the night."

"It didn't run away," I replied, shrugging my backpack off and pulling open the top drawer of the desk. When I produced the list from the depths of its disorganization, Carla clasped her hands over her heart like she'd just witnessed a magic trick.

"Oh, it went to spend some quality time with you."

"You left it out on the counter," I said, smiling at her theatrics despite myself. "I swiped it before the cleaning crew showed up last night."

"My hero," she said, patting my hand gently as she took the slip of paper. "What am I going to do without you when you graduate?"

"Probably lose a lot of our regular patrons, for one."

Carla's smile told me I had walked into a trap. "Well, seeing as you're still here, why don't you do your best to keep them happy?"

I let her shoo me over to the fiction section, knowing full well there was no point in resisting. It wasn't that I disliked helping people—quite the opposite, actually. I loved helping Mr. Morris pick out a new book for his book club every month, and it had become a sort of game for me to try to recommend a thriller to Mrs. Baker that she hadn't already read.

The only problem was that once I started talking to someone, it was impossible not to get looped into the constant stream of gossip that kept Saint Juniper in a permanently judgmental chokehold. There was always some conflict to publicize or rumor to dissect with stage whispers and unsubtle laughter. For the last week, all anyone had talked about was our mayor's divorce and some new boy who'd just moved to town. And all week, just like every week, I'd done my best to ignore it.

I didn't exactly blame them for trying to stay entertained. Without the manufactured drama, the most interesting thing about Saint Juniper was that nothing interesting ever happened at all. But the predictability wasn't all bad, at least not in my book.

I liked that my life had a certain kind of order to it. I knew the sun would cast long beams of light across my bedspread by ten forty-five a.m., but I would be long gone by the time the smell of warm cotton filled my room, even on my days off. I knew I would run into some family friend by early afternoon who would ask about my sister, Grace, and I would have to recite that yes, she was doing great, yes, she was still dating that nice guy she'd met in her master's program, and no, she was not engaged yet. I knew I would pick up my phone when I got lonely after sunset, and instead of texting my friends, I would type whatever I was thinking into my notes app, lock my phone, and go to sleep.

I knew in perfect detail what the rest of my summer was going to look like, because it was going to look a lot like the summer before and the summer before that. Half of it would be spent at the library, more to pass the time than anything else, and the other half would be spent mostly on my own.

The only thing that would be different this summer was that I'd be trying to figure out college applications and my entire future before it closed in on me. Which was why, by the time I finished helping patrons and made my way back to my desk, there was no longer any point in ignoring the glossy pamphlet tucked into the front pocket of my backpack. When I pulled it out, I felt a sharp stab of panic the second my eyes landed on the University of Vermont logo.

It had been sitting on the kitchen counter when I went down for breakfast that morning, long after my parents had already left for work. I wasn't sure it had been left there purposefully until I flipped it open and saw the section my dad had marked off with a bright yellow sticky note: *Excellent pre-law program*. I had no idea three words could instill so much anxiety in my heart in so little time, but you learn new things every day.

I sighed from behind my post at the front desk, shifting uncomfortably as the battle between the humidity from outside and our overzealous air-conditioning started to make me feel sticky. For the first time in as long as I could remember, the muffled quiet of the library felt a little bit suffocating.

Slumping over the counter, I rested my forehead against the cool, flat surface for just a moment.

"I don't pay you to nap," Carla chirped as she flitted behind me, balancing a truly shocking number of books in her arms as usual. Every time I begged her to use a cart, she simply waved me off.

I turned to look at her, lifting my head off the counter just enough to press my cheek against the cool spot where my forehead had just been.

"Not napping, just thinking," I murmured. "And technically, you don't pay me at all."

"Well, I can't argue with that," she conceded, squinting at the spine of one of the books teetering at the top of the pile in her hands. "Carry on with your thinking, then."

"Actually, do you—" I started, then realized I had absolutely no idea what I wanted to say.

Carla paused. "Do I what?"

Honestly, it hadn't occurred to me to ask for Carla's advice until just then. I wasn't sure how much she could help, but she had known me for three years, which was more than I could say of the college counselor I'd get assigned once I started classes in the fall.

"Do you think I have what it takes to go pre-law?" I blurted, instantly regretting the way I'd phrased the question.

Carla's eyebrows shot up, which was either a very good thing or a very bad thing. I studied her face to try to make the distinction as she set the books on my desk. "Of course I think you have what it takes," she said carefully. "Your grades are good enough to get you into any program you'd like, I'd imagine."

"Why do I feel like a 'but' is coming?"

Carla peered at me over her first, or second, pair of readers. The tortoiseshell pair was still sitting on top of her head.

"You're not asking for advice," she said. "You're asking me to tell you what to do, and I won't do that no matter how much I like you."

She was right, of course. It wasn't fair of me to put her in that position when I didn't have the first idea of what I wanted to do. I was nothing like Grace or any of my friends, who didn't seem to doubt themselves half as much as I constantly doubted myself. Every time I tried to wrap my head around my future, all

I could see was a lifetime of other people's expectations scribbled on bright yellow sticky notes.

"I'm sorry," I said, wanting nothing more than to crawl back into bed and start the day over, this time without impending college-related doom to ruin my mood. "I don't even know if I want to stay in Vermont for college, let alone what to do while I'm there."

I must have done a terrible job of concealing how deflated I felt, because Carla placed a warm, weathered hand on my shoulder. "How you see things now may not be how you see them forever. Just try not to get in your own way."

"Well, how am I supposed to do that?"

"If we went down that rabbit hole, we'd be here all day."

"I *am* here all day."

Carla studied me carefully, and I realized a moment too late that I had walked into another one of her traps.

"Not anymore," she announced, nudging the books piled on my desk in my direction. "I can't have you stewing here all afternoon with that sour face. People will think I'm treating you poorly. Take these over to Wolf's Head Middle School. The librarian there is expecting them before classes start."

As I packed the books up and got ready to leave, my conversation with Carla played on a loop inside my head. Getting out of my own way wasn't exactly my strong suit, and the idea that this was just the tip of the iceberg when it came to my next move made me feel even more lost than before.

By the time I loaded the books into the trunk of my car, the drizzle from the morning was turning into a downpour. Flooding was a serious issue on the roads leading into Wolf's Head, and even though summer storms were a constant, the county managed to be spectacularly ill-equipped for them regardless. I definitely wasn't in the mood to take any chances, so my only option was to brave the winding back road that led right into the thick of Saint Juniper's Folly.

The tourists who popped into Saint Juniper for leaf peeping every year always got a kick out of the valley's name. The original settlers chose to call it La Folie, a warning that only a fool would try to enter the valley again after a group of French explorers had disappeared into the wilderness without a trace. Any sensible person could guess that they had probably just joined the Sokoki tribe that lived in the valley, but that version of the story didn't seem to please the historical society. Either way, the name and its implicit warning stuck.

The light dimmed as I started my descent into the valley, the crowds of towering pines and thick cover of foliage overhead sheltering me from the blustering winds of the incoming storm. Underbrush crept so far onto the road that it narrowed what could barely be called two lanes on a good day into only one usable one, and an incoming layer of mist didn't make navigating any easier.

The valley always made me a little bit anxious. I wasn't *really* afraid of it, not like some people in town who swore they'd seen things out in the woods or clung to small-town legends about sasquatches and werewolves and haunted houses. I never believed the silly stories even when I was a little kid.

There were some real stories of tragic deaths in the area that were more troubling to me. After too many hikers had fallen to their deaths in the heavily wooded bluffs and yawning ravines, the sheriff's department posted dozens of No Trespassing signs along the solitary trail into the valley. The signs never did much to deter high school kids from getting drunk in the woods before homecoming, or even more ridiculous, trying to find proof of the scary stories we'd heard around campfires for the better part of our childhoods.

But what made me uneasy about the valley was harder to pin down. I figured it scared me in the same way that deep water scared me: it was too quiet, too vast, too unknown. The incredible sense of remoteness was both terrifying and hallowed in its peacefulness. The arc of the sky felt broader there, the clouds hung a little bit lower, and the air always felt charged with possibility. Something about it made me feel a little bit invincible, and that scared me more than anything.

Maybe that was why I ended up flying down the back road into Saint Juniper's Folly a little faster than I should have, with the woody scent of the earth after fresh rain pressing in through my open driver-side window, and the remnants of the humid morning chill sending goose bumps up my arms.

Maybe that was also why I didn't see the tree lying in the middle of the road until it was too late.

One second I was rounding a bend, and the next my hands twisted on the steering wheel as if they had a mind of their own. Sapling branches scraped the nose of my car as I came to a jarring stop.

I stared numbly at the fallen tree, trying to level my skyrocketing pulse, then I turned my engine off altogether. The car felt suffocating to my adrenaline-addled mind, so with shaky hands, I grabbed my backpack and popped my door open.

But as I stumbled out of the driver's seat and onto the rainsoaked asphalt, a shape caught my eye just past a thicket at the edge of the wood. Beyond the iridescent light that filtered through the canopy, a grizzled tree stood twisted and splintered in the strangest way I had ever seen.

The blackened tree must have been a white ash, though it was disfigured nearly beyond recognition. It looked oddly burnished in the afternoon light, stripped clean of bark and split along its massive trunk in hypnotizing patterns. Whatever damage had been done was probably decades if not centuries old, because the tree stood taller and broader than any other I'd seen. There was a noble sort of triumph to it, so much so that I almost felt I didn't deserve to stand in its presence.

A thrush warbled at me from a nearby branch as I ventured closer, but its reedy song felt dissonant and wrong. The world was a little bit tilted off its axis. The valley could sometimes have that unsteadying effect for no particular reason, making me feel indescribably small, distinctly human, and alarmingly vulnerable at the same time. And now more than ever, it didn't feel random.

By the time I came within arm's distance of the tree, a heavy sense of dread had gripped me in earnest. The lush forest pulsated around me in an almost sickening way. Every shifting leaf and creaking branch scraped like nails against a chalkboard. A chill raked wickedly up my spine and turned into a violent shake by the time it reached my fingertips.

I took an unsteady step back, closed my eyes, and tilted my face up to suck in a deep breath. But when I opened my eyes again, I froze. Because just as penetrating and heavy as the weight of a human's unwavering gaze, I could feel the tree staring keenly back at me.

Hysteria rose so fast in my chest it threatened to choke out the little air I still had in my lungs. I was going to be sick. The forest spun around me, and I reached out to steady myself, hand brushing the scarred bark.

That was when I heard the screams.

They crowded into my ears all at once, one shriek overlapping the next with an intensity my brain couldn't comprehend. It was someone sobbing, choking, crying out for help. I bolted into the woods at full speed, aiming for the direction of the strangled voice.

My feet sank into the rain-softened earth like quicksand, the slick pull of mud against my shoes slowing me down as I flung myself into the densely packed foliage. Saplings' eager branches pulled at my clothes and tore at my face, and I couldn't tell if they were leaving trails of dew or drawing blood. I was so focused on the screams it didn't matter.

Between one gasping breath and the next, an errant root poking out of the ground caught my foot midstride and threw me to the ground so suddenly it knocked the wind out of me. My hands slipped in the mud as I struggled to push myself up onto my forearms, and the smell of tree bark and rotting leaves from the forest floor threatened to choke me.

Just as I rose to my feet to take stock of my surroundings, a foreign object appeared through the low-hanging mist, and my heart stuttered to a painful stop. I wondered if my eyes were playing tricks on me, but the hard angles of a turret were unmistakable, as was the dull glint of cloud-deadened sun off a second-story window. The hair on the back of my neck prickled as I stumbled forward, coming to the edge of a small meadow.

I had heard about an abandoned house in the woods so many times the stories had all but lost their meaning. Every year, kids would claim to have broken in or seen a ghost hovering by one of the windows. To be honest, I had never even considered that the house might be real, let alone look so fearsome.

The turret I first saw through the gloom made it difficult to tell how many stories tall the house was, though it had to have been at least three or maybe even four. The house was all harsh angles and unexpected details, so spectacularly unsymmetrical and imaginative that I could hardly make sense of what I was looking at. The wood siding was painted a deep shade of crimson, draped in ivy and weathered from exposure to the elements. A dilapidated front porch wrapped around the side of the house, adorned with intricately carved columns and trim coated with flaking black and gold paint.

Everywhere I looked there was crumbling, ornate woodwork that felt entirely out of place surrounded by the roughness of the valley. The house was impossible as it was breathtaking, yet solid in all the ways the rest of the day hadn't been. In a moment of bizarre clarity, I thought about my cell phone sitting in the cupholder of my car and wished I had it so I could take a picture.

I couldn't be sure the screams had been coming from inside the house, but its presence was too conspicuous to think otherwise. I listened hard for signs of life as I inched closer, but beyond the steady beat of rain against the roof and my own frenzied heartbeat hammering in my ears, the property was quiet as death. I clung to the straps of my backpack, which I had managed to hang on to during my wild run through the woods, and every twig that cracked under my boots echoed like a thunderclap as I edged around the perimeter of the house. I circled it like a live animal, not wanting to get too close for fear it would lunge out and snap at me.

Where the wraparound porch ended at the back of the house, an enormous greenhouse extended into what must have been the backyard. Its iron framework was even more intricate than the eaves at the front of the house, though most of the glass panes were broken, and those that were intact were streaked with grime and fogged from the humidity. An iron door marked the entrance, barely hanging on by a single rusted hinge.

The greenhouse was a mess of dirt and broken pottery, old vines snaking over almost every square inch of space while new buds nestled in the rain-dampened dirt. I was so busy straining to see through the eerie greenish light inside that I nearly missed the too-still boy leaned up against one of the windowpanes. His olive skin and tangle of dark hair acted as camouflage against the backdrop of browning leaves, but a small gold hoop he wore in one ear caught my attention. Well, that and his hands, which were caked with the deep reddish brown of dried blood.

My first irrational thought was that I had just seen a ghost, and my second was that I had just found a dead body. I would say my blood ran cold, but that's not really how it feels when you're profoundly alone and witness something that sucks the humanity right out of you.

Once when I was on a field trip to Devil's Gulch as a kid, I wandered away from my group and stumbled across a moose carcass in the thick of the woods, splayed out at my feet on a pile of dry brush. There was no gore, just the unearthly stillness that was entirely unfit for a place normally so full of life. I remember it felt like the entire world had stopped, like the wind was blowing right through me.

I felt the same way standing at the entrance to the greenhouse. My feet were rooted in place even though all I wanted to do was run. I opened my mouth to call for help or make any noise at all, but the shock had lodged itself somewhere deep in my chest and was holding my voice captive along with it.

And then the boy opened his eyes—perfectly hazel and perfectly alive.

"Who the hell are you?"

CHAPTER 4
JAIME

THE FIRST THING I noticed about him was his hair, the color of butterscotch, a blond so gold it almost looked bronze in the fog-dimmed light of morning. The second thing was his eyes, pale blue-green that would have seemed cold on anyone else but looked strikingly clear and honest on him. The third was that he looked like he was about to faint, and I definitely couldn't have that.

If I hadn't felt like absolute death, the way his jaw dropped when I opened my eyes would've been genuinely hilarious. I knew I looked like shit, but first impressions were never really my strong suit. Neither were second impressions, actually. I think I was just more of an acquired taste. But I couldn't risk scaring off the only hope I had of survival, so I shut my mouth and waited for him to calm down.

"I thought you were dead," he said, letting out a shaky breath. "You scared the crap out of me."

"Sorry, not dead yet," I croaked, my voice sounding hoarse and foreign to my own ears.

I hadn't spoken out loud for days. *God, how depressing.* I would've laughed if I wasn't sure it'd feel like a razor blade in my throat. Instead, I made the equally stupid mistake of trying to sit up, concealing the wince that followed poorly enough that the boy's face twisted in concern.

"Are you all right?" he asked, taking a nervous step toward me. His face went white as his eyes flicked down to my hands. "Oh, god. Is that blood?"

I looked down, turning my hands over to inspect the dark red streaks dried across my knuckles and under my fingernails. I guess it did look gruesome out of context, but to be honest, I had forgotten it was there.

"Don't worry, it's not fresh."

He gawked at me, clearly not appreciating my sparkling wit even in the face of great adversity. Rude. "That is really not as reassuring as you think it is."

I sighed. This, I thought, was the exact type of person I had not wanted to show up. This guy was clearly a wimp. He was dressed in a predictably granola way for what I assumed was a Vermont native, but his grey Henley was caked in mud, and his knee was skinned through a tear in his jeans. He was handsome enough it was annoying, but in a nonintimidating boy-next-door kind of way. He looked like he could be the star of *Saint Juniper: The Musical.* But beggars couldn't be choosers.

"Listen, I don't have the energy to explain all this, but I'm stuck," I said. With my head pounding the way it was, I could barely string a sentence together, let alone make sense of my situation to this guy. "Here, I can show you."

I moved to push myself off the ground, but I hadn't realized how lack of sleep, food, and water would make every tiny movement feel like I was rubbing sandpaper against my joints. By the time I stood up straight, my vision had almost blacked out, and the look on the boy's face told me I wasn't hiding it as well as I thought I was.

Before I could think to stop him, he rushed forward to help me. In the moment his hand should have connected with mine, his body ricocheted back like he had hit a brick wall. He fell hard onto the muddy ground, clutching the spot where his outstretched arm had connected with, well, nothing.

"What the hell was that?" he gasped, his eyes tracking my movement as I leaned heavily against the spot where the door should have been. Just like the first day I had been in the house, the shoulder of my T-shirt flattened like it was pushing up against glass.

"I have no idea," I said, willing my voice not to shake as I blinked the stars from my eyes. "When I found this place, I just wanted to look inside for a second, but when I tried to leave, I was trapped. I tried everything, even breaking a window, which is how I wrecked my hands. I didn't want to waste my drinking water by washing them, so there you have it."

I figured, as he was knocked flat on his ass having the existential crisis of a lifetime, that the SparkNotes version would do. He didn't need to know that the reason I was out there was because Saint Juniper had gotten under my skin. He didn't need to know that whatever awe I'd felt when I first stumbled into the house had slipped away when I realized I was stuck, replaced by a terror so expansive I was afraid I would choke on it. He didn't need to know that I had rammed up against the invisible barrier enough times for my shoulder to turn black and blue, or that I'd shouted until I didn't have a voice or the energy to keep going. And he definitely didn't need to know that once I'd tried everything, I was so busy freaking out that I hadn't realized until a full day later I might starve to death if nobody found me.

To his credit, he didn't seem to be losing his marbles as much as I thought he would. He was just gaping at me, at the green-house, at the whole scene, like staring would make it any less ludicrous.

"This is . . . it's . . ."

"Impossible?" I offered.

"I mean, yeah," he said, finally rising to his feet. I hadn't noticed before since his face wasn't at eye level, but he had a smattering of freckles across his nose. When his eyes focused on me again, his expression changed. "Wait, how long have you been here?"

"I'm pretty sure it's been four days," I replied, glancing away when he looked appropriately horrified. But then he pulled a sandwich and bottle of water out of his muddy backpack, and it felt like the closest thing to a miracle I had ever witnessed.

"If I pass this to you, will it go through the, uh, the thing?"

I shrugged. "There's only one way to find out."

The boy straightened and tossed the sandwich to me first. It somehow managed to pass through just fine.

"This is all I have on me right now, but I can bring more tomorrow," he said. I already started digging in to the food in my hands, but at the same time, the idea of a complete stranger taking care of me kind of made me want to crawl into a hole and die. "It was really lucky that I heard you when I did. Thank god you called for help."

I swallowed a bite of food and stared back, not sure I'd heard him right. "I didn't call for help."

"I heard screaming and ran here from the road. You're really telling me that wasn't you?"

If it was anyone asking other than this overgrown Boy Scout, I would have thought they were pulling my leg. The truth was, the last few days in the house had been a blur, and most of that time I'd felt like I was losing my mind. There were a couple of moments I had woken up at night thinking someone was talking to me, but I thought I was just hearing things because of the starvation. Maybe the voice wasn't just in my head after all.

The boy must have interpreted my long pause as something other than immense confusion, because he narrowed his eyes again. "Are you messing with me?"

"Dude, does any of this seem like a joke?"

"Well, it's my first time hearing voices. I need a minute to process."

"Join the fuckin' club," I grumbled, unscrewing the cap of the water bottle and taking a long swig. I instantly felt the pressure inside my head start to ease up.

"I just don't get it. I know people who have bragged about finding and breaking into this place, but I've never heard about anything like this happening."

"I get that you're at the denial stage right now, but I'm gonna need you to skip ahead to acceptance so we can be on the same page."

"But don't you think there has to be a logical explanation for this?" he said. It irked me that he was acting like he had a better handle on the situation than me, like I hadn't spent the better part of a week agonizing over it on my own.

"Do you have high blood pressure?" I asked in a tone so snide I knew it could annoy a saint. "You should get that checked out."

"I don't know how you're can be joking right now," he snapped. "Isn't someone back in town wondering where you are?"

My stomach lurched, an acrid, familiar wave of anxiety washing over me. He had no idea what a loaded question that was, or what a terrible time I had chosen to go missing. He had no idea how wrong he was for assuming anyone cared, and there was no way I was letting him go down that rabbit hole.

"*You* know where I am."

"Yeah, but I mean someone like your parents," he replied. "It's been four days. Don't you think they want to know you're safe?"

"I already said no, okay?" I said evenly, taking a step back from the entrance of the greenhouse. "Just drop it."

"Why are you being so stubborn? They're probably worried sick about you."

His words struck some dissonant chord that left me emotionally stranded halfway between sorrow and anger. That was, after all, the exact reason I had come to Saint Juniper in the first place. To live with a family friend I hadn't even known existed until two months prior—someone who might finally worry about me more than I constantly had to worry about myself. But I'm sure I burned that bridge when I wandered off and got stuck. If there was one thing I knew for sure, it was that she wouldn't lose sleep wondering where I was or what I was doing. No one ever did.

"You know what," I said, gathering the water bottle and what was left of the sandwich in my hands. "You ask too many questions. From now on, you're limited to one a day."

Before he had the chance to sputter a reply, I'd already turned on my heel and slipped out of sight. Ducking under the vines hanging from the roof of the greenhouse, I made my way into the game room at the back of the house.

I didn't realize how fast my heart was beating until I pressed my back against one of the flaking black walls and finally had a second to breathe. An ancient pool table with feet carved into lion's paws squatted on an unbelievably ugly rug, and on the far wall, mounted animal heads looked back with glassy eyes and unsympathetic stares.

"You can't just walk away in the middle of a conversation," the boy called from the clearing. I let out a huff of hollow laughter in reply, and a raven from some nearby branch cackled back.

As the moody silence of the house settled around me, I started to wonder if the boy had actually left. But then, just when I was sure he was gone for good, I heard him speak up again.

"I'm coming back tomorrow morning with food," he said, sounding exasperated but resolute. "You better be ready to talk then."

I let myself slide down the wall and come to a crouch on the floor, not sure if I was relieved or more terrified than before. I could hear the boy wrestle with the underbrush at the edge of the clearing, and as his footsteps faded into the ambient noises of the forest, I forced myself to imagine him heading back to what must've been a perfect home in a perfect neighborhood and never coming back.

I didn't want to think there was a chance things might turn out okay, but a tiny, annoying flutter in my chest told me I was already hoping this boy hadn't given up on me, that maybe I didn't have to figure everything out on my own. So just as quickly as it came, the fear of nobody ever knowing I was trapped was replaced with the fear that somebody knew but might not think I was worth saving. And I didn't even know his name.

CHAPTER 5
TAYLOR

"I CAN TELL YOU'RE stewing," Anna said, peering at me over her iced matcha. Her top matched the shade of her drink perfectly, and I wouldn't have been surprised if she'd planned it. "No stewing allowed during coffee, that's the rule."

"I'm not stewing," I lied, pulling my thoughts away from the jumble of questions I had about the valley. Anna narrowed her eyes.

"Now you're stewing *and* lying. Disgraceful. Excuse me," she called out, flagging down the barista from across the café. Everyone who worked here had been suffering our presence every week for the better part of the summer, so I only felt a little bit mortified when he actually sidled up to our table. "Can you please tell her to stop stewing?"

"You heard the girl," he joked, clearing my empty glass and tucking a coffee-stained kitchen towel into his apron pocket. "No stewing allowed on the premises."

"Oh my god, I wasn't stewing. I was just thinking."

"You've never formed a coherent thought before," Anna said, grinning over her glass. "What inspired you to start now?"

I glared between her amused expression and the barista's barely restrained smile.

"This place is a nightmare," I said as the barista retreated behind the counter, chuckling as he went.

Anna was right: no stewing was the only hard-and-fast rule of our weekly catch-up sessions. Even though our shifts at the shop overlapped, neither of us felt like we could vent or gossip as much as we wanted when Elias was always hovering. After all, if I thought the chip on Elias's shoulder about witchcraft was bad, it was nothing compared to how he'd reacted when I told him I'd hired a psychic without asking him first.

I met Anna at the beginning of the summer purely by chance, striking up a conversation with her when she was bored out of her mind working a booth at our county fair. I initially mistook her for being much younger than me, with her round cheeks, golden hair, and big brown eyes, but once we got talking, I realized we were only a few months apart in age.

We were thirty seconds into a reading when she sat back, saying she couldn't finish because she never did this type of thing with friends. It struck me as an odd thing to say to someone you'd only known for five minutes, but as I got up to leave, she slipped me her card. *One touch and I'll tell you your future* was embossed on the front.

"You might need this in a bit," she said, then waved me off as I stared back and forth between her and the small piece of card-stock in my hand. "I'll see you when I see you, okay?"

That same night, I went home to find my dad pacing the living room, on the phone with his sister back on the island. He was telling her he couldn't lend her any more money, then abruptly took her off speakerphone the second he saw me in the doorway. I called Anna the next morning and offered her a spot in our shop, and after making a very compelling case to Elias about how she could help pull in more regular customers, it was a done deal.

I appreciated her companionship more than I thought she knew. After my mom's memorial in the spring, I had been prepared for the "how are yous" to flood my inbox. But I'd had no idea how quickly they would dry up, or how my friends would stop coming to me with their problems because they figured I had enough of my own. I still hadn't figured out if Anna was hanging out with me out of pity or genuine friendship, but I would take what I could get.

"All right, spit it out," she said, tapping her fingers on the tiny table we'd grabbed by the window. "What's got you all daydreamy?"

I chewed the inside of my cheek for a beat. Anna knew how I felt about the valley, about my parents' warnings, and about my mom's muddy jacket. But I wasn't sure how to begin unpacking the unsteady feeling I'd gotten last night, or what it meant. Dark, ominous energy like that could come from a wounded animal or a lost spirit, but in the light of day, I couldn't be sure it was either. What if the sound I heard was just a lone coyote or someone goofing around?

"I was wondering," I started, "how do you know for sure you're tapped into some magical intuition? I mean, instead of it just being the placebo effect?".

"I'm not sure if I know how to describe it, honestly," Anna replied, her eyes drifting to the window behind me. "If I touch someone normally, I can guess how they feel or what they're going through, but it's just a hunch coming from my own mind. When I'm using my power, I get this sense of clarity that comes from *their* mind instead. Does that make sense?"

I nodded, sitting back and watching her take a sip of her drink. Our powers were similar in the sense that her clairvoyance and my ability to perform witchcraft were natural gifts we'd been born with. Anna didn't have any formal training as a psychic, but she'd been able to improvise until she got the hang of her skills. It was a pretty simple process—touch, see, repeat.

In a lot of ways, I envied her for being able to just feel things out on her own, no pun intended. It wasn't until my mom died that I realized how few practical skills I had when it came to magic, and how hard it was to teach myself. There was a time in my life, back when we lived in Boston, when I was always tinkering with witchcraft. I'd watch and mimic my mom perform minor spells and purification rituals. And sometimes, when she got hired to cleanse a space or help a lost spirit cross over, she would even take me with her.

But I never took notes as she explained which herbs amplified which energy, or paid close enough attention when she walked me through complex spells. I thought I had all the time in the world to learn from her when I got older, when I wasn't busy with schoolwork and friend drama and normal preteen worries.

I had no way of knowing that as soon as we moved to Wolf's Head, Elias would start saying that following in my mom's footsteps was too dangerous. That practicing magic would put a target on my back in a small town, and nothing I said could make him change his mind.

Without proper guidance, trying to understand what my witchy intuition was telling me about the valley felt near impossible. It was just another thing I wished I had asked my mom about when I still had the chance, and now I felt totally lost.

Anna must've been able to tell I was lost in my thoughts again, because in a rare display of seriousness, she leaned over the table and locked eyes with me. Her long blond hair came dangerously close to taking a dip in her drink. "Now tell me what's really bothering you."

"It's the valley," I said, voice low. "I think something weird is going on."

Anna's honey-colored brows pulled together. "The usual weird, or a new kind of weird?"

"New kind of weird," I replied. "I was practicing tapping into my sixth sense yesterday, reaching out to see if I could feel anything. And last night, I thought I heard something, or someone, calling out from the valley."

"I mean, that definitely sounds like *something*," she said, swirling the half-melted ice around her glass with a paper straw. "Are you going to try to go back?"

I sighed, sinking back against my chair. I knew that question was coming next. The only time I had ever disobeyed my parents' warning was after copious amounts of peer pressure my sophomore year. My friends managed to convince me that sneaking into the valley at midnight with a bottle of cheap tequila was a great way to start the school year, but I only managed to hike about a half mile in before I got a terrible feeling about the whole thing and bailed. I still had no idea if that was my sixth sense or plain old guilt from rebelling against my parents.

"Maybe. No. I don't know," I said. "I can't tell if this is real or if I'm just driving myself crazy over nothing."

"Have you thought about bringing it up with your dad?"

I let out a huff of defeated laughter. "You know he'd just stonewall me."

"I get that you don't want to push him, but you're a whole-ass adult. It's not like he can ground you."

"Spoken like a true gringa," I said with a grin, then dodged the straw wrapper Anna threw playfully in response. "Not everybody hit the cool parent jackpot where they let you do whatever you want."

"They only behave because I trained them well," she beamed, and I knew she wasn't really joking. From what she'd told me, her parents had needed time to take her gift seriously, but they'd turned out to be pretty supportive when all was said and done. "Can you please at least *try* to break your generational curse of being painfully emotionally repressed?"

I sighed. "If I say yes, will you buy me another cold brew?"

"Deal," she said, practically leaping out of her seat.

———

By the time Anna and I made it to the shop, we were a handful of minutes late for our afternoon shift. Elias barely looked up from his spot behind the register when we burst in, but I could tell he'd been waiting for us. His keys were lying on the counter. Anna greeted him and scurried into the storeroom before he could lecture us on proper time management.

"I know, I know," I said, scooting past him to get to the stairs. "We lost track of time. Just let me go change and I'll be right down."

Elias hummed in acknowledgment, attention still glued to the stack of receipts he had been sifting through when we walked in. I thought I had avoided a confrontation, but I only made it up three steps before he cleared his throat.

"You know I don't like you hanging out with her outside of work," he said.

I stopped, one hand on the railing, and resisted the urge to roll my eyes. "Are you saying I can't be friends with her? I'm eighteen, not eight."

"I'm not saying that," he replied evenly. "I just don't want her putting any crazy ideas in your head. She treats that power of hers like a party trick. She's careless, and I don't like it. Magic is—"

"Dangerous, I know," I finished dully.

I turned to face him, but the argument I'd been planning to make died on my lips when I saw how tired he looked. He hadn't been getting much sleep in the past few months—I could hear him pacing around the apartment when I should have been asleep too—but his tan skin looked even more sallow than usual. I watched silently as he pocketed his wallet and keys.

"I'm heading out for the night. Be good, okay?"

"Always am," I murmured back.

Truthfully, if Elias knew what I did on Friday nights while he was in Burlington playing dominoes with his buddies, he'd never have left me alone. The only bar in Wolf's Head was a few blocks south of us, and Anna and I had learned that if we kept the lights on late enough, we could reel in dozens of drunk people for readings—people who wouldn't be caught dead at the shop in broad daylight. It was a brilliant way to generate extra cash for the shop and for Anna pocket more tips, and what Elias didn't know wouldn't kill him. I was just hoping he didn't find out and kill me first.

Those long nights were some of my favorites. Every so often, while Anna was doing her readings, I'd sneak into the back of her booth from the storeroom and listen. If I angled my body just right, I could peek through the swathes of velvet and gold-foiled drapes while still staying hidden.

But most of the time, I took those few nights of freedom to put a Cheo Feliciano album on the ancient record player and study magic outside the confines of my cramped bedroom. I'd pull up a forum online or flip through my jumbled notes, refreshing my memory so I could keep my mind sharp even if I wasn't casting spells out in the real world.

But that night, no matter how hard I tried, I couldn't seem to focus on the words in front of me. A storm was brewing on the horizon, and there was a sharp, thrilling energy in the air that reminded me of my mom. When I was a kid, she always said people would try to tell me I was made of sugar and spice and everything nice, but Bishop women were made of pure lightning.

She taught me there was power in storms, power that went much deeper than the raw force you could see on the surface. We'd collect rainwater in little glass jars on the kitchen windowsill, then charge it in the light of the new moon to use for healing. Once, back when we lived in Boston, I saw her heal a stray kitten with a broken leg with just a few laps of that water from her palm.

When a peal of thunder rumbled down from the mountains, it was all the invitation I needed to push away from the counter and find an outlet for my jumpiness. I quickly lit a bundle of mugwort and pine needles to smoke-cleanse a handful of black obsidian for protection from negative energy. After I was done, I started to walk in slow circles around the bookshelves and racks of potions, placing the obsidian where I thought the room needed it for balance and letting the smoke fill the room. That was where Anna found me around eleven p.m., after she finally managed to shepherd her last customer out of the shop.

"Purify me, Taylor," she said, flinging her head back and her arms out wide. "Mama needs to be cleansed."

I stifled a snort, ushering her to the center of the room. "I got you, just stand still. Was it really that bad?"

"'Bad' doesn't even begin to cover it," she said, pouting as I circled her, wafting the spirals of smoke so they curled around the ends of her hair and the slope of her shoulders. Since she was more than a head taller than me, that was the highest I could reach. "He kept trying to play footsie with me while I was doing his reading. I was like, dude, this is a place of business. Take it back a notch."

I paused mid-waft. "You should've told me he was giving you trouble, I would have kicked him out. Plus, I don't think smoke-cleansing protects against douchebags."

"Well, what's the point of magic if it's not douche-proof?" she asked, drifting over to the register to tally her spoils for the night. We only had a half hour before last call, but it looked like we'd brought in a pretty good haul.

"If I ever manage to figure it out, I'll definitely let you know."

"Well, you better whip up something quick. I'm gonna need it to keep the frat boys away from my dorm," she replied, then froze when she realized what she'd said.

In her defense, college talk wasn't strictly off-limits. But she was always careful not to mention it around me. I'd never asked her to tone it down on my account, but I think she knew on some level that I was still bummed about postponing my freshman year to stay in Wolf's Head. The whole topic was an ember glowing hot and uncomfortable in my chest, and the right gust of wind could easily make it catch flame. But it felt silly for me to be upset over something that nobody had asked me to do, and it felt even sillier to have her walk on eggshells around me to compensate.

"That's not a bad idea, honestly," I said, and Anna brightened. I crossed to the counter so I could extinguish my bundle of herbs. "Maybe if I send you a care kit for warding off evil spirits, it can do double duty for keeping creepy men out of your business."

Anna shot me a smile that was only a little bit strained. "That's the dream. And by the spring I'll be the one sending you care kits to your dorm."

Something twisted painfully in my chest as I pressed the still-smoking leafage into a clay dish on the counter. When I sent in my deferment, I figured I'd only take one semester off to help my dad sell our remaining stock. But that was before I found the note in my mom's jacket, and before this thing with the valley grabbed hold of me.

Another thunderclap echoed down the street, closer than the last. I could see the wheels spinning in Anna's head as she watched me, so it was no surprise when she spoke up again. "You're still planning to start in the spring semester, right?"

I knew it made sense to leave Wolf's Head and move on with my life. But part of my mom was still here. Not just in the grief that sat like a film over every memory I had in town, but also in the secrets she'd left behind. It would've been easier to just focus on the future instead, pero la familia no se deja. Of all the things my dad had repeated to me over the years, why did that have to be the one that stuck?

"I'm not sure, but I'll figure it out," I said, trying to sound nonchalant, but it came out tense.

"Listen, I didn't mean—"

"Do you have any trash back there?" I interrupted, jutting my chin in the direction of the storeroom. "I think the bin up front is full. I can take it out before it starts pouring."

Anna nodded, and I slipped behind her to collect the bags. By the time I returned to the shop floor, Anna seemed determined to make things less awkward, even though I was pretty sure it was my fault the conversation had gone sour.

"I'm sorry," she said, picking at her cuticles like she always did when she was nervous. "You know I'm never judging, I just want you to be happy."

"I know," I said, and I really did think she was telling the truth. If there was one thing I could be sure of, it was that Anna would always be honest. "This is a me thing, not a you thing. Trust me, you don't need to apologize."

Anna offered me a sheepish smile, but she was still fiddling with her fingers. I didn't think anything of it at the time, but I reached over to give her hand a quick squeeze. Her eyes widened when I did, and a look crossed her face that I couldn't identify.

Suddenly she looked down at the bags I was holding. "Let me take those out for you."

"What? Seriously, Anna, we're good. I promise."

"No, that's not—" she started, then tried to tug one of the bags from my hands. "Seriously, I got it."

"Dude, relax," I replied, waving her off as I nudged the door open with my shoulder. "I'm sure someone else will stumble in here after last call. Just stay put."

Anna opened her mouth to say something else, but the door swung shut behind me before I could make out what she'd said. I hadn't realized how much the wind had picked up, but the massive elm tree next to the shop was swaying back and forth enough to make me dizzy. My curls whipped around my face as I walked to the alley at the end of the block, trash bags in tow.

The clouds were drawing closer by the second, but the storm-charged air wasn't the only thing raising the hairs on the backs of my arms. My mind was buzzing again, vibrating with the same persistent sense there was an invisible hand tugging at the edge of my consciousness. I was still standing in the navy shadows of the alleyway when the screams started again.

They were bloodcurdling and relentless, and they weren't just some far-off sound I hadn't noticed over the racket of the oncoming storm. They were an electric shock to my system, as startling as a slap in the face and as sudden as a flock of birds taking flight.

The voice was loud enough that it drowned out the sound of my sneakers hitting the sidewalk as I scrambled from the alley and ran south. It bounced off the pavement and the stout buildings that lined the narrow road, only getting louder when I rounded the corner to a quieter side street.

I skidded to a stop at the end of the block, trying to pinpoint where the screams were coming from. And it was there, under a cascade of light from the nearest streetlamp, that I realized I had followed the voice to the edge of the valley. There was no denying it was real now, not the pull I felt or the voice I heard. My heart was stuck in my throat, and my feet were rooted to the ground.

"Watch where you're standing—I'm trying to walk here," growled a man from just over my shoulder.

I whipped around, expecting him to be as startled as I was, but all I saw in the dim light was an indignant expression and the glow of a cigarette hanging out of his mouth. I mumbled an apology and ducked out of the cloud of smoke that hung around his shoulders.

Another group of people were chatting across the street, looking equally unconcerned. The screams should've been loud enough to make them stop in their tracks, but they just kept walking like nothing had happened. When I finally turned my attention back to the valley, it was silent.

I hurried away from the edge of the forest in a daze, my mind reeling. But by the time I saw the shop's white siding and black shutters at the top of the hill, I knew I needed to find out more.

The door jingled when I shuffled back in through the entryway, and Anna was still standing exactly where I'd left her.

"Did something happen out there?"

When I met her eyes, she didn't look confused by my expression or worried about what had taken me so long. Instead, she seemed apprehensive. Expectant, almost.

"No," I lied, shooting her an empty smile. "The storm is just starting to pick up, that's all."

CHAPTER 6
JAIME

I THOUGHT, LIKE AN idiot, that because I finally had some food and water in my stomach, I'd make it through the night without hearing any voices.

I was wrong.

My head felt clearer than it had in days, so I figured it would be safe to drift off to sleep in a second-story bedroom. Like the rest of the house, the room was fully furnished and decorated in matching hues of intricately designed wallpaper and heavy velvet drapery. I curled up on the velvet loveseat at the far end of the room, thinking it would be less creepy than climbing into the gaudy four-poster bed decked out in emerald fringe.

But the second I closed my eyes, a chillingly familiar voice pierced the air.

"Jaime? Where are you?"

My eyes flew open, searching the flat blackness enveloping the room, but nobody was there. It took what felt like hours for my pulse to stop racing, then for my eyelids to get heavy. But as I finally drifted off, it happened again.

"Come on, Jaime. It's not funny anymore."

And again. *"If you're not out by the count of three—"*

By the time the sun started to rise, it was almost a relief to give up on sleep completely. In the early hours of morning, darkness clung to the edges of the room. The furniture huddled together in unfamiliar shapes, and there was one shadow in the corner that looked particularly out of place. Blinking the sleep from my eyes, I got up from the couch and squinted into the murkiness.

And that was when the shadow lunged.

Panic shot through my veins as a spectral hand clamped around my wrist and dragged me out of the room. I tried to scramble away, kicking and shoving as hard as I could, but the woman's grip was like iron. Her silver-streaked hair covered her face as she pulled me up the stairs.

"Stupid boy," she hissed, hauling me in front of the third-story window I'd broken when I first tried to escape. "I thought you understood that you can't leave."

"I'm sorry, I didn't mean to—"

My breathless plea became a scream when she pressed her nails into the open cuts on my palms where the broken glass had slashed me. Hot blood snaked down my wrists, and stars threatened to white out my vision completely. But just when I thought I couldn't stand the pain any longer, the woman let me go.

I spun away from the window, gasping for air and cradling my hand against my chest. My eyes raked the shadows enveloping the hall for any sign of her, but it was like she had vanished into thin air. If it weren't for the aching open wounds on my hands, I might've convinced myself it was just a nightmare born out of paranoia, or some by-product of almost starving to death. My legs were numb, but I managed to race back down the stairs to the ground level.

When I saw a figure hovering in the front doorway, I was afraid the woman had come back to finish the job. Instead, by some strange miracle, the boy from the day before emerged from the shadows of the porch like a mirage.

"Whoa, what's wrong?" he said, his eyes searching my face before dropping to my blood-slicked hands. "Okay, that is definitely fresh. What the hell is going on?"

Between how petrified I felt and how shocked I was that he'd shown up, I couldn't think of anything to say other than "I think I just saw a ghost."

"I'm sorry, *what?*"

"I kept hearing things. I thought I was going insane." I babbled, adrenaline still coursing through me. "And then this lady came out of nowhere. I don't know how it's possible, but she did. I think she was mad that I broke a window trying to escape."

"Okay, don't panic," he said, though he didn't sound particularly composed himself. He fished a water bottle from his bag and rolled it into the foyer. "Wash the cuts first—you can't afford to get an infection out here."

He watched numbly while I rinsed my hands, wincing as the water stung the open wounds.

"So," he tried, once my breathing had slowed. "You're being haunted. In a house. A haunted house."

"Don't say it like that. It makes it sound fake."

"Everything about this sounds fake," he said, "but I promise I believe you. If you're sure that's what you saw, it's the only lead we have on why you're stuck."

For the first time since I'd woken up, I was able to take a full, deep breath. "So what are we supposed to do? Unless you have a medium on speed dial, we're shit out of luck," I said, more as a pitiful joke than a real suggestion, but the look that passed across the boy's face made me pause. "Wait, what's that face?"

The boy chewed his bottom lip. "I don't think it's worth mentioning."

"If you don't tell me and I go full Paranormal Activity while I'm in here, that'll be on you."

"It's not much," he said, shooting me a wary look, "but there is an occult shop a town over from here."

Under any other circumstances, I would've loved that I had a roof over my head and a space where nobody could breach but me. After bouncing between six homes in seven years, this house could've been the most stable home situation I'd had since, well, ever. Making lemonade out of the world's shittiest lemons was kind of my specialty, but not when there were ghosts involved. If there was ever a situation where I had to admit I needed help, this was it.

"You have to go," I said, and the boy grimaced.

"I don't think you understand. It's, like, a souvenir shop for tourists," he said, and for the first time, I thought I detected a little of that Saint Juniper judgment in his voice. "It's highly unlikely I'll find anyone who can help us there."

"Any help is good help," I said, but he still looked torn.

I racked my brain trying to think of how to get him on board. Unfortunately, the only thing I could come up with was sincerity.

"Listen, I haven't asked for a single thing from you so far, but I'm asking now."

The boy leveled a stare at me. It was the same look he'd given me the day before, the kind that felt like it cut all the way down to the quick of my soul.

"I'll go, but on one condition," he replied, and my heart dropped. "You have to let me know who you're staying with back in town."

It took everything in me not to groan out loud. I should have known there was going to be a catch.

"Nobody," I lied. "I'm not from Saint Juniper. I'm just passing through."

He let my fib hang in the air between us for a beat before swatting it down.

"That's not true. I didn't put two and two together when I saw you yesterday, but you must be the new kid that's joining our class in the fall. Everyone in town has been talking about you," he said, matter-of-fact. "You said I had one question for the day, right? Well, this is it—tell me the truth."

"Or what, you're gonna let me rot to death in here?"

"No, god no," he said, and the appalled look on his face told me that was the furthest thing from his mind. "I'm just trying to keep you safe."

"Don't you have anything better to do than bother me?"

I meant it mostly as a joke, but something tightened around his eyes that made me pause.

"No, not really," he said, crossing his arms. "This town has a crime rate of zero percent, so the fact that your face isn't plastered all over the local news when you've been missing for days doesn't add up."

A shard of panic spiked behind my lungs. I didn't exactly envision Michelle organizing a search party to come and find me, but considering how little wiggle room the foster system gave when it came to runaways, I did have a ticking time bomb hanging over my head to get out of there in one piece.

"What are you going to do if I tell you?"

"Nothing you don't want me to do," he said evenly. "I just don't want things to get any more complicated than they already are. Not to get too dark here, but if something happens to you, I need to know who to tell."

Damn, he was good. I considered lying again, but I didn't think that would get me anywhere. I was quickly learning that he was as stubborn in practice as I was in theory, which was probably why we wanted to strangle each other. I sighed.

"My parents aren't in the picture," I started, careful to edit out the details he didn't strictly need. "I've been in foster care for the past few years. I just moved back here like three weeks ago. I'm staying with a friend of my mom's, Michelle."

The boy's eyebrows shot up, but he reined his expression back to a neutral place in record time. He must've known that peppering me with more questions wouldn't be a smart move, because he held his tongue, thinking for a bit before he spoke.

"I can go talk to her if you want."

"And say what?" There was no way she'd be sitting by the front door, wondering why I hadn't been home in time for dinner. If anything, she probably thought I was just like my dad, that I had bailed the second things got a little bit tough. "It's not like you can tell her where I really am, and without that, it'll just sound like I ran away."

"But what if I don't tell her?" he ventured. "I can say you're staying at my place, just until we manage to get you out of here. That way she won't get suspicious, and we won't have to worry about anyone else getting involved."

I was surprised by how much he had thought this through. It wasn't the worst idea I had ever heard, but I still wasn't sold.

"And what if we can't break me out? You'll be leaving a trail right back to you if anything happens to me."

The boy studied my face with the most sincere expression I had ever seen. "That's a chance I'm willing to take."

I had done such a good job of throwing any maybes and what-ifs about my failed fresh start out the window the second I got stuck in this stupid house. It felt unfair on a cosmic level that a boy with eyes like sea glass and a smile like summer that seemed so good, too good to have anything to do with me, was giving me hope when I didn't want it at all. Some rancid part of my brain wanted to nuke the whole conversation like I'd done the day before, angry that he had managed to back me into a corner.

As a last-ditch effort, I said, "She's basically a complete stranger to me. I don't think she's going to care one way or the other."

"Even if she doesn't, we might as well try. At this point, what do you have to lose?"

Trusting another person was a luxury in my book, one that I'd never really had the emotional credit to afford, but something about this guy was making me want to change my mind. None of this would guarantee a happy reunion or a roof over my head if I managed to get out. But his plan wasn't half bad, and if he was willing to put his neck on the line to make it work, then I could get on board.

I held his gaze for as long as I dared, then sighed. "Okay."

His eyebrows shot up again, but this time he made no effort to reel in his excitement. "Wait, really? You're not messing with me?"

Ugh, I hate this guy. Why did he have to care so much? Why did he have to look at me like that? Had I not suffered enough in life?

"Ask again and I'll change my mind."

"Nonono, this is good," he said, and I could tell he was already making plans inside his head. "I can handle this."

I rolled my eyes for an excuse to peel them off him. "Well, good luck finding her. Her address is on my phone, but it's been dead since I got here."

Truthfully, I'd been stuck in the house for a day and a half before the screen flickered to black. In the rare moments I was able to get even one bar of service so deep into the valley, I didn't have anyone to call for help even if I wanted to.

"I'll bring you a power bank at some point. Just give me the best directions you can," he said, earnest and laser-focused in that way that made my face feel hot. "I'll find it, I promise."

As I squashed down my discomfort, I realized I finally had the opening I needed. "You know, I would feel a lot better accepting help from you if I knew your name."

"Oh, right," he said, like he'd forgotten we had skipped a few steps between being strangers and . . . whatever we were. "I'm Theo. Theo Miller."

Theo, I thought. *TheoTheoTheo*. It suited him. "I'm Jaime Alvarez-Shephard."

"I know," he said, then quickly backtracked. "We went to elementary school together before you moved. I didn't recognize you at first, but I do sort of remember you now."

I peered at his face, but like always, my memory of that time in my life felt like a black hole. "I don't remember you."

"That's okay, it was a long time ago. It's nice to re-meet you, Jaime," he said, repeating my name out loud, just like how I wanted to repeat his. I was surprised by how little I hated the sound of it coming out of his mouth.

As I talked through everything I could remember about Michelle's house, I watched in fascination as Theo started to pull things out of his backpack like a handsome type-A Mary Poppins. He tossed items to me one by one—half a loaf of bread, a Tupperware full of rice, one metal fork. I was about to poke fun at him for the random assortment of items he'd chosen to bring, but it dawned on me that these were probably the only things he could nab from his house without anyone noticing. Instead, I silently assessed what might be the easiest for me to eat since my stomach still wasn't settled from my brief tango with starvation.

"I'm thinking this should have you set for the next few days at least," he said, tossing me a bag of pretzels. "Do you need me to bring you anything specific from Michelle's place?"

I automatically opened my mouth to reject his offer, then shut it again. I was so focused on survival that I hadn't even considered making the place a bit more livable. Basic personal hygiene was still kind of important, I guessed.

"A change of clothes would be great."

"Easy enough," he said. "Anything else?"

I mulled it over for a beat, weighing how embarrassing it would be to ask for what I actually needed. "Okay, and deodorant. And a toothbrush. And soap," I listed, crouching to scoop up a can of tuna that had slipped off the top of my pile and clattered to the floor. *It's Fresh!* was emblazoned on the label in seafoam-green print. Why would they need to specify that?

"Sure, I can do that," he said, and when I looked up from the tuna, he seemed mildly perturbed. "How do you even take showers out here?"

I had just been using rainwater from the greenhouse, but I couldn't resist messing with him when he gave me an opening like that.

"That's a very personal question," I said, putting a hand to my chest in mock offense. "How dare you ask me that."

"Jaime."

"I can't believe my only hope of survival is the local pervert," I said wistfully.

"Please stop." He zipped his backpack shut as he rose to his feet. "I'm guessing you feel okay if you have the energy to annoy me, but I have to head to work now. Are you going to be all right while I'm gone?"

"Probably not." I sniffed, leaning my head against the doorframe. "I'll be standing right here for the rest of the day, clutching my handkerchief as I wait for you to return from war."

If looks could kill, Theo's would have decapitated me on the spot. "I thought we were making progress with the back talk. Can you please just answer the question?"

"Yes, *Mom*. You don't need to baby me, you know. I was fine before you came along."

Theo gave me an exhausted look. "You literally almost died. Twice."

"Really," I said, "that's neither here nor there."

As I watched him descend the porch steps, I almost wished I had dragged the conversation on a little longer. The second he slipped beyond the trees, I would be alone again, trapped in this place and in my own mind.

The eerie silence I dreaded settled on the house again, and I knew that only time would tell if I could trust Theo as much as he clearly wanted me to. But all of a sudden, before I'd even had the chance to resist, it felt like the two of us were in this mess together.

CHAPTER 7
THEO

I WASN'T SCHEDULED TO work the next day, so I took my dubious instructions and misplaced optimism and decided to cruise around town, waiting for the house Jaime had described to jump out at me. Whatever scraps of sunshine we'd gotten to enjoy the day before were long gone, and the sky was gray as death as I started to circle the south side. By early afternoon, the humid air that pushed up against me through my driver's-side window said a deluge wasn't completely off the table.

After nearly two hours of nothing but the low rumble of my tires on blackened asphalt to keep me company, I was starting to doubt that I'd ever find Michelle's house. I even considered getting out of my car and taking a lap on foot while the weather held, but I figured it was already a miracle the neighborhood watch hadn't called the sheriff on me, and I didn't want to push my luck.

I pulled over to the side of the road to check the map on my phone for the fortieth time, turning the radio down like that would somehow amplify my sense of direction. The crisscross of semifamiliar streets felt impossible to untangle on my phone screen, so I squeezed my eyes shut and leaned my forehead against the steering wheel to collect my thoughts. With my eyes closed, questions about the house in the woods wouldn't stop buzzing around my mind. I hopped from one impossible topic I'd been avoiding to another, somehow landing squarely on the worst one of all: Jaime.

Though I didn't want to admit it, something about Jaime had definitely gotten under my skin. He was distracting, and I hated distractions. In fact, I had lived my entire life up until that point almost completely distraction-free. My mom always told me I had an incredible sense of duty, whatever that meant. In reality, I'd mostly been laser focused on staying out of trouble and getting good grades just because I felt like it was expected of me. Not just by my parents, or because of the intangible pressure that came from having a successful older sibling, but by everyone. The universe, maybe.

I also knew good grades might mean a scholarship to any school I wanted, which would mean finally leaving Saint Juniper and getting to live an unobserved life for the first time ever. So I figured keeping my head down was a win-win, so long as I didn't factor in my personal feelings of existential dread.

But if there was one thing that could break my focus, it was the uncanny knack I had for noticing sad people and not being able to rest until I fixed them. It wasn't just people who felt a little blue, it was people who were sad on some fundamental level. Sad with nowhere to go but sadder. It was the type of sadness that could keep for years. Maybe it was a little like the sadness I felt myself.

I saw it in my parents, and in their strained relationship, more often than I wanted to admit. I very intentionally did not think about it, because if I did, I would feel compelled to fix it. But for whatever reason, Jaime was a different story. Even though the brief conversations we'd shared had made me want to rip my hair out, between the cracks in that big attitude of his, I could have sworn he was terrified. I saw it in the way he looked surprised when I showed up at the house the day before, like he didn't believe I was actually coming back for him. I saw it in the distrust that filled his eyes when he tracked my movements like a world-weary tiger in a cage. I saw it most when he couldn't seem to look me in the eye when I gave him anything, and it upset me more than I wanted to admit.

The selfish part of me nagged that the last thing I needed was something or someone to tie me to Saint Juniper when I was so close to being rid of it completely. But despite all logic and Jaime's best attempts to push me away, I did feel a grudging responsibility for him. I knew he didn't care about me—at best, he found me amusing, and at worst, he found me insufferable. Asking me to deliver a message to Michelle wasn't an olive branch by any means, but I couldn't help wondering if maybe in his own infuriatingly stubborn way, he was trying to let me in.

When I finally sat up, I noticed it had started to drizzle. I squinted through the droplets collecting on my windshield, my eyes locked on a cul-de-sac where I swear there hadn't been one before. There, at the very end of the narrow roundabout, sat a pale yellow house with glossy black shutters, just as Jaime had described.

As I pulled into the driveway, I realized I hadn't even considered whether Michelle would be home. Still, I jogged up to the front door, unreasonably excited that finally something was going my way. It might not have been in the realm of haunted mansions, but I'd still take it.

I rapped my knuckles on the front door four times. Nothing. I lifted the tarnished knocker and tried again. I was almost convinced I needed to come back some other time when I heard someone slide back the deadbolt on the other side of the door.

I wasn't sure what I was expecting, but the woman in front of me wasn't it. Her brown hair was pulled into a loose braid that collected at the hood of a well-worn sorority sweatshirt. Though I couldn't make a guess at her age, she definitely didn't look old enough to be the guardian of a seventeen-year-old. As I squinted at her through the mesh of the screen door, she gave me a none-too-subtle up-and-down in return.

"Are you Michelle?"

"Who's asking?"

Well, all righty then. She and Jaime might not have been related, but they certainly had the same artful communication skills.

"Theo. Theo Miller. I'm a, uh, friend of Jaime's."

Her eyebrow twitched. Maybe it would have been more accurate if I'd said *The guy you're supposed to be taking care of is an enigma who likes to bully me, and I only tolerate it because I'm trying to keep him alive.*

"A friend of Jaime's," she repeated, but there was something unexpectedly mean about the way it was delivered. It sounded more like she was saying *Jaime doesn't have friends.* "You're welcome to come in, but you won't find him here."

"Oh, I know," I said, giving her a smile that most adults couldn't resist. She resisted. "Jaime is actually staying with me right now. I hope that's okay."

I was surprised to hear her laugh a bit—a humorless puff of air—as she popped the screen door and shuffled aside to let me in. I followed as she led me through a narrow entryway and into a small carpeted living room that opened into a kitchen. The space was cozy enough, decorated in shades of blue, the walls hung with framed photos from baptisms and family reunions.

"A bit late for that, isn't it?" she asked, motioning for me to sit next to her on the couch. I almost felt guilty before I realized she meant her comment as a slight to Jaime, not me. "For all I know he's been dead in a ditch the past week."

Stellar parental instincts. I shifted uncomfortably on the couch. This conversation was more like navigating a minefield than the easy in-and-out I'd been expecting.

"Well," I started carefully, "that's why he wanted me to come by and let you know he's all right."

"Listen, I can tell you're a nice kid," she said. The way she pronounced her vowels told me she'd been born and raised in Saint Juniper. "But Jaime is not nice. I know he didn't tell you to come here."

She wasn't necessarily wrong, but the way she said it rubbed me the wrong way. "I thought you'd want to know."

"Oh, honey, it's not your fault. This is just what happens when you're not brought up right. Believe me, that boy wasn't raised up, he was dragged up," she said, sounding shockingly indifferent as she leaned forward to pluck an abandoned mug off the coffee table. "I don't know why I ever expected him to have manners in the first place."

I didn't want to argue for fear of being rude, but hearing those things about Jaime and his childhood when he wasn't there to defend himself felt like crossing a line. It was starting to make a lot more sense why he'd been so hesitant to tell me the truth.

"Um?"

"I figured there's a reason his parents didn't stick around, you know. When Samantha got pregnant so young with that guy, I knew it'd be a disaster," she prattled on. "You can't keep trouble from coming, but you don't have to give it a chair to sit on. That's what I've always said."

"Then why did you decide to take him in?" I asked before I could stop myself.

"It's what God wanted of me," she said thinly, taking a sip from her mug. Then, over the rim, she shot me a conspiratorial look. "The money doesn't hurt either, so I'm not complaining."

How I managed to keep my eyes from popping out of my head was a mystery. I stood up from my seat before I fully registered what I was doing.

"Would you mind if I go into his room and grab some of his things?" I blurted.

Michelle seemed unconcerned by my outburst. She simply nodded toward the hall leading off the kitchen. "Second door on the left. There's not much there, though."

She wasn't lying. Jaime's room was small and dark, with all the basic dressings of a bedroom but none of the character to suggest that a real human being lived there. It struck me as odd that the bare walls were painted navy blue. Jaime did not seem like a navy blue kind of person. A lamp on the bedside table was the only source of light besides a small window, and I flipped it on as I took stock of the space.

Every shirt strewn across the floor was some shade of black or gray, and seeing his bed pushed up against the wall somehow struck me as very Jaime. I'd noticed he had a habit of sitting with something against his back, whether it was a wall or a doorframe. I idly wondered if it was a by-product of growing up in spaces that weren't really his, always having to look over his shoulder.

Truth be told, standing alone in his room, the main thing I felt was embarrassed. Not for him—I didn't know Jaime well, but I was pretty sure he'd knock me out cold if he ever got the sense I pitied him. Instead, I was embarrassed for myself, for forcing him to let me into this part of his life even if his situation demanded it.

I had been so sure I was going to prove him wrong, that Michelle actually did care what happened to him, that I hadn't stopped to consider I might be the only person he had in his corner. Now that I could see that was the case, I was determined not to let him down.

Grabbing what looked like a brand-new duffel bag lying on the floor, I tried to gather everything he could possibly need without completely upending his personal belongings. There was a large trash bag in the corner, but rifling through it didn't feel right somehow, so I delved into the closet instead. There wasn't much, but I grabbed what I could: a handful of band tees, some flannel shirts, three nearly identical pairs of black jeans. Moving to his dresser, I shoved a handful of socks and underwear into the bag too. Even though I was completely alone, my face heated. I tried to tell myself this was probably going to embarrass him more than it embarrassed me and put it out of my mind.

When I emerged from Jaime's room, Michelle was still sitting on the couch exactly where I'd left her. She got to her feet to walk me to the door, though it seemed to be more out of distrust than politeness. Just as we were about to reach the front door, she piped up again.

"You know, Jaime can stay with you as long as he wants, but he has to be back before the DCF visits."

I blinked at her. "Before who visits?"

"The Department for Children and Families. They're going to do their post-placement visit at beginning of September," she replied. "Jaime knows all about it. He's been in the system long enough that I'm sure he has all this stuff memorized."

Yeah, I thought, *no problem at all*. It was already mid-July, so I just needed to forcibly extract a guy I barely knew from some supernatural Victorian death grip by the end of next month. Super simple, super straightforward.

"It really is a shame a nice kid like you is getting involved with him," she said, likely misreading my worried expression as regret. "Be careful, now. Trouble follows that boy around like nothing I've ever seen."

"I think I'll be fine," I said with a tight smile, and started to retreat down the stone walkway to my car.

I only made it a few steps before she called out one last time.

"Don't get too attached. There's nothing in Jaime that keeps him in one place for long."

If I hadn't been so irate on Jaime's behalf, I probably would've laughed at the irony. Instead of saying anything, I turned and raised a hand to wave goodbye. When I looked back over my shoulder, I realized Michelle had already shut the door between us and gone inside.

———

The day felt different by the time I reached the Wolf's Head town limits. I had driven straight through the valley to get there, and with the forest wrapped around me and the conversation with Michelle settling inside my head, a small part of me wanted to stop by the house and talk to Jaime first. I wanted to ask why he hadn't told me about the DCF visit. I wanted to ask if Michelle was an outlier or if all his foster homes had been like that. But more importantly, I wanted to get him the answers he needed. So I drove on.

I didn't visit Wolf's Head often, but when I did, it always felt like a breath of fresh air. I knew most people in Saint Juniper didn't feel the same—most people called the town quaint, but they definitely didn't mean it in a nice way. Where Saint Juniper had its perfect landscaping and colorful boutiques lined up on Main Street, Wolf's Head had a jumble of earthy coffee shops, thrift stores, and hole-in-the-wall takeout spots. They didn't draw nearly as many tourists as we did, but that was why I liked it. It felt real, and that was a novelty to me.

The winding one-way streets eventually confused me enough that I had to find street parking and search for the occult store on foot. I definitely didn't realize from the map on my phone that Avalon Apothecary was at one of the highest spots in the whole town. From where I was wandering, I could see the Green Mountains even more clearly than I could back home. When I was younger, I used to imagine that the arcs of the mountains in the distance were the backs of sleeping wolves, monsters huddled together to keep warm in the unforgiving night. Now I wasn't so sure it was just my imagination.

I was so distracted by the view I almost passed the shop by accident. It looked more like a house than a place of business, all white siding and black shutters sitting staunchly under the shadow of a huge tree.

A bay window gave me a peek at the lush interior. But looking inside only seemed to confirm my fears that this place was phony. A pair of antlers here and a potion there pulled my attention, as did the herbs hanging from the ceiling. It was interesting, sure, but I wasn't sure how legit any of it was. There were so many trinkets and showy relics I hardly knew where to look.

I sighed as I reached the entrance, spotting a girl through the warped glass of the front door. Candlelight bounced warmly off her tawny skin, and she wore a frilly baby blue shirt that looked like the top half of a dress on the cover of a romance novel. A cascade of bronze curls that hung all the way down to her waist obscured her face as she pulled her phone out from behind the counter.

I crossed my fingers in my pocket and pushed through the door, a bell tinkling merrily to announce my arrival.

CHAPTER 8
TAYLOR

"WATCH HIM," ELIAS SAID curtly beside me.

He said the same thing every time a suspicious-looking teenager walked through the door, but when I put down my phone to size up his latest suspect, I couldn't for the life of me figure out why Elias would be on high alert. The boy was without a doubt the most unintimidating person I had ever seen.

His high cheekbones, wide eyes, and small, upturned nose were terribly cute, but the way he was slouching told me he probably didn't see himself that way. When he reached up to push a lock of rain-dampened hair out of his eyes, the sleeves of his shirt fell back to reveal pale arms punctuated by a constellation of freckles. With his hair mussed up from the rain, he looked more like a puppy that'd just gotten out of the bath than a threat.

Even though he looked ridiculously out of place in our little shop, I could tell he hadn't wandered in by accident. He looked like he meant business—well, as much like business as you could look with a face like that.

I retreated to the storeroom to find Anna. It was the first shift we'd had together since working late Friday night and hearing those screams, and I still wasn't sure if her reaction when I came back to the shop had been her trying to tell me something or if I was just projecting. It wasn't like her to keep her thoughts to herself, so I figured if she was even a little bit suspicious, she would've already asked all about it.

"Hey," I whispered as I rounded the corner, but the second I did, I saw there was no way in hell she could have heard me. She was chomping on gum and swaying back and forth with her earbuds in, music blasting loud enough it made my ears ring from three feet away. I reached over and pinched her, and she jumped as if I'd shocked her.

"Warn a girl, will ya?" she said, popping an earbud out.

"That was the warning, you goon," I said, reaching over to turn the volume down on her phone myself. "There's a kid out there, he kind of looks like a pushover. I think he's from Saint Juniper. You should try to get him to pay for a reading."

She blew a bubble and popped it obnoxiously.

"First of all, *you're* a kid," she said, capturing the hand that had pinched her moments before and spitting her gum directly into my palm. "Second, I'll see what I can do."

Before I could remind her that we were basically the same age, Anna had floated out onto the floor of the shop. It still amazed me how she could switch from the Anna I knew to her powerful mystic persona in five seconds flat. I'd seen her turn hesitant tourists into paying customers with that charisma more times than I could count. Even if she hadn't been a good psychic, she could definitely feel proud of being an accomplished actress.

I busied myself organizing inventory until I heard the distinctive scrape of Anna's chair. She'd made short work of convincing him. I could hear the soft murmur of their voices before I even had the chance to pull up a stool.

It usually wasn't too hard to piece pre-reading chitchat together, but when I peeked through the folds of the thick fabric at the back of her little lair, I got the sense I'd missed an essential part of the conversation.

"Ghosts are off limits. I'm a psychic, not a medium," Anna said tersely. From my vantage point, I could only see the edge of her face behind the half-melted candles and hodgepodge collection of crystals, but she didn't look happy.

The boy blinked innocently. "What's the difference?"

"The difference," Anna replied, "is that I can tell your future, but only yours. Take it or leave it."

He scratched the back of his neck as he mulled over her offer, but I could barely sit still. It wasn't every day someone came in with a ghost problem. It might have been a massive coincidence, but with the screams from the valley fresh in my mind, I wasn't so sure.

"I guess it couldn't hurt since I'm already here," the boy murmured, and in silent reply, Anna placed her palm faceup in the center of the table. He seemed more like he was looking down the barrel of a gun than at a girl's hand, but after a pause, he placed his hand in hers.

He was still pretty stiff as Anna closed her eyes and took a few deep breaths, her face going slack like it always did at the beginning of readings. Based on what she had always told me, Anna needed a little time to sift through the muck inside people's heads, to separate their hopes for the future from the future itself. When her eyes locked with the boy's again, the shift in energy was almost palpable.

"Things are definitely changing for you, aren't they?" Anna asked, eyes flicking between their hands and the boy's skittish expression. "You've already been thrown off balance. You don't have the power to fix it, and it's bothering you. You're not used to feeling this helpless."

It was a generic enough statement, but the boy seemed to recoil a bit. "I—I don't know about that."

"You're approaching an intersection," she said, closing her eyes and tilting her head as if she were trying to hear some far-off sound that was just out of earshot. "Not just in your life, but in multiple lives."

"Which lives?" he asked, leaning across the table. I found myself leaning in too, until Anna leveled him with a warning look that was searing enough to make even me hold my breath.

"I told you, I'm not a medium. You have enough to worry about on your own, holding on so tight to everything. I get the sense that if a match were lit between your fingers, you'd rather get burned than let it go. But catching fire doesn't stop the heat. The truth always catches up with you eventually."

In the booth, the boy's brows drew together, his expression mirroring mine as I tried to follow Anna's meaning. "What?"

"Don't worry, you're not going to be terrified forever," she said, releasing his hand and sitting back in her chair. "Do you believe me when I say that?"

The boy stayed stock-still, leaning over the table with his hand extended toward her. He looked like he had been set adrift. Heartbreakingly quiet, he replied, "No, not really."

Anna pushed away from the table, getting to her feet. "Well, you don't have to believe me for it to be true."

"Wait, that's it? You barely told me anything," he said, standing up so fast he nearly upended the table.

Anna held back the velvet curtain to the shop floor. "I told you everything I saw."

Defeated, the boy paid for his reading and exited the booth, and Anna followed. A minute later, she slipped back into the storeroom, and I pounced.

"What the hell was that?"

Anna hardly made eye contact with me as she settled back into her usual perch, picking up her earbuds like the reading hadn't been the most interesting thing to happen all summer. "What was what?"

"That reading. I mean, *hello*," I said, shocked she wasn't going to give me even a hint of a reaction. "What did he ask you before you guys went into the booth? Also, you know I appreciate the showmanship, but what happened to customer service?"

Anna shrugged, still not looking up from her phone, and I felt excitement begin to bleed into frustration. This was right up my alley and she knew it, but she was icing me out. I wanted to grab Anna's shoulders and shake her, but if the boy was still in the store, I could just get the answers I needed from him myself.

"Whatever. I'm going to go see if that guy needs help," I mumbled, turning on my heel.

"Wait—" Anna started, but when I turned back, she seemed to be at a loss for words. There was that odd look in her eye again, and even though I hadn't been able to place it on Friday night, I recognized it now. She knew something I didn't. I waited for her to continue, but she glanced away. "Forget it."

Thankfully, the boy was still in the shop when I left the storeroom. He was eyeballing our small collection of books on the far wall when I sidled up next to him.

"Have you checked this author out? He's pretty legit," I said, plucking a book off the shelf behind him and handing it over. "I'm Taylor. I heard you might need some help."

The worried crease between the boy's brows softened, and his eyes, which were shockingly light up close, brightened instantly.

"I do, actually. But I was hoping for something a little more substantial than a book," he said, then surprised me when he ducked his head closer to mine. In a much quieter voice, he asked, "Does anyone here know how to deal with ghosts? I tried asking your psychic, but she seemed upset that I asked. Am I missing something? Is ghost stuff, like, a big trade secret?"

Pulling back a bit, I searched his face for an inkling that he was messing with me. Even though I could tell he had no idea what he was talking about, he looked dead serious. I decided to bite.

"Can you be a little more specific?" I asked. "What kind of ghost are we talking about here?"

"The angry kind," he said, matter-of-fact. My mind darted back to the otherworldly screams I'd heard coming from the valley, and my pulse hiccuped. "I was hoping to talk to someone who had experience with that type of thing. I mean, not that you don't have experience. I don't know your professional history with ghosts—you look very knowledgeable."

"Believe it or not, I am," I said, which might have been a bit of a stretch. Relief flooded his face immediately.

"Oh, thank god. I really don't want to go back empty-handed."

"Go back where?" I asked, and I could tell the boy understood what I was asking. I didn't want to know where he was from, I wanted to know where the ghost was.

He held my gaze, and I could see the gears turning behind his eyes as he sized me up. Just when I started to fear I had pushed him too far, he said the two words I had been hoping for all along. "The valley."

No. Fucking. Way.

"You spend a lot of time there?" a voice asked from behind me, and I nearly jumped out of my skin.

Elias appeared beside me out of thin air, and I watched in confusion as he held a hand out for the boy to pass the book back. After hesitating for a second, the boy obliged. I wondered silently if Elias had been listening the whole time.

"Depends on what you mean by a lot," the boy said, fiddling with his ear. My god, he had a horrible poker face.

"Just what it sounds like," Elias replied. The non-question hung awkwardly between the three of us, and I shot Elias an annoyed look that he ignored. If his and Anna's goal was to lose customers today, they were doing a real bang-up job.

"Oh," the boy replied reluctantly, "I guess so, yeah."

"Well, you'd better be going," Elias said coldly. "It looks like the rain is going to pick up. Wouldn't want you to have trouble on your ride home."

Elias's face was stony as ever, but the skin was taut over his knuckles from how tight he was gripping the book. Apparently, it was on me to break up this fever dream of a conversation. Not being able to stand the weird macho tension anymore, I plucked the book from Elias's hands.

"You can come with me. I'll ring you up," I said to the boy, ushering him over to the far end of the shop.

I tried to play it cool, but my brain was a jumble of cartwheeling thoughts. This boy, or whatever issue he had going on, could be the connection between the questions I had about my mom and the screams I had heard. Between that and the bizarrely cold reaction he had gotten from Anna and Elias, there was no way I was letting him walk out of my life. In a snap decision, I grabbed a pen from behind the counter and scribbled my number on the back of his receipt.

"Does this look okay to you?" I asked, angling the receipt so he could see it but Elias couldn't.

The boy's eyebrows pulled together, and I realized a second too late that he had misinterpreted my offer. He looked so bewildered I honestly thought he would turn around and walk right out of the shop.

Rolling my eyes, I pulled the receipt back, scribbled a bit more, then showed it to him again.

i'm trying to help you, dummy

"Oh, that's fine," he said, visibly relaxing as I tucked the receipt into the book jacket.

He caught my eye again as he gathered his purchase, mouthing *thank you* before he turned to leave. By the time the bell on the door rang for the second time that afternoon, Elias had disappeared from the shop floor.

CHAPTER 9
THEO

THE GRAYISH HAZE FROM the day before had yet to be chased away by the morning light, and the house, along with its unwilling occupant, seemed even gloomier than usual. The duffel bag I had hauled into the forest lay abandoned at Jaime's feet.

"I'm sorry, you did *what*?"

"Can you at least double-check that I got everything you need before you chew me out?" I asked, but Jaime only responded by fixing me with an even more acidic glare than the one he was already shooting my way.

In retrospect, I probably shouldn't have brought Taylor up before I'd fully debriefed him on my visit to Michelle's house. The second Jaime heard I'd found someone to help us, any hope of asking him the mountain of questions I had about foster care flew out the window. At first, he seemed excited by the prospect of having a helping hand. But his mood turned sour when I mentioned Taylor was our age, and it got even worse when I told him I'd already invited her to check the house out for herself.

"This is so not happening," he said, running a hand through his hair to push the dark, messy waves away from his face.

"I know it's not ideal, but you told me to get help, so I got it," I said, sounding more confident than I actually was. "I thought you'd be happy I sorted everything out for you."

"Well, big shocker here, I'm actually not thrilled you broadcasted my location to the first person you saw."

"I didn't give away any details about you or the house. That's the whole reason I'm going to pick her up myself. She has no idea where you are."

"Still, there has to be someone better we can find," Jaime said, turning away to rub a hand over his face. "I thought you were gonna get, like, adult supervision, or an actual professional."

Technically, he did have a point there. I was still a little skeptical that Taylor was legit, and I had no idea what to make of the odd experience I'd had at the occult shop. But whatever doubts I had were far outweighed by the DCF visit looming ahead. If Taylor was my only shot to get Jaime out in one piece before his time was up, I was willing to take that chance.

My worries were only amplified by the dark circles under Jaime's eyes. He probably thought he was hiding his exhaustion well, but I could tell he was running on fumes. The rough burn of his voice was almost as ragged as the first day I had found him, and in the dimness of the morning, he looked completely drained. The darkness of the foyer seemed to be swallowing him whole.

"Did you see her again last night?" I asked quietly. "The ghost?"

Jaime shook his head, but he still looked queasy thinking about it. "Not really, not like the other day. I keep thinking I see her out of the corner of my eye, but I can't tell if it's real or if I'm just seeing things because I'm paranoid now."

"That's all the more reason to give Taylor the benefit of the doubt, right? You were the one who said any help is good help," I noted as gently as I could, knowing that what I was about to say next would probably feel like a punch in the gut. "We don't have time to mess around. Not with the house, and not with the DCF."

I watched Jaime's face twist into an even deeper frown as my meaning hit home. "So Michelle let the cat out of the bag, huh?"

"Why didn't you tell me about the visit?" I asked, not unkindly.

"Because if they show up and I'm not with Michelle, there's nothing you can do to keep the cops from getting involved. I'll be declared a missing person, and if they find out you had something to do with it, you're screwed."

"If anything, that's why you should have told me sooner. We barely have two months to figure this out."

"I didn't know how to bring it up without freaking you out," he said with a sigh, but before I had the chance to glean an ounce of goodwill from his comment, he added, "You're high-strung enough as it is. The last thing I needed was you jumping down my throat more than you already were."

"I wouldn't have jumped down your throat," I replied sternly.

"Well, if it wasn't that, then you probably would've run for the hills," he said, nudging the duffel bag with his foot and looking anywhere other than my eyes. "You're cookie-cutter Saint Juniper, I didn't expect you to understand. Still don't."

For a second, I wasn't sure what to say. I didn't think it'd mean much to Jaime if I told him that it didn't matter, that nothing about him made me want to run for the hills, and I actually felt the exact opposite. So instead, I said, "We already went over this. You have to tell me what's going on or I can't help you. We're in this together, so no more secrets, all right?"

As Jaime considered me, the silence that settled over the property was nearly palpable. Other than the sound of leaves shifting in the distance, you could have heard a pin drop.

"Fine," he finally replied. When his eyes met mine, the unguarded look I'd caught before still lingered, but it was gone again in an instant. "What, are you waiting for me to make a pinky promise with you or something? I thought you were leaving."

It took most of the walk back to my car to rid myself of the urge to strangle Jaime, and the rest of my journey into Wolf's Head to convince myself that trusting Taylor was as good an idea as I had made it sound.

I still wasn't sure why the shop owner and the psychic had seemed so bothered by my presence the day before, so I parked a few blocks down to be safe. Just as I began to wonder if she was going to show, I heard a rap on my passenger-side window.

Taylor, holding two takeaway coffee cups and looking oddly chipper, waved at me through the glass. I unlocked the door and watched as she popped into the passenger seat like she had done it a thousand times.

"Here," she said, holding out one of the cups with a hand full of silver rings. Her corkscrew curls were pulled away from her face, and she smelled of cinnamon and something pleasantly woody, just like the occult shop. "This is my way of apologizing for the early call time. The shop opens at eight and I didn't want Elias to see me sneak out."

I gladly accepted her peace offering, taking a sip before peeling away from the curb. "Elias, is that—?"

"The shop owner, who also happens to be my dad."

Oh, duh. When I thought back, they did have the same curls, round face, and large, dark eyes. The only reason it was harder to see the resemblance was Taylor's face was open and expressive, whereas Elias's was very much the opposite.

I thought about asking why he had all but kicked me out the day before, but I didn't want to cross a line. Instead, I asked, "You call your dad by his first name?"

"Not to his face," she replied, turning to look out the passenger-side window as we drove south, reaching the outskirts of Wolf's Head. "Also, I appreciate the cloak-and-dagger thing as much as the next person, but are you gonna eventually tell me where we're going?"

"There's an abandoned house on the west side of the valley," I said as we rolled up to a stop sign. "I don't know if you've heard of it, but a lot of kids from Saint Juniper have tried to find it and break in."

"Yeah, but I thought it was just some dumb urban legend," she said, arching a brow at me. "You're telling me it's not?"

"It's very real. I could try to explain the issue with it, but I think it's better if you see it for yourself."

The sun flickered behind a cloud as we entered the valley, and Taylor's attention was pulled to the edge of the forest. "Well, into the belly of the beast, I guess."

When I glanced over, her expression was unreadable. "Not an outdoorsy person?"

I was surprised when she let out a little laugh. "Yeah, you could say that."

Taylor's demeanor shifted as we drove farther into the forest, and by the time I parked my car at the side of the road and started into the valley on foot, her nervousness was almost palpable. I wasn't sure how to comfort her, or even how to ease my own nerves, so I trotted next to her and pointed out errant roots and muddy spots to avoid on the forest floor. The patterned sundress she was wearing was hardly the ideal gear for a hike, but her combat boots let her manage well enough.

The looming pines seemed to grow taller the farther we walked, and the mossy floor absorbed the sound of our footsteps to the point where the silence was unnerving. And then, as soon as we stepped within sight of the house, Taylor's jaw dropped. I waited for her at the edge of the meadow, watching her expression shift from incredulity to fear and back again. I followed her gaze, tilting my head to take in the scene, and goose bumps broke out on my arms like I was seeing it for the first time all over again. I wasn't sure if it was the house itself or the spirit haunting it, but everything about that place made me want to run. It seemed like Taylor was having a similar reaction.

"When you said a house in the woods, I didn't think you meant this," she whispered.

"Don't worry," I replied, "it gets weirder."

When we made it to the porch, Taylor paused. "Can we go in?"

"Not exactly," Jaime piped up, sliding from the shadows inside the house in a bone-chilling way I hated. Next to me, Taylor went rigid.

"You've got to stop doing that—you're going to give someone a heart attack," I scolded, but Jaime was too busy sizing up Taylor to care.

"You seem normal," he said, crossing his arms and leaning against the doorframe like that was a regular thing to say to a complete stranger. "What's your deal?"

"Wow, nice to meet you too. My *deal* is that my mom was a witch," Taylor said. After hesitating for a moment, she added, "And I am too."

My eyes flitted to Jaime, sure he was going to give me the *I told you so* look I'd been dreading, but he actually looked a little impressed. I turned to Taylor, who also seemed way too casual about all this.

"Wait, you're not joking?" I asked.

"I'm really not," she replied.

"What exactly does that mean? Being a witch," Jaime inter-jected. "Like, do you ride on a broom under the full moon and cast spells and stuff?"

"No to the broom, yes to the spells. It's a gift that's been passed down through my mom's bloodline for generations," Taylor rattled off. "We pull energy from nature to connect with spirits. Mostly dead ones, but living ones too, if they need our help banishing negative energy. Short of conjuring objects out of thin air, there's a spell for almost anything. It's all catalogued in grimoires that are usually passed between family members."

"Fair enough," Jaime said simply. Then, pointing to me, added, "He's gonna need time to process."

I nodded sheepishly, and Taylor laughed a little, turning back to Jaime. "So, what's your deal? I heard there was a ghost problem."

It didn't take much time to fill Taylor in. With a little prod-ding, Jaime explained how he was trapped, and he even let Taylor press her hands up against the barrier herself. She listened intently as he described the ghost, about how she had attacked him and cut his hands.

"And the one thing she keeps repeating is that I can't leave," he said, wrapping up his recap. "Like, yeah, lady. I get it. Trust me, you've made your point."

"Ghosts tend to be a little heavy-handed. It's kind of their whole thing, given they only exist because they have unfinished business," Taylor replied with a chuckle. "But overall, hauntings are pretty straightforward. First, there are ghosts that are sad. They might make lights flicker and doors slam, but they're harmless, and it's pretty easy to help them pass over to the other side. Second, there are ghosts that are pissed off. Whatever unfinished business they have makes them want to nuke everything."

"Okay, so she's the second one?" I ask.

"Bingo. They're a little harder to get rid of, but not impossible. If we want her to pass over to the other side, we need to figure out why she's so pissed and fix it, or make it up to her somehow."

"You did break that window," I muttered, then noticed the dark look Jaime shot in my direction. "What? I'm just trying to help."

"Dude, don't be a narc."

"You two have a beautiful friendship, have I mentioned that?" Taylor said, taking in the scene with obvious amusement.

"We're not friends," Jaime scoffed. I was unprepared for the pang of disappointment that followed his jab, and when I tried to catch his eye again to see if he was being serious, I didn't quite manage. "From what I can tell, tons of kids have trashed this place over the years. I don't think a single broken window would qualify me for eternal house arrest."

"You're right, that's not exactly a big-ticket item," Taylor said thoughtfully. "It'd probably be better to figure out who she is and how she died. That's usually where the drama is."

The fact we had a plan, or at least the beginning of one, made me feel like a massive weight was off my shoulders. But there was something that'd been bugging me since the day before, and I finally felt like I could ask.

"I hope this doesn't come off wrong, but why are you so eager to help us?" I asked, turning to Taylor. "What's in this for you?"

"Ah, right," Taylor said, turning to look across the meadow. "I've felt there was something off about this place for a long time, but I couldn't put my finger on it. And then my mom passed away in the spring, and I know for a fact she came to the valley before she died. I don't know how or why, but I think something is going on here that may help me find some answers."

"I'm sorry, I had no idea—"

"Don't be," she said quickly. "You pulling me into this might finally bring me the closure I'm looking for."

Jaime caught my eye and gave me a nearly imperceptible nod that said *I trust her*, and I decided that I did too. "So, where do we start?"

"We need to figure out who this woman was and how she died," Taylor said.

"I volunteer at the library, and my mom is the chair of the historical society. With all those resources, I'm sure we'll be able to find something," I said. "We can start with the history of the house and go from there."

Taylor nodded, but the tension hadn't left Jaime's shoulders.

"Isn't there anything I can do to protect myself while I'm stuck in here?" he asked.

"I can bring some stuff by tomorrow and try to banish some of the negative energy for starters," Taylor said, eyes wandering to the carvings around the front door.

"That's all you can do?"

"Hopefully, that's all you'll need for now," she said. When she looked back at Jaime, the expression on her face sent a shiver up my spine. "In the meantime, try not to get on her bad side."

CHAPTER 10
JAIME

I WAS ABSOLUTELY, WITHOUT a doubt, on this ghost's bad side. And the sick part was that for once in my life, I was actually trying to behave.

Even though I was dying to poke around the house, half out of genuine curiosity and half because I needed a distraction, I listened to Taylor and left everything untouched. I didn't rifle through the pantry outside the porcelain-tiled kitchen, and I didn't move the creepy tarnished silverware and wax-speckled candelabras from the dining room table set for a dinner that had never happened. I'd learned my lesson from the window, and I wasn't aiming for a repeat. That was why when I found a locked door on the third floor, I didn't dare try to jimmy it open. See? Very respectful.

Even so, the ghost was still lurking at the edges of my mind's eye. I could actually feel her in the house, more than I ever had before. Sometimes I thought I could see her, in my peripheral vision, but the second I turned to look, she was gone. It kept me in a constant state of panic, even when the sun was shining.

Night was a hundred times worse. Every time the sun started to set beyond the pines, the darkness that followed felt like a threat. Because no matter how vigilant I was during the day, I couldn't seem to keep her out of my dreams.

Sometimes I dreamed of my childhood home, the tiny single-story house the three of us had shared until it all fell apart. It was the home my dad had left pockmarked with fist-shaped holes in the drywall and my mom had flooded in an ocean of tears, so really it wasn't a home at all. I dreamed of the dark, tight spaces I would hide in to feel safe as adult-sized chaos erupted around me, of slammed doors and strained conversations poorly muffled by too-thin walls.

Other times I'd dream I was in the house in the woods, but I was even more trapped than I was in real life. I'd dream I was running down a hall that never ended, or falling down the stairs without being able to figure out which way was up and which was down. And the ghost was always there, leaning in to say the exact same thing: "You can't leave."

After two weeks, the days I spent in the house started to bleed together. I could only be sure time was passing because the cuts on my hands turned from scabs into shiny purple scars, and because Theo and Taylor visited me daily. They came rain or shine, which was the only reason I wasn't surprised when I heard them making their way through the woods on a blustery, pitch-black Wednesday morning.

The forest was completely transformed in the rain, lush and intimidating and jungle-like. A storm had blown in just a few minutes earlier, and rain pelted Theo ruthlessly as he fought through the massive ferns on the edge of the clearing. By the time he got to the porch, he was sopping wet. I was shocked that Theo, the most chronically overprepared person I'd ever met, had been caught off guard by the deluge. I only understood why a second later when Taylor emerged behind him, shielded from the storm by his blue umbrella. I felt a twinge in my stomach at that, but pushed it down before I had to look the feeling in the eye.

"She didn't know it was going to rain this morning," Theo panted, hands clasping his knees as he caught his breath.

"No shit. You look like a wet dog," I observed, trying not to let my eyes linger too long on how his hair, soaked from rain, was clinging to his forehead. "I'd invite you in to dry off, but, you know."

It took a second for my joke to hit home. When it did, Theo was still catching his breath, so he simply held up a middle finger in response. Of all the things in the world that could brighten my mood, I did not think Theo flipping me the bird would be one of them.

"Shouldn't you be at work?" I asked, stepping back from the door as he shook the rain from his hair. Without the sun as a guide, it was hard to tell what time it was, but it definitely seemed too early for him to be done with his regular shift.

"Took the day off," Theo said, pulling a stack of soggy papers out of his backpack. "I did bring you more reading material, though."

"My hero," I said, not entirely joking, as I caught a stack of photocopies of the *Saint Juniper Daily Messenger*.

It turned out being stuck in a haunted house that was slowly driving you insane was pretty boring without Wi-Fi, so I'd offered to help research in my ample free time. I was on obituary duty, keeping an eye out for sketchy deaths, while Theo and Taylor were focusing more on the house itself. I flipped through the photocopies as Theo unpacked my haul for the day and nudged it across the threshold. He'd also brought a flashlight, two cans of tomato soup, a blanket, and a liter of water.

"I'm still not sure how to start narrowing things down," Theo said with a sigh. "There's no way we can sift through so many files in so little time."

"What about the architecture?" I volunteered without really thinking, and Theo paused.

"What do you mean?"

"There's no way this type of crap"—I pointed at the intricate carvings on the eaves of the porch—"was in style for more than a handful of years. Maybe you can use it to pinpoint the year the house was built and go from there."

Theo scrutinized the carving, and when he turned back to me, his face had brightened. "That's an amazing idea, actually."

"I'm known to be brilliant from time to time."

That reply won a smile from Theo and, annoyingly, a small flutter from somewhere deep in my chest.

"All right, nonbeliever," Taylor said to Theo, shooing him away from the doorframe. "Step aside and let me do my work."

"I don't think that's fair," he grumbled, but retreated anyway. "I told you, I am trying to wrap my head around all this. Promise."

"Sure, sure. You're still the Dana Scully of the group, though," Taylor teased, and Theo scrunched his nose in response. Clearly, it wasn't the first time he'd been the butt of that joke, and there was that little pang of jealousy again, except this time I couldn't catch it before it turned sour.

I knew Theo was spending time with Taylor purely out of necessity, and that the whole reason he had even met her in the first place was because he was worried about me. Still, I had only just gotten used to the idea of the two of us being in this thing together, and I wasn't particularly keen on that changing. And maybe I didn't love that they had inside jokes.

"Does that make you Mulder?" Theo replied to Taylor.

"Obviously not," I interjected. "I'm Mulder. She's one of the feds."

Taylor shut me up by tossing me a bundle of herbs tied together with twine. "First of all, how dare you. Second, if that means I'm the boss, then I'll take it."

I flipped the herbs over in my hands, inspecting the tightly packed leaves as I went to retrieve a matchbook from the kitchen. Taylor had spent the last few days helping me smoke-cleanse the property. She'd explained that the smoke from healing plants had the potential to banish some of the negative energy in the house. Needless to say, I hadn't seen any results.

"How is this different from the last one you did?" Theo asked once I'd returned.

"It's a different combination of herbs," Taylor replied evenly. She already had a shallow plastic bowl balancing on the porch railing, collecting rainwater so I could douse the bundle once I was finished. "Cedar and rosemary wrapped in bay leaves. It's about as close to 'hey, sorry you're dead' as you can get with herbology."

Ditto, sorry you're dead, I thought as I held a burning match to the tip of one of the leaves. It took a moment for the fire to catch in the merciless humidity, but once it did, the smoke that wafted from the herbs was thick and fragrant. I began my slow lap around the ground floor, starting with one of the two sitting rooms that mirrored each other on either side of the entryway.

"How's everything with the ghost going?" Theo called from the door. I was glad he couldn't see my face fall when he brought it up.

"Uh, it's going," I called back flatly.

"That's code for not very good, right?" Taylor called, and I snorted.

"Pretty much," I said once I'd finished my lap. "I haven't touched anything, but she won't leave me alone. It's like, get a hobby or something. I can't possibly be that interesting to watch."

"You really hit the jackpot with this place, huh?" Taylor said, and I grimaced in response. She slid the bowl of rainwater over the edge of the threshold, and I put out the smoking bundle of herbs with one sizzling dunk. "How did you even end up out here in the first place?"

"It's not a very good story."

Taylor and Theo exchanged a look, and I knew what she was going to say before she opened her mouth. My strict one-question-a-day rule had dissolved into a kind of a game with us. Every time I resisted a conversation, Theo or Taylor would use it as a hall pass to get me to talk.

"I'm cashing in my question," she said. "Spill."

Of course, I could have just shot the questions down. But being on high alert with the ghost was starting to chip away at my sanity, and I'd take any opportunity to extend their visits by a few minutes if it meant less time on my own. That, and I was starting to notice I didn't really mind them asking.

So in the hushed chaos of the storm, I told them about my two weeks in Saint Juniper. I told them about how quickly my nerves had worn thin, and how when I felt like I couldn't breathe, the valley had called to me.

"You felt like it was pulling you in?" Taylor said with a frown. "You didn't mention that before."

"I mean, I guess. Is that important?"

"It might be. What did it feel like?"

"Uh, I don't know. It felt sort of jittery, like adrenaline or a runner's high or something," I said, noticing that Theo was leaning in too, though I'm not sure it was for the same reason. He tended to do that, listen a little bit too closely to whatever I was saying and look at me a half a second too long. But this time, instead of making me restless, his attention felt more like a comfort than anything else. "Like I said, I was really stressed. Maybe it was just anxiety. I remember feeling the same way growing up, like I was under a microscope all the time. Granted, I don't know if it was because my parents were never married or because I was the only Mexican kid within a fifty-mile radius or what, but the pressure was too much. It still is."

For a split second, I worried I had shared too much. The tense, mythical atmosphere of the forest hung around us for a moment before Taylor broke the silence.

"I had a hunch you were Latino too," she said. When I shot her a questioning look, she grinned and pointed a finger at her own face. "It's the eyebrows."

"Well," I said, "maybe if I had a little less eyebrow, then I wouldn't be here."

We looked at each other for a beat, then burst out laughing. The conversation didn't feel nearly as heavy as it was before, and I was grateful she had managed to break the ice.

"If I feel suffocated in Saint Juniper, I can't even imagine how bad it must be for you," Theo said once we finally calmed down. I could tell he wasn't just saying that to placate me, but it still surprised me.

"You feel that way too?"

"Not in the exact same way, but yeah. Everyone here has known me since the day I left the hospital. If I sneeze the wrong way, everyone in town knows in under an hour," he said, hugging his knees. I hadn't even considered that Theo would understand how I felt, but when he put it that way, it made sense. "Most of the time I just fantasize about the day I can get out of here."

"I don't blame you, man. Saint Juniper seems brutal," Taylor said. When my eyes met hers, I was surprised by the kindness behind them. "I'm not surprised everyone was flocking to you like fresh meat. Wolf's Head isn't as bad, but it's still a small, ridiculously white town in Vermont. People will find a reason to make you feel small no matter what, but you didn't deserve that."

"Thanks," I blurted out before I lost my nerve or my fleeting desire to be polite. "It makes me feel a little better that it's not just me."

But right when I thought the conversation was over, Taylor spoke up again.

"Is that why you go by Jaime?" she said, pronouncing my name *jay-mee* instead of the Spanish way, *high-may*. She must have noticed I tensed, because she held her hands up in response. "I'm not judging, I swear. You gotta do what you gotta do."

"It's complicated," I replied, suddenly fascinated with a hang-nail on my index finger. "Also, you already used your question."

Out of the corner of my eye, I saw Theo lean in. "Can I ask it as mine?"

"No, you can't ask two loaded questions in a row. It's against the rules."

"That's not fair," he said, brows drawing together so the near-permanent crease between them got much deeper. If I hadn't known better, I would have said he was pouting. "What am I supposed to do instead? Ask who your celebrity crush is?"

"I guess. It's River Phoenix, by the way," I replied with an easy smile. "See, I can be honest."

Theo looked totally lost. "I have no idea who that is."

"Google it," I said, but Taylor had pulled my attention away from the conversation. She was staring at the sky, which had faded to a dangerous shade of cobalt. "Worried about the roads flooding?"

She nodded. Both she and Theo looked genuinely sad they had to leave, and I may have been genuinely sad to see them go. I watched them gather their things, but just as Taylor braced herself to head back out into the storm, Theo told her he'd stay behind and meet her at the car. Once she retreated into the woods with his umbrella, Theo turned to me.

"I haven't mentioned foster care to Taylor, but I think she should know about the DCF visit, given we only have a month or so left to figure this out," he said. I wasn't sure what I was expecting him to bring up, but I felt a little disappointed regardless. He quickly added, "If it's all right with you, of course."

I nodded carefully. "I'm cool with that. You can fill her in."

"Okay, I will, then," he said, fiddling with the hair at the nape of his neck. "By the way, I think that was the most I've ever heard you talk in one go. Earlier, when you were telling us about moving. It was nice."

My stomach did a flip entirely without my permission. "Yeah, I guess it was for me too."

Truthfully, there was even more I wanted to talk to him about when it came to foster care. I had spent the entire day Theo was visiting Michelle wondering what she'd say to him, what he'd think of her house, of my stupid empty bedroom. I was sure he'd see the garbage bag I'd dragged back and forth across state lines more times than I could count and think I was pathetic.

But of everything he brought me after the visit, none of it came from what was packed away in that bag. When I finally built up the nerve to ask him how it had gone, Theo just confirmed that he'd told Michelle I was safe and grabbed some of my things. I was too anxious to ask for more info, so I just left it at that.

It was probably for the best that I didn't know, but I also had to wonder how much Michelle had told him about my time in foster care. I didn't necessarily want Theo to know all the gory ins and outs, but for some odd reason, I felt this intense need to explain myself to him. Or, god forbid, open up.

"The clothes you brought me from Michelle's place are awful, by the way," I blurted. *Nice, very smooth.* "How did you manage to only grab the worst clothes I own?"

"I did my best," Theo shot back, but I could tell he was trying not to laugh. "Speaking of, I brought you one more thing."

After rummaging through his bag, he tossed me a power bank.

"What's this?"

"It's for your phone, so you can text me if you need anything. I wrote our numbers on the back."

I turned the block over in my hands and sure enough, there they were on a little yellow Post-it. I resisted the urge to run my thumb over the neatly printed numbers next to his name.

"Thanks," I said awkwardly. Then, thinking better of being civil, "I'm not going to text you, though."

Theo had already turned to go, but when he glanced back, the knowing expression on his face made my heart pinch in a way that felt dangerously close to affection.

"I know," he replied. "But that's what friends do. Save it anyway."

Before I could think to argue, he jogged off into the woods, disappearing as quickly as he'd materialized. Long after he left, I still had the Post-it note with his phone number in my hand.

CHAPTER 11
TAYLOR

AS THEO PLOPPED YET another book about Vermont history onto the massive stack of titles in front of me, it was a little hard not to feel like I was trapped in the world's longest detention.

I had been sitting at one of the dark wood tables at the back of the library for the better part of the afternoon, and other than getting double vision from reading so many books, I hadn't accomplished much. It was a godsend we were at least able to narrow our search down to a few years. Per Jaime's suggestion, we compared the intricately carved woodwork to a dozen architecture websites and figured out that the house had to have been built between 1880 and 1900. Even then, there was a lot of history to sift through with very little else to go on.

Theo must have just finished helping a patron and bought himself some time to rest, because he slumped down into the chair to my left. Even though I had lived in town for five years, I had never actually set foot in the library before. The space was nice enough that I almost forgot why, until a woman approached the table with a tall stack of books in her arms.

"There's a girl up front who needs some help finding her summer reading," she said. "Bit of a bold approach to wait and request your books at the end of July, but be a doll and help her out?"

I realized belatedly this was Theo's supervisor, Carla. It took a second for her to notice me, but when she did, her eyes focused on my hair first, then eventually made their way to my face. I resisted the urge to smooth my curls down. I knew I should have done something with them before I left the house, but after breaking two hair ties in fifteen minutes, I'd cut my losses.

"And who do we have here?" she asked.

"Taylor Rivera Bishop," I said, but she still wasn't quite looking *at* me. "Nice to meet you."

Theo didn't seem to notice anything odd about our exchange. Truthfully, this was one of the reasons I didn't like taking up space in public, at least not in Wolf's Head. I hated this kind of attention, the kind that felt like people were looking at you as an object instead of a person. It made me want to disappear. Hell, it made me understand why Jaime *did* disappear.

"I've got a history question for you, if you have a minute," Theo said to Carla. "Do you know anything about Saint Juniper in the late eighteen hundreds?"

"If you're suggesting I was alive back then, I might have to fire you," she said with a smile.

"Oh, hardly. You don't look a day over a hundred and ten," he replied, then neatly dodged her when she tried to whack him with one of the smaller books in her hands. "If I wanted to do a little research about landowners in Saint Juniper, like who owned the land my house was built on, where would I find that?"

"If you really want to do a deep dive, you could probably ask a historian at one of the colleges in Burlington," she started, then shifted gears when she saw the dubious look Theo and I shared. "We also have a registry of deeds on the library intranet. Why don't you start there? Get the information straight from the horse's mouth, so to speak."

Theo chewed his lip, lost in thought, and as usual, his facial expression betrayed him. Carla's eyes flitted between us, and she peered at me again with barely concealed curiosity.

"Are you getting him into trouble?" she asked.

"What? No," Theo floundered as I tried to stomach the sting of her accusation. "We're doing . . . a summer history report. Very aboveboard."

Seemingly satisfied by that answer, Carla disappeared into the nonfiction section to help a patron, and Theo led me over to his desk. I watched, a little deflated by the interaction, as he pulled the registry of deeds up on his work laptop. He clicked through to filter by year, selected 1880 through 1890, and—

"Six hundred results?" I read off the screen. "Are you kidding?"

"Well, according to the dozen history books I read this morning, there was a huge influx of immigrants moving up to Vermont back then," he said with a sigh, tapping the screen. "Oh, great. And the only way to search is by address, which we obviously don't have."

The lack of information we had on the house was starting to make our whole investigation feel impossible. But as Theo scrolled aimlessly through the list of deeds, I realized maybe we didn't need an address after all.

"Wait, do you think you have access to old maps on here?"

"I mean, probably. But I've only been to the house on foot. I don't think I'd know where it is from a bird's-eye view."

"But I think I do," I said excitedly. "My mom drew a sort of map before she passed. It might have been directions to the house. If you pull up a map, I could try to compare them."

After a few minutes of clicking around, Theo did manage to find a collection of old maps through the town hall site. Most of them were in tatters by the time they were scanned into the system, and some had faded to the point that we hardly recognized our own towns. But then, on a map from 1892, the erratic lines marking streams and pathways actually started to look familiar. And there, about four miles south and three miles west from the southern edge of Wolf's Head, a title was scribbled across the page.

"The Blackwood Estate," Theo read. "Kind of ominous. That has to be it, right?"

"I mean, it's definitely fitting."

He turned to me with a megawatt smile. "Now we have a name and a year. We can double-check the newspapers to make sure we haven't missed anything, and I'll ask my mom if I can look through the files from historical society too."

"Sounds like it's worth a shot," I said, smiling back.

"God, I'm so relieved," he sighed happily, melting into his chair a little. "We finally have some good news for Jaime."

Cute, I thought. "You said you two didn't know each other before all this, right?"

"Right. Well, technically we went to elementary school together for a few years, but Jaime says he doesn't remember." Theo tilted his head toward me. "Why do you ask?"

"No reason," I said with a shrug. After searching my face again, Theo turned his attention back to the map, clicking through to print us both a copy.

Theo seemed to spend a lot of time worrying about Jaime, and worrying in general. I figured that was why he insisted on coming with me to the house every day even though I told him I could manage on my own. But it was sweet how much he cared, and I was relieved we had good news too.

I hadn't quite figured Jaime out yet, because the more time I spent with him, the more he surprised me. One afternoon, we'd been huddled together at the greenhouse entrance tying protection spell bags to entrance points of the house. Theo had gone out into the woods to clear some brush off the path we usually followed to the meadow, and when it was just the two of us, seemingly out of nowhere, Jaime asked me about my mom.

"You said she was a witch too, right?"

I nodded, tossing him one of the little sachets filled with sage and sea salt. "She taught me everything I know. I just wish I'd had more time with her."

"Does all this make you miss her more, or does it make things easier?" he asked.

The question startled me so much that the first thing that popped into my head was the truth—it was a little of both. I almost said that the entire time I'd been preparing the bags for him, it had felt like she was in the room with me. But I didn't want him to feel guilty, and I couldn't say all that and hold myself together at the same time. Instead, I just said, "She would be happy if she knew I was helping you."

The heavy silence that followed made it clear he'd noticed that I didn't answer his question.

"It doesn't really stop, though, does it?" he asked after a pause, reaching up to tie the sachet to the exposed iron framework at the door. With his chin tilted up like that, I couldn't see his face. It would have been hard to tell what he was feeling, but the roughness in his voice gave it away. "Missing her, I mean. There are days it's a little quieter, or it takes a different shape, but it's never really gone."

Again, I didn't know what to say. I thought about shutting down the conversation, but I couldn't remember the last time I'd been able to talk with someone who understood loss on that level. Most people I tried to talk to just treated grief like sadness, so I learned to keep my thoughts on it to myself. But somehow, he seemed to get it.

"Yeah, pretty much," I replied. "Everyone says the last stage of grief is acceptance, but that's a load of crap. I miss her every second of every day. She's still my first thought when I wake up and my last thought when I go to sleep, you know? How could I accept she's never coming back?"

"I don't really know. It's like, sometimes you're drowning, and sometimes you're treading water, but you're never really on land," he said, tightening the knot on the spell bag. "It's not that you accept they're gone and you're suddenly okay with it, you just end up accepting that not being okay is your new normal."

For a few beats, I just looked at him. Somehow, this person I'd only just met had made me feel more seen than any of the friends I'd kept for years. "Are your parents—?"

"No," he said simply. "Not dead, just gone."

We had moved on to tie the next sachet, and Theo and I eventually headed back into town, but that conversation played on a loop at the back of my mind for hours after the fact. Theo eventually told me about foster care, and it felt like the pieces of Jaime were beginning to fit together. He also told me about the DCF visit hanging over their heads, and now, mine.

But the more I learned about the house, the more questions I had. My mom had known about Blackwood and made the trek into the valley, so she must have been able to feel the ghost's presence like I had. But if that were true, why hadn't she helped it pass to the other side? I didn't have any of the answers I needed yet, but I knew I had to find them quick if we wanted to get Jaime out of there in one piece.

CHAPTER 12
THEO

WHEN I SAW THE number of file boxes packed into every square inch of our small, dim basement, I nearly turned around and went back upstairs empty-handed.

"The boxes are organized by year," my mom said, wiping her hands on a kitchen towel as she met me at the top of the basement stairs. I'd fibbed that I wanted to get ahold of as many primary sources as I could before starting APUSH in the fall, and she was more than happy to let me use the files. "If you're interested in this kind of thing, maybe you could join the historical society yourself after you graduate."

"Yeah, maybe," I murmured, not wanting to temper her enthusiasm. "It might be a little weird if I end up going to school out of state."

"Well, who knows if that will happen," she said breezily. "And it doesn't mean you can't come back and help out every once in a while. I'm sure everyone would love that."

"Your mother is right," my dad chimed in from behind her, settled in his customary spot on the sofa with his nose buried in the same book on World War II that I could have sworn he'd been reading for the last three years. He didn't look up to fully join the conversation, and my mom hardly spared him a glance. "People will expect you to stay involved. Plus, something like that would look good on your résumé."

Leave it to him to bring up post-grad when I wasn't even out of high school yet. I nodded along, my mind drifting back to the boxes in the basement. Just a few weeks earlier, applying to college had actually been my biggest problem in life. Now I was basically a glorified ghost hunter harboring more secrets than I could keep track of. For once, my own future wasn't the scariest thing on my mind.

There was no way I was going through the files in the dank basement, so I decided to move them into Grace's room instead. She was four years older than me, and her room had been vacant since she'd left for college. I was pretty displeased she'd made it out of Saint Juniper before me, even if it was just by benefit of being older. Plus—not that I would ever admit it to her—I missed her company much more than I expected.

High school might've been easier if she'd been there to help me. No doubt my parents' relationship would be going smoother too. She was the glue that held us all together, and things always felt a little fractured when she was gone. The pieces fit together again when she came home for Thanksgiving or Christmas, but they'd fall out of place as soon as we dropped her off at the airport. I couldn't truly be mad, since she had her own life now, on her way to getting her master's at one of the best universities in the country with a boyfriend who adored her.

If she could have seen me sprawled out on her old bedroom floor wading through historical documents for a complete stranger, she probably would've thought I'd lost my mind. That, or she would've jumped in to help me. Or maybe both.

I spent way too long sifting through the photographs, letters, and articles, making my way through nearly half of the boxes before I finally came across something useful. It was a photo of Blackwood dated 1896, so grainy I had to squint to make sure it was actually the same house. The estate was stunning in its heyday, but the front door was flung open, and there were thin ropes cordoning off the porch. It looked like a photo from a crime scene, but when I turned it over, there were no details written on the back to give it any context. Still, it didn't feel like a total dead end. At the very least, I got confirmation we had the right place and some kind of crime had happened there.

Eventually, I grabbed the rest of the files from that year and migrated to my bedroom, planning to keep searching for information on Blackwood until I got tired enough to sleep. The window behind my headboard was cracked open, and the cool night air carried in the sound of crickets chirping as I settled onto my bed.

I barely had time to dig into the next group of files before my phone buzzed, half buried under a pile of papers. When I fished it out and unlocked it, I was surprised to see that my friend Sarah had sent a string of photos to our group chat. She was visiting her extended family in Germany, and it was one of the only check-ins I'd gotten from her the whole month. But summers were usually like that: quiet, a little lonely. Most of my friends from school were traveling with their families, but my dad didn't like to take time off for something as impractical as a vacation.

It was hard not to feel a bit envious. Sarah was out stargazing in the mountains while the only things I had to look at were the string of twinkle lights woven through my headboard and the massive pile of research at my feet. But once the moment of jealousy passed, I felt a little silly. After all, the company I'd been keeping lately was far from boring.

Ever since I'd talked with Michelle, things had felt different between me and Jaime. He wasn't nearly so prickly, and we were actually starting to have real conversations. There was a small chance I was beginning to enjoy spending time with him. The only downside was that gave my mind more material to pick over when it drifted in the middle of my commute or a particularly boring shift at the library. Instead of replaying our arguments, I found myself thinking about the picture-perfect profile of his straight nose when he refused to look at me, or the cut of his cheekbones, or the sound of his voice in the morning, deep and quiet and surprisingly rough.

My phone, which I had all but forgotten about even though it was still in my hand, brightened again as Sarah sent another selfie. Clicking on the photo, I tried to look at her in the most neutral, unbiased way I could manage. She was pretty, I had always known that. Objectively, lots of girls were pretty. But objectively, lots of boys were pretty too. I mean, that was just a matter of having eyes, right? It wasn't the kind of thing that should have sent me spiraling.

But for some reason, the thought that Jaime might be pretty made me want to bury my head in my pillow. I hadn't been able to pinpoint why he was so attractive at first, but at some point, I realized it was because everything about him was in abundance: the long hair, the thick lashes and brows, the full lips, even his big personality. There was so much to take in and, in turn, so much to be confused about. I tried my best to untangle the butterflies in my stomach from the purely factual image of his face inside my head and, predictably, failed.

It didn't help that his celebrity crush comment had been bouncing around my head like a pinball all week. I hadn't thought much of it in the moment, but then I did look up River Phoenix. When I saw he was a guy, my stomach did a somersault. Technically, who Jaime was into shouldn't have even mattered. But I found myself wanting to know for sure whether it was an offhand joke or a moment of honesty where he was trying to tell me something. If he was being serious, would that make things more or less complicated for me?

I wasn't so dense that I didn't realize how daydreaming about Jaime probably did mean something, no matter how much I wanted to deny it. Even if it was subconscious, charting the hours between when I had seen him last and when I would see him next was . . . well, it was notable, to say the least. I wondered idly if I'd ever know what it felt like to be sure of anything.

"You're still up?"

I flipped my phone facedown on my bed before I had time to consider how suspicious it would look, and my mom, who had materialized in my bedroom doorway, raised a brow at me.

"No—I—I mean, not really," I stammered. *God, what is wrong with me?* "I'm going to sleep soon. Why?"

"Your father and I are heading to bed. I just wanted to say good night," she said carefully.

"Oh, well, good night," I squeaked. With one more glance at my phone, my mom retreated down the hallway.

Her appearance had snapped me out of my overthinking daze, enough that I finally organized the nest of papers spread across my comforter and moved them to the desk at the far end of my room. My phone buzzed again, and I scooped it up on my way to the bathroom, thinking it was another message from Sarah. I paused in the hallway when I noticed it was from a number I didn't recognize, and it wasn't until I read the message that I knew it was from Jaime: *i found something, come to the house asap*

I read the message again, then a third time, a thousand thoughts flitting through my head at once. At the speed my pulse was racing, it might as well have been a booty call instead of the world's vaguest text. But knowing Jaime, something significant must have happened for him to text me in the first place.

I peered down the hallway. There was no light leaking out from under the door to my parents' room. Odds were my dad was already asleep, and even if my mom wasn't too, I seriously doubted she would notice if I was gone for a few hours. I had always secretly wanted a reason to sneak out of my house in the middle of the night. Up until that point, I'd never considered it would be to meet up with a boy.

I turned on my heel and went back into my room before I talked myself out of it. Skidding to a stop in front of my mirror, assessing whether I could afford to go out the way I was already dressed. I made the executive decision to change out of my faded, ratty The Strokes T-shirt and into a sweatshirt that didn't have nearly as many holes in it. Nothing could be done about my hair, which was the case almost every day of my life.

I had long before taken the screen off my window so I could sit on the roof and watch the sun set during the summer. But when I moved to open it, I paused. Jaime really was taking over my life in more ways than one, and I was scared by how little that scared me. Giddy energy bubbled up in my chest as I braced my hands against my window frame, looking out into the indigo night. Fireflies hung suspended in the cool summer air, and for a moment, it felt like time had stopped. *Am I really doing this?*

But as soon as I asked myself the question, I knew the answer. After seventeen years of playing by the book, maybe it was time for me to actually start living a little.

CHAPTER 13
JAIME

A FEW MINUTES PAST eleven p.m., I heard a noise out in the depths of the woods that I knew meant trouble.

The forest came alive at night in a way that always set my nerves on edge. The wildlife got more restless, and the shadows and movements out in the valley made me feel even more trapped than I did in the daytime. Add my anxiety about the ghost into the mix, and I felt worse than trapped. I felt like I was being hunted.

I had been curled up on one of the couches in a second-story bedroom, knees tight to my chest, when I heard the first rustle. And then another, and another, until the rustle was less of an isolated incident and more of a steady disturbance. This didn't seem like a fox or raccoon foraging for a late-night snack. Then it hit me—those sounds were too big to be made by an animal, but just the right size to be made by a human.

I got up and stared anxiously into the darkness from the second-floor window, and the darkness stared rigidly back. At first I didn't see anything, but then the silver beam of a flashlight cut through the night and my nerves all at once. My heart leapt into my throat, fear taking hold of me with an iron grip.

I scrambled into one of the other bedrooms, which was a bit worse for wear compared to the rest of the house. For once, I was grateful for the mess. I found a piece of debris, a length of crown molding that had ripped away from the wall, and decided it would be good enough to wield as a bat. There was a good chance it wouldn't inflict any real damage, but it could at least give someone a mean faceful of splinters.

I readied myself for a fight as I crept down the staircase and into the foyer. The light from the flashlight cast a soft white glow under the front door, so I figured the trespasser had made it to the porch. I took a deep breath, flung open the door, and froze when I saw a familiar mop of strawberry-blond hair and a startled set of blue-green eyes.

"Theo?" It came out more like a squeak than a question. "What the actual hell, man? You scared the shit out of me!"

"What do you mean? You literally texted me to come over," Theo said, his eyes following my makeshift weapon as I moved it off my shoulder. "Were you going to *hit me with that?*"

"Yes, I was going to hit you with this. I thought you were a creep! It's the middle of the night. What are you doing out here?"

"You said ASAP," he said, voice rising in exasperation as I stifled a laugh. "That means as soon as possible. How else was I supposed to interpret it?"

"I don't know, like, as soon as the sun is out. Plus, I didn't even think the message went through. I tried sending it hours ago, but my phone said it was undelivered." I tossed the piece of wood in my hands aside. I could tell he was still a little mad by the furrow between his brows, so before I lost my nerve, I added, "I'm glad you came."

Theo rolled his eyes, but his little smile told me that all was forgiven. "Since I'm here, the least you can do is show me what you found."

After so much fuss, I almost felt embarrassed to show him. But I retraced my steps to the bedroom anyway, and when I returned with one of the photocopies of the newspaper Theo had given me, the excitement on his face made it all feel worth it.

"I read through the papers you brought me," I said, crouching down to slide the photocopy across the weathered wood of the porch. He followed suit. "Check this out."

I watched as Theo shined the flashlight onto the paper, his eyes tracking across the smudgy print of the 1896 edition until they landed on the right paragraph. It was just a few lines in the "local intelligence" section of the paper, but I'd nearly shouted when I found it.

Mrs. Josephine T. Harris, who had been in failing health for the past three years, died on Sunday shortly after she set out for the Blackwood Estate. She leaves behind a husband and son, to whom her widespread reputation for kindness and unvarying integrity will be some consolation, we trust, for their heavy bereavement. An investigation will be conducted into the unnatural manner of Mrs. Harris's demise.

"I know it's vague," I said, squinting down at the paper in the bluish glow of the flashlight. "But it's something, right?"

Theo nodded, eyes still glued to the paper. Then he did the one thing I didn't want to admit I was hoping for: he looked up and smiled at me like we had just won the lottery. "This is *amazing*," he said, and I had a hard time keeping myself from grinning back. "I found a photo of Blackwood that looked like some old-fashioned crime photo. This must have been why."

I nodded. The relief on his face was the reason I'd texted in the first place. Finding something good would help ease the pressure on Theo to find answers, and I was happy I could finally pull my weight with our search. And sure, I also might have sent him the message just because I needed an excuse to text him, but that was beside the point.

"If Josephine died here, she's probably the one who's haunting the place. If I can find more info on her, maybe Taylor will have enough material to do her magic and get you out of here," he said, then paused. "Why did you only text me, though?"

If it hadn't been Theo who asked, I would have thought I was being teased. The genuine curiosity on his face was the only thing helping me keep my composure enough to cover my ass.

"You came to mind first, I don't know," I mumbled. Then, because self-sabotage was my specialty, I blurted, "Why, do you like her or something?"

Theo went from puzzled to entirely nonplussed in a second flat. "No, do you?"

I blinked at him. "She's not exactly my type."

"What's that supposed to mean?"

"Well, for starters, I like guys," I retorted, and instantly regretted it. Not because I didn't want him to know, but because I hadn't had time to think before it came tumbling out.

"Oh," Theo said quietly. I searched his face for any sign of disgust, but the only giveaway he was even a little surprised was that one of his brows twitched. Then, by some miracle, he just shrugged. "All right. I can show her tomorrow if you want."

"Uh, thanks," I said. His reaction, or lack of one, didn't stop my pulse from racing a hundred miles a minute. I decided to change the subject before I dug myself into an even deeper hole. "How did you manage to duck out, by the way? Aren't your parents gonna kill you for staying out late?"

"They were asleep when I left. As long as I'm back soon, I doubt they'll notice I'm gone," he replied, sinking down to sit against the doorframe, opposite the side I usually hovered around.

I settled in too, more grateful for his company than I'd ever have admitted outright, and the evening quickly devolved into a venting session about Theo's parents. Part of me always thought hearing about his life in Saint Juniper would leave me feeling resentful, but it never did. It was a bridge, a window into the life of someone I was starting to care about more than I'd ever thought I could. It was like walking past an open window and hearing soft laughter from inside. *Oh, so that's what I've been missing.*

Theo's life was far from perfect, I knew that now. His mom was well-meaning and sweet, but tried to keep the peace so much that Theo barely felt like she was being real with him. His dad was a Saint Juniperite through and through, so concerned with appearances that he was hardly present in any way that mattered. He was a lawyer by profession and personality, and it seemed Theo butted heads with him the most.

"I guess the cashier at the general store mentioned I've been buying a lot of my own food recently, so the other day my dad cornered me and told me to stop," Theo said. "He didn't even care why I was buying it, he just went, 'People are going to think we're neglecting you.' Can you believe that?"

I let out a long whistle. "A very admirable bid to gain entry to the elite Disinterested Dads Club. I'm actually the sitting president, but you can be the treasurer if you want."

"Well, that sucks," Theo said, "but at least we have something in common, right?"

Technically, he was right, but something about that observation startled me. I'd spent most of the time I'd known Theo assuming he couldn't possibly understand anything about my upbringing, a sort of knee-jerk jealous reaction whenever I met anyone who seemed more normal than me.

"Yeah, I guess we do," I said tentatively.

"I've never heard you talk about your dad," Theo said, but it sounded more like a question than a statement.

I shrugged, not sure if he could even see me in the dark. "There's not much to say. He bailed on us when I was really young, I wouldn't even be able to remember his face if I didn't look like him myself. He didn't teach me shit about my heritage, not that it really mattered anyway."

"I'm sorry," Theo started, but I just shrugged again.

"When I got matched with my first social worker, she told me it'd be easier if everyone just thought I was white. Families are more likely to foster a white boy with an easy-to-pronounce name than a brown boy, y'know?"

When I'd told the social worker I was Mexican, she had looked puzzled. *But only half*, she'd said. With a few clicks, she changed the ethnicity in my file to White/Caucasian. *Trust me, you'll thank me later.*

"Is the system like that for everyone?" Theo asked.

I thought about how young I was back then, how I'd swung my legs back and forth in the chair as I sat and waited for my file to be processed, and how little I'd understood about that pivotal moment in my life.

"Most of the time, it's worse," I replied.

And then some of the pieces of my story I had packed up tightly for ages started to unfold. I finally told him about foster care—*really* told him—and about how lucky I was that none of my homes were dangerously bad, but they weren't good either. I told him how relocating back to Saint Juniper was my last chance for normalcy before I was on my own, and how I didn't want to be chewed up and spat out by the system like my foster siblings were once they turned eighteen.

Theo listened intently the entire time, hugging his knees to his chest and resting his head against the doorjamb as he peppered me with more questions. And then, a little past midnight, he asked me the one thing I didn't want to answer.

"What about your mom? What's she like?"

A hollowness settled in my chest as Theo waited patiently, and I thought long and hard before I answered him.

"She's really pretty, from what I remember. Beautiful, actually," I said quietly, then paused.

I knew I could steer the conversation wherever I wanted from there. I could go on about how I had her nose or how she sang me to sleep on stormy nights, but I didn't want to. Talking about her like that would just be a collection of half-truths, and I didn't want to give Theo half-truths anymore. When I got up the nerve to say what I needed to say, I could feel the words burning me up like acid before they came out of my mouth.

"She dumped me at a shopping mall. Most common place to abandon kids, apparently. I didn't realize what was happening, because she didn't say goodbye, she just kept saying she was sorry." I saw Theo lift his head from the door out of the corner of my eye, but before he had the chance to react, I added, "She always acted like there was something wrong with me."

"What? Why?"

"I don't know, honestly. Maybe she could tell I was gay before I figured it out myself. Maybe there's something else wrong with me that I don't even know about."

Theo sounded strangely upset. "I wish you didn't talk about yourself like that."

"There's no point in sugarcoating it," I countered, but there was a lump in my throat that was winning before I could even think of swallowing it down. "It was like, she fucked up her life having me so young, and I wasn't even a good consolation prize. I don't know if I ever saw her happy, and I think it was my fault."

"Jaime—"

"It's true, don't tell me it's not just to make me feel better," I said, turning my face away from him. "By the time she left me, it just felt . . . I don't know. It felt like she was doing both of us a favor."

"Jaime," Theo said softly. "Look at me."

I knew it was a mistake the second I glanced over. The expression on Theo's face pushed me over the edge of an emotional cliff I hadn't realized I was standing on until it was too late. Something in me that had been waiting to break for years finally splintered apart. I could feel the edges of it tearing at me from the inside out. It wasn't a clean break; I feared it wouldn't set right, that it would never heal and I would feel jagged and ruined forever.

"You know, I've realized a lot of kids worry that their parents love them but don't particularly like them," I breathed into the darkness, squeezing my eyes shut to stop their stinging. "But I don't think my mom ever even loved me in the first place. I don't think anyone ever has."

For a moment, the night was so quiet I could hear the second hand on Theo's watch ticking. My heart was hammering in my chest, and part of me was afraid he could hear that too.

"I'm sorry," he whispered, and I could tell he meant so much more than just those two words alone.

We sat in silence for a little while, and Theo let what I'd said hang in the air between us undisturbed. I was thankful he didn't try to comfort me. I had been thankful for him every second since I'd met him. Not just for saving my life, but for conversations like this. For helping me feel like I wasn't completely on my own. When I looked over at him, though, his brows were pulled together doing this pinched, sad little thing I hated. He looked heartbroken.

"I'll give you an extra turn," I said suddenly, willing him to stop looking at me that way. "Another question. You get a free turn."

Theo hummed thoughtfully, and I could sense we were in that space between sleeping and waking where you could say anything. A voice in the back of my head told me he probably shouldn't stay, that the house was dangerous so late at night and that he would get in trouble if he didn't head home soon, but I ignored it.

"Can I ask you something you might not want to answer?" Theo asked after a pause.

"It's never stopped you before."

"How did you know—" he started, then paused so long I almost thought he had fallen asleep. When he spoke up again, his voice sounded different. "How did you know you liked boys?"

The question felt like it was way out of left field, but I figured there was some connection in Theo's head and I had just missed how he got from A to Z in the silence. Did him asking mean what I thought it meant?

"Jaime?" Theo asked anxiously.

"I'm thinking." After mulling it over for a beat, I decided to tell the truth no matter how cringy it sounded. "I think I kind of always knew, but it clicked because the love songs on the radio started to make sense. They felt so corny if I imagined they were about girls, but if I thought about boys, it was a whole different story. It was just this feeling of knowing exactly what I wanted. Does that make sense?"

Theo stayed silent, and I held my breath waiting for his reaction. But when he spoke again, it wasn't what I expected. "I'm not sure if that type of feeling is meant for someone like me."

My first instinct was to argue with him, to tell him that he was a million times more deserving of that type of feeling than someone like me, but I didn't. Instead, I said, "You don't know until you know."

Theo nodded, and I could tell his brain was a hundred miles away. I squinted through the darkness to try to make out his expression, but it was lost in the blackness of the night. I was glad he hadn't made fun of my answer, but I tried not to get too hopeful about him asking in the first place. Hope was something I wasn't used to having, and I knew I was hoarding it when it came to Theo. I worried it was bound to catch up with me in the end.

"Hey, Jaime?" Theo murmured.

"Yeah?"

"Do you think we'll still be friends once you get out of here?"

Theo asked it with a perfect innocence that only he could manage. It didn't feel like a weighted question, just like he was thinking out loud. I wanted to say we weren't really friends, but for the first time, it felt like I'd be lying. If anything, it felt a little like we had gone past friends into something else entirely. So instead, I replied, "It would be a little weird if we weren't."

Theo didn't say anything in return, but I swore I saw the ghost of a smile on his face as my lids became heavy.

———

When I drifted back into consciousness hours later, my face felt pleasantly warm. For some strange reason, my first thought was that Theo had his hand on my cheek. When I peeled my eyes open, I realized it was only the warmth from a beam of sunlight.

But Theo *was* there, hair was tossed wildly across his forehead and eyelashes looking nearly translucent in the morning light. His mouth was slightly open, but instead of looking like a mouth breather, he looked peaceful. Perfect. Of course he would look like that when he was sleeping. Clearly, the universe wanted me to suffer.

For once, I was glad the barrier was there. If it wasn't, I might have done something stupid like reach out to touch his hair, or trace the spot on his temple where his freckles met the edge of his hairline. Instead, I stared at him a minute or two longer than was strictly necessary, then decided to wake him up.

"Theo?" His eyelashes fluttered and I tried again, louder. "Theo, wake up."

His head shot up at record speed. "What's wrong, what happened?"

"Nothing's wrong," I said, settling back to watch him panic. "I mean, it's morning. You slept here last night, so if that qualifies as something wrong, then sure."

"Oh my god," he said, jumping to his feet. It truly amazed me how quickly he could get worked up. "Oh god, my parents are going to kill me."

I silently watched him scramble to collect his things. Then, because I couldn't resist, I asked, "Is it just me or does this kinda feel like you're doing the walk of shame?"

"Don't start with me," he shot back, fixing me with a searing look. I smiled sunnily. "I'll see you later if I'm not grounded for life."

I waved him off and watched in amusement as he pushed through the underbrush until his silhouette faded into the trees. I was too tired to make my way upstairs to sleep on the sofa, and the daylight felt safer than the shadows inside the house, so I stretched out in the beam of long golden light shining into the entryway. I dreamed of sunlight and Theo well into the afternoon, my hands still itching to touch his hair. I didn't realize it until later, but that was the first time in weeks I had been able to sleep through the night.

CHAPTER 14
TAYLOR

I DIDN'T WAKE UP on Friday planning to commit petty theft, but you know what they say: life comes at you fast.

It all started with a text from Theo. *Major breakthrough*, it said. *Stop by the library later if you have time.* I probably should have been happy he was making progress, but with the date blaring at me from my lock screen, all it did was add fuel to the fire that was already burning under my ass. August 1. One month until the DCF visit, one month to unravel Jaime's mystery and figure out what the hell the valley was hiding from me.

For the last week, I had been turning my house upside down looking for a connection between Blackwood and my mom. I searched through every junk drawer and cabinet for another scrap of paper or missing piece to explain what she'd been doing out there, or who could have wiped the house clean. I came up with a whole lot of nothing.

And on top of that, I was starting to suspect that the ghost haunting Jaime was even more complicated than I initially thought. One thing that struck me as a little odd was how Theo was able to pass food through the barrier. As far as I remembered, if a ghost sealed you in, nothing could go in or out. But that was the problem: I couldn't *really* remember. I needed my mom's grimoire. It was the only way I could feel prepared once it came time to help the ghost pass to the other side. Without it, my only references were the books we sold at the shop, and I tried to inconspicuously peruse the bookshelves every chance I got. When I got the text from Theo, I made a beeline for the shelves to double-check for any books I had missed.

I was still lost in thought staring at the spines when Elias sidled up next me.

"Sometimes I think you like to raise my blood pressure on purpose," he said, placing the last of our astrology guides on a shelf I couldn't reach. "Don't hover around the books. Customers won't come over if you do."

"Hovering isn't a crime. Or is reading too risky for you now?"

He sighed. "We're not having this conversation again," he said, heading back to the register. I followed.

"If I promise not to do any witchcraft at all, can I take a peek at Mom's grimoire? I just want to see something really quick."

"No, you can't. That information is dangerous, and if you use it, you'll just be putting another target on your back," he said. "You could have such a good life if you just put this behind you. *We* could have a good life. Why do you want to hold onto the past?"

"Because learning about witchcraft is my birthright. It's a part of who I am as much as anything else," I replied, trying my hardest to keep the combative edge out of my voice.

"Birthright" was the word my mom had always used to describe my gifts. It was the same word that was thrown around every time my parents argued in the last few years. I had pressed my ear against the seam of their bedroom door to try to listen in a dozen times, but I was never able to piece the conversations together.

"That's where you're wrong," Elias said, dragging a hand down his face. "You can't control how people treat you because of your heritage, but you can control this."

"Please don't talk to me like I'm a baby. I know I'm not like everyone else in this town. I have eyes."

"Y tienes sentido común, pero no lo estás usando, mija. You're lucky you don't see it as an issue, but you're . . . you're . . ." I waited for him to pick out the word he was looking for. "You're sheltered."

I was, maybe for the first time ever, totally speechless. Sheltered wasn't my classmates saying they were as dark as me after summer vacation. It wasn't my homeroom teacher scowling when she heard me speaking Spanish on the phone after class. It wasn't a white friend coming over after school, seeing my dad in the front yard, and asking me if he was the gardener. But I would never tell him any of that, not if it fed his complex. "If I am sheltered, whose fault is that?"

The bell over the door jingled, announcing the arrival of a new customer.

"That's enough," Elias said, low enough that the woman who just walked in wouldn't hear. "I don't want to hear about this again."

Absolutely classic, I thought as I turned on my heel. The shitty thing about fighting on the clock meant I couldn't go get some fresh air to cool off, but I could leave Elias alone on the shop floor to fend for himself with a stranger, and that was almost as satisfying. I used every ounce of the extra weight my heavy boots afforded me to stomp loudly into the storeroom.

Anna looked up from the tarot deck she had spread out in front of her. "Elias being Elias again?"

"You guessed it," I said, slumping into the chair next to her.

Normally, I would have vented to her about the fight. But ever since the day Theo came to the shop, Anna had been much more reserved. We hadn't been joking around like we usually did, and I couldn't tell if it was something I'd said or because I hadn't been spending as much time with her as I usually did.

I almost opened my mouth to ask her point-blank, but I wasn't sure I had the energy for another strained conversation. Instead, I shimmied my phone out of my back pocket, and the screen lit up. Theo's text was still there waiting for me, and I stifled a sigh. Elias was probably never going to see things from my point of view, and with the clock ticking for Jaime, I didn't have time to see if he would.

As Anna pulled another tarot card next to me, I thought about the conversation we'd had over coffee. *I get that you don't want to push him, but you're a whole-ass adult.* I'd made fun of her for it then, but maybe she was right. The only thing that stopped me from taking matters into my own hands was Elias's disapproval, but I already had all the disapproval I could possibly get. If I wanted answers, I couldn't ask for permission or wait around for them to fall into my lap. I had to go out and get them myself.

I pulled up the text conversation with Theo, typed out a message, and hit send before I lost my nerve. *Want to help me with a top-secret mission?*

Three dots popped up on the screen but then disappeared. Maybe this was a mistake.

"Are we on for our usual Friday night mayhem?" Anna asked, pulling another card. It was the Tower reversed. "I could probably use the tips."

"Actually, I'm not sure," I murmured, watching as the three dots popped up again. When a new message came through, I scooped up my phone in a second flat. It read, *Are we in Mission: Impossible now?*

Ew, hate Tom Cruise, I typed back. *I don't fw Scientologists.*

Three dots again, then another message from Theo. *What does "fw" mean?*

"Who are you texting?" Anna asked, hand hovering over the cards she'd pulled.

"No one," I said, quickly typing out another message. *Don't worry about it. Will you help or not?*

There was another long pause, and I thought for sure I had pressed my luck for the final time. But just before I tucked my phone into my back pocket to head onto the shop floor, it buzzed again. *What time do you need me to be there?*

CHAPTER 15
THEO

WHEN I LEFT THE valley the morning after I accidentally slept over, I wasn't intentionally trying to avoid Jaime. I barely had time to think while I was racing home. And just as I suspected, slipping back into my house unnoticed proved to be impossible. I only made it to the base of the stairs before I heard someone in the kitchen.

"Theo, a word?" my dad called.

Ugh. Why did he have to choose that specific morning to take his time leaving for the office? I padded into the sunlit kitchen, where my dad peered at me over the top of his newspaper. "What's up?"

"I trust you stayed out all night for a good reason," he said flatly, his icy eyes boring into mine. People always said my eyes looked just like his, which I never really liked to hear. "This isn't something I'm going to have to worry about, is it?"

I tried hard not to fidget. "Um, no?"

"Were you with . . . Hmm. Remind me, which is the girl with the blond hair?"

Of course my dad wouldn't remember the name of my friend of nearly ten years. "You're thinking of Sarah. And no, I've told you multiple times she's in Germany for the summer."

He set his paper down then, which meant I had officially reached DEFCON 2.

"I'd watch your tone if I were you. I think I'm cutting you an awful lot of slack, all things considered," he said in his best courtroom voice. "I ran into Mrs. Baker the other day, and she said you've barely been at the library the past few weeks. If you start shirking your responsibilities, people will notice. People will talk."

"I know that," I said tersely.

"I understand you want to have your fun. I did too when I was your age. But I don't think I need to remind you that this type of behavior can't continue when the school year starts. Do I?"

For the first time since I'd left the house in the woods, my mind flitted back to Jaime. It wasn't that I took what my dad said literally—with the DCF deadline, I wasn't thinking I would be sneaking out weeks into the fall semester. But the time I spent with Jaime was changing me, and maybe I would have to leave the person I was with him behind at the end of the summer too. My dad continued to stare at me expectantly.

"No," I replied. "No, you don't."

That conversation alone wasn't enough to shake me up, at least not completely. The simple thing that ended up doing me in was the playlist I put on for my drive to work.

As I drove, my mind wandered. I wasn't thinking of Jaime directly, but I could feel his presence at the edge of my mind. Between the intimate conversations the night before and drifting off to sleep with the sound of his voice wrapped around me, it was like he was everywhere all at once.

Before I even realized what I was doing, I found myself replaying the night in time with the song playing from my beat-up stereo system. I was searching through the lyrics just like Jaime said he'd done when he was younger, willing them to give me some kind of hint as to how I felt and what it meant.

The second I realized what I was doing, I tried to rein myself in, but of course, it didn't work. My feelings for him were a crooked, hapless kind of affection that didn't have limits, and they galloped ahead of whatever logic had carefully fenced them in before. It was like a piece of me had been let loose, and I worried I would never be able to hold it in my hands again.

But I wasn't ready to put a name to those feelings. That would mean rearranging everything I knew for myself to make room for something new, which was terrifying beyond belief. Someone with more courage than me might have crossed that bridge no problem—someone like Jaime, maybe—but I wasn't sure I could wrap my head around it even if I tried.

So when I got Taylor's cryptic text, it caught me at exactly the right moment, when I desperately needed a distraction from . . . well, everything. I managed to make it through work and the rest of my day without overthinking myself into a crisis, which felt like a real win. But when I parked across from the shop that evening and spotted Taylor out front, I wasn't so sure agreeing to help her with zero context had been the best choice.

"I told you, we're not open late tonight," she said, trying to make eye contact with a man who was having a little trouble staying upright. Even from a dozen feet away, I could smell alcohol wafting off him. "The psychic isn't even here."

"I thought *you* were psychic," he slurred loudly as I locked my car behind me. "You look like you know things."

Taylor shot him a look that would have been searing if he could see straight enough to notice it. "I do know things. I know that we're closed, and your wife is going to be pissed when you get home smelling like a distillery."

I was already making a beeline for the shop entrance, but before I had the chance to lend Taylor a hand, the man decided he wasn't going to press his luck and started to wander off.

"What was that about?" I asked, peering after him as he disappeared into the shadows at the end of the street. Taylor let out a sigh I could tell had been building up for a while and shepherded me inside, locking the door behind us.

"On Friday nights, Anna and I usually stay open late and do readings while my dad is out of town," she said, turning the sign on the door to Closed and shutting off some of the warm lights. "We usually get all the overflow from the bar down the street, but obviously we don't have time for that tonight."

"Right," I said, already feeling a bit out of my depth. If I had even half the confidence she did about disobeying her dad, I wouldn't know what to do with myself. "Speaking of, are you going to tell me what we're doing here, or do I have to stay in suspense?"

Taylor dropped her shop keys on the counter and paused at the register, her face half concealed in shadow. "We're going to steal my mom's grimoire."

I blinked at her. "When you say 'steal,' that's just an exaggeration, right? Please tell me it's an exaggeration."

"Borrow with the intent to return." She motioned for me to follow her upstairs to what I assumed was their apartment. When I didn't move, she turned to face me and planted a hand on her hip, the universal signal of imminent peer pressure. "This whole ghost situation is more complicated than I originally thought."

"Complicated how?"

"Some of the stuff Jaime told us doesn't add up. Like, why can food pass through the barrier but we can't? Also, why she would single out Jaime from all the people who've broken into that house in the past?" she said. "The information in that grimoire is way more helpful than anything I could come up with on my own. If you want to help get Jaime out of that house before the DCF comes knocking, getting our hands on it is our best bet."

At that one ridiculously simple argument, the part of me that wanted to get back in my car and head home quieted. We only had a month left to figure this out, but even with all my jumbled-up feelings for Jaime, I couldn't walk away from the opportunity to help him.

"Fine," I said after a pause. "As long as you're sure we won't get caught. I don't need to be on your dad's bad side any more than I already am."

Taylor shook her head as I followed her up the stairs. "God, I can't believe you're more nervous than I am. The grimoire has to be packed away in my dad's office or something. We'll be in and out quick, I promise."

Taylor led me down a long hallway and to her dad's office. But when she turned the lamp by the door, I wasn't sure how quick our job would be. Loose papers and receipts were strewn across his desk, and boxes of inventory were piled high in each corner of the small room. I hesitated at the door, questioning again whether any of this was appropriate, but another sidelong look from Taylor gave me the extra nudge to follow her into the room.

I started looking through the boxes at the outside edge of the room while Taylor painstakingly sifted through the clutter on the desk. As we searched, I filled her in on what Jaime and I had found, both the newspaper snippet and the photo from the historical society.

"Josephine Harris, huh?" Taylor repeated. "It's great that we have a name, but it sucks that the historical society couldn't provide any context. What's the point of even having a historical society if they're going to be that useless?"

"I know, right? I was looking at more files this morning, and there's nothing that even mentions we were a station on the Underground Railroad. The whole thing is just another way everyone is living in their own little bubble, as far from the truth as they can possibly get." I sighed, more to myself than to her. But Taylor paused, and I looked over at her sheepishly. "Sorry, too heavy?"

"Nah, not too heavy at all," she said, considering me with barely concealed curiosity. "Theo Miller, I think I may have underestimated you a little."

I was so taken off guard I nearly laughed. "What makes you say that?"

"I dunno. What you just said, the fact you even agreed to come help me out in the first place," she said, moving to the bookshelf next to where I was squatting. "I assumed when I met you that you were going to be stuck-up. Or like—"

"Cookie-cutter Saint Juniper?" I suggested dryly.

"Yeah, kind of."

"Jaime said the same thing not too long ago, you know."

I caught the sympathetic look Taylor shot me out of the corner of my eye, but didn't feel like I could meet it. "I'm sure he doesn't feel that way anymore," she said.

"I hope not," I murmured. Taylor opened her mouth to say something else, but I changed the subject. "Is there a reason you're sneaking around behind your dad's back? I would have thought having a witch for a daughter would be an asset in his line of business."

"He doesn't see it that way. To him it's just a liability," she said, shaking her head. "He doesn't want me to learn any more than I already have. Says things would be harder for me if people knew, but I don't buy it."

"How so?"

"I don't know, it's like Jaime said the other day. It's not easy to live here even when you're not the villain in a Goosebumps book. In my dad's mind, if people caught wind that I'm a real witch and not a commercialized fake, they'd chase me out of town with pitchforks or something."

I glanced over at her, and her face was grim. I could tell this wasn't just some surface-level struggle; it really bothered her.

"Sounds like you're damned if you do and damned if you don't. I'm sorry things are like this with your dad," I said, moving to a new section of the bookshelf. "And I'm sorry if I've ever made you feel like witchcraft is ridiculous. This is all new to me. I guess I've never really believed in anything like this."

Taylor caught my eye and smiled a little as she walked over to a small closet at the far end of the room. "Hang out with me long enough and maybe I can change that."

I smiled back. "Taylor Rivera Bishop, I think I may have underestimated you too."

Whatever she was going to say in response stopped halfway out her mouth as she pulled the closet door open. What should have been a walk-in closet was blocked off with a solid wall of cardboard boxes and clear storage bins. I could tell by the look on Taylor's face that the books, candles, and other items packed inside must have been her mom's.

"Maybe I'll be able to deliver on that promise sooner than I thought," she said.

CHAPTER 16
JAIME

IT STARTED WITH THE feeling I was drowning. My face was pressed into something soaking wet that was too soft to be the edge of the couch cushion I usually used as a pillow. I fought to open my eyes, pressing my hands down into the dampness and feeling moss curl around my fingertips rather than velvet. Recoiling from the unexpected sensation, I shoved away from the ground, flailed for a moment, then landed hard on my back.

Rain pelted my face as I made out the basic shapes of trees painted in sickly, sallow hues of green. I was out in the woods, finally free, but it felt wrong. There were shadows reaching out for me, grabbing at my shirt and tugging at my hair. Rivulets of rain trailed down my neck as I turned to face them, but I froze as a voice rang out in the night.

"Jaime? Where are you?"

I immediately took off through the forest, desperate to get away from the shadows and back to Blackwood. I knew where it was instinctually, though something in the back of my head told me that couldn't be possible.

"You don't have to hide."

The shadows snatched at my heels, dragging me back just as a structure pierced through the impossibly low clouds bordering the clearing. But instead of Blackwood, it was the tiny single-story home I had grown up in on the south side of town, dropped into the forest like it had always been there.

"It's safe, I promise."

I kicked and scrambled my way to the front door, where a dark figure was waiting for me. A crack of lightning illuminated her ghostly face, her chestnut hair. Josephine stared down at me with a cold, self-satisfied smile.

"Let me back in," I choked, my voice breaking as I gasped for air. I scrubbed my eyes, frantically wiping away the rain and turning back to look at the shadows closing in. "Please, I don't want to be out here anymore."

"Do you finally understand?" Josephine asked. "It's not safe out there, so you have to stay. You can't leave. You shouldn't leave. Not now, not ever."

When I jerked myself awake, it took me a second to realize that the rain pelting the sitting room window was real and not imagined. I sucked in a few giant breaths, but the humid summer air only drove my panic deeper into my gut, seeping under my ribs like a poison. Josephine's warning and the oddly familiar words that had rung out in the forest echoed in my mind.

I fumbled for my phone between the seat cushions and shielded my eyes when the screen momentarily blinded me. The time read 12:23 a.m. I couldn't remember falling asleep downstairs, so I must have drifted off sometime late in the afternoon while I was waiting for Taylor and Theo to show.

I still hadn't heard from Theo since he'd slept over. In the darkness, our conversation that night had felt untouchably honest. It had felt like I was invincible. But in retrospect, I couldn't believe how much I was letting myself play with fire.

Liking Theo didn't scare me. I had survived enough one-sided crushes to know it wouldn't be the end of the world if he didn't feel the same. What did scare me was that I was starting to feel like things might not be one-sided after all. It scared me how much I hoped it wasn't just my imagination, because if I started thinking he would eventually meet me in the middle, I'd be a goner.

Clicking through to my messages, I typed out a text, my eyes still adjusting to the bright light of my screen. My thumb hovered over the send button. I read the message once. I read it again.

are we okay? i thought you were coming over today

I held down the backspace key until the entire message was deleted and let my head flop back against the couch's armrest. Overthinking things was pathetic, but I didn't exactly have anything better to do. I didn't want to assume he was avoiding me, but it was hard not to wonder if spending the night had been too much for him. If *I* had been too much for him.

I sat up and stared at my phone screen again. This time, I typed and sent a shorter text: *what's up?* The words *Message not delivered* blinked next to the text bubble, and I let out a sigh. I got up from the couch thinking I might be able to get a signal if I went up to the third floor, but a rustle outside stopped me in my tracks.

Over the steady drum of rain pelting the roof, two excited voices echoed through the forest. Relief flooded through me. Taylor and Theo must have come after all. I was seconds from rushing into the entryway to greet them when I heard an unfamiliar voice, and then another.

"Pass me the lighter," the stranger slurred, and I stopped in my tracks.

"You can't light up with one hand when you have booze in the other," a girl giggled. "You'll burn the place down."

"Might as well," he replied. "Who's gonna care if I do?"

Before I could understand what I was hearing, the front door slammed open with the force only a kick could deliver. The only fear that haunted my waking moments more than any nightmare was becoming a reality: someone else had finally found me, and they weren't there to help.

CHAPTER 17
TAYLOR

THE BARE LIGHT BULB overhead took a minute to reach its full brightness, but the closet was still so dim that Theo and I had to hover at the door and squint to make out what was what.

The smell of dust and warm cotton filled my nose as I peeked at a bin of my mom's old clothes. Flashes of maroon silk and worn denim and black velvet hit me with a tidal wave of nostalgia that I pushed down as best I could. *This isn't why you're here*, I reminded myself sternly, my resolve already on dangerously thin ice.

"Where do you think he put it?" Theo asked quietly beside me.

I made sure the lump in my throat was under control before I responded. "Your guess is as good as mine."

A pile of cardboard boxes in the back of the closet marked *MISC* seemed like a decent enough place to start. My mom had never left her grimoire unattended, not even for even a few minutes, so I only had the barest memory of the brown leather-bound book to guide my search. I gave Theo the best description I could, and we dove in.

To anyone else, these boxes were full of disorganized junk. But I saw the meaning and value behind every memento and saved scrap of paper. There was a tarnished necklace I'd gotten her from a vending machine on a road trip, a handful of the hair ties she never seemed to have enough of, a pot of her favorite lip balm that reminded me of sticky forehead kisses.

In the months since my mom had passed, I'd made it my mission to keep my chin up. But being surrounded by her things was the ultimate test, and I was dangerously close to failing. Just like Jaime and I had talked about, coming to terms with my mom's death wasn't a difficult process, it was an impossible, soul-crushing mission I wasn't sure I'd ever successfully complete. In that little walk-in closet, her absence was inescapable, and if Theo hadn't been there, I might have slammed the door shut and run.

But then my fingers brushed a leather-bound spine, and I paused. Wedged between a stack of envelopes and a map of Massachusetts, there was a thick notebook, falling apart at the seams. As I pulled it gingerly from the clutter, I recognized the strange, labyrinthine etchings on the cover. I'd never gotten a good enough look at them to puzzle out what they represented, but now I could clearly see that the twists and curls were the edges of a storm cloud wrapping around the branches of a massive tree.

I cracked the grimoire open and started to leaf through it, equal parts invigorated and shell-shocked. In the dim yellow light, I could barely make out the writing that spiraled tightly across each page, traversing the margins and squeezing between drips of candle wax. The handwriting toward the front of the book wasn't my mom's. As I flipped through the pages, it was slowly overtaken by a different style, then another, then finally by my mom's distinctive chicken scratch.

Two-thirds of the way through the book, I stumbled across a page that was blank save for a small inscription in my mom's handwriting.

From this page on, the laws of nature require blood for power.

"What," I whispered with feeling, "the actual hell."

I ran my fingers over the words once and then moved over them again, each vowel indented into the soft paper by the pressure of a hasty pen. I knew right away what the writing meant: there was blood magic in this grimoire.

Bloodshed in spellcasting wasn't a foreign concept to me. My mom had told me about witchcraft through different time periods and cultural traditions, so I knew blood sacrifice wasn't as sinister as it seemed on the surface. It was just incredibly volatile and hard to do safely. Without a proper measure of the power you were siphoning, spells could quickly go awry. And in all the times my mom had told me about magic that powerful, she'd never once made it sound like she practiced it herself. Keeping a secret like that was a very Bishop thing to do, but knowing that didn't make it feel like any less of a kick in the chest.

"Hey, I think you should take a look at this," Theo said, voice tight.

Impulsively, I flipped back to an earlier page in the grimoire. I didn't have time to process what I'd just seen, let alone explain it to Theo. But somehow, what he had to show me was even more shocking.

From the depths of one of the boxes, Theo pulled out a skeleton key. It was oddly ornate, with intricate patterns forming around a stylized letter "B" at the bow. It took me a second to place it, but key's tarnished color and the curve of its designs were too familiar.

"Call me crazy," he started, "but doesn't this look a little like—?"

"Like it came from Blackwood," I finished.

"Jaime said there was a door up on the third floor that's locked. What if this opens it?"

Before I had the chance to respond, a sound from the shop floor below made us both jump out of our skin. It was the unmistakable sound of the bell jingling that told me if we didn't move fast, we'd be caught red-handed.

CHAPTER 18
JAIME

WHEN THE FRONT DOOR slammed open, my first instinct was to duck behind the couch. My second was to call Theo.

My phone was in my hand in an instant, call trying to connect as the intruders whooped and stomped into the entryway. It rang once, twice, then blared an error sound in my ear. *Call failed.* I mashed the End Call button so hard I thought I might have blown out a pixel on the screen.

Even from a dozen feet away, the smell of alcohol wafted off the intruders and into the living room. I whipped my head back toward the chaos and managed to catch the last pair of boots disappearing beyond the edge of the foyer. By some miracle, the group tumbled down the hall toward the game room, away from the sitting room, where I was hiding.

Sucking in a deep breath, I steeled myself, then made a mad dash for the stairs. The darkness hid me well enough that I managed to stay out of sight, and the excited shouts from the group below covered the sound of steps creaking as I sprinted to the top floor. But it wasn't long before I heard them thumping up the stairs too, chattering loudly as they came. I darted into the only bedroom on the third story, shutting the door behind me and slumping against it to catch my breath.

With my back against the door, I tried to send a series of panicked messages to Theo:

someone found the house

Message not delivered.

this is not a drill

Message not delivered.

where are u???

Message not delivered.

are u ducking kidding me

Message not delivered.

*fucking

Message not delivered.

I would've flung my phone across the room if the circumstances had been different, but I settled for shoving it into my pocket as the intruders' voices ricocheted through the house. Of course the one time I really needed Theo, I wasn't able to reach him. My mind pinballed unhelpfully between a hundred different questions as I tried to make sense of how these strangers had made it past the barrier.

I turned to press my face against the seam of the door, straining to make out what was happening. I could hear doors being flung open below me, but it sounded like part of the group had reached the third story. A rattle and some chatter at the end of the hall made me think they were clustered around the locked door I'd given up on trying to break into for fear of angering Josephine. A vortex of raw anxiety and a sick sense of protectiveness over the house twisted in my gut like a knife.

But they must not have been able to get it open either, because their interest in the mystery room didn't last long. Footsteps approached the room I'd holed up in. I skittered away from the door, whirling around to take stock of the furniture and find a place to hide. The armoire at the far end of the room barely looked big enough to fit me, but I jumped in and closed the doors as tightly as I could anyway. It smelled horrifically musty, and I almost gagged as I heard the door to the bedroom slam open.

"No way," boomed a voice on the other side of the too-thin armoire door. Something sloshed onto the ground, so I could only assume the guy had brought his drink with him. "Can you believe this?"

"Ugh, this is way too creepy for me," said a girl, her voice faint enough that I figured she hadn't even stepped all the way into the room. "I wanna leave, okay? I'm serious."

"Come on, don't be a baby."

I racked my brain for a way to get them off the property. My mind darted back to how skittish I'd been when I first found the house, and an idea popped into my head. I sent up a silent prayer to any god that would listen, raised my hand against the armoire door, then dragged my nails down the rough wood. It made the exact bone-chilling noise I was hoping for, one that raised the hair on the back of my neck even though I was the one making it. For a moment, there was silence.

Then the girl let loose an earsplitting shriek, the boy bellowed, and the two of them booked it faster than I'd expected. They shouted to their friends to get out, wrangling the group down the stairs at what sounded like breakneck speed.

I burst out of the armoire and ran to the window on the far side of the room. And like a goddamn miracle, four figures ran from the house and into the woods.

Adrenaline still pumped through my veins, but I was frozen. I stood stock-still at the window for what felt like ages, straining to hear even the tiniest noise that would suggest they were coming back. I stood there long enough for the hollow, colorless light of the moon to emerge from behind the clouds. Still, I couldn't seem to wrap my head around what had happened.

When I finally drifted away from the window and down the hall, I followed the dirt and leaves tracked across the threadbare carpets and down the stairs to the foyer. The front door had been left open in the intruders' rush to leave. I moved to close it but paused with my hand on the doorknob.

For a split second, I wondered if I should test the barrier again. Maybe if those people were able to leave, so was I. With my heart in my throat, I slowly lifted my hand to the threshold.

Then two cold hands landed on my shoulders, fingers digging into my skin hard enough to bruise.

Jerking back from the door, I whirled to look behind me, but nothing was there.

"I thought you understood you can't leave."

I spun around again to find Josephine in the doorway, a jagged shape illuminated by the light of the moon. The front door slammed shut behind her, and when the lock clicked into place on its own, a horrible chill raked down my spine.

"I'm sorry," I said breathlessly, scrambling back onto the stairs as she took a step toward me. "I understand. Please don't hurt me."

Josephine's mouth twisted into a grimace as she came closer. "I won't, but they will. Everyone in that godforsaken town. You won't survive out there, and you know it."

"I know, I'll stay, just don't hurt me," I begged again, heart stuttering in my chest, but Josephine wouldn't stop. I shrank back, raising my arms to shield my face, but the icy fingers I expected to close around my wrists never came. The only noise in the foyer was the sound of my own ragged breathing, and when I finally lowered my arms to look around, Josephine was gone.

I curled into myself on the stairs, every muscle in my body clenched so tight I couldn't stop shaking. I didn't move for a long time, hugging my knees to my chest and waiting for the terror to subside, but it wouldn't budge.

I hadn't been thinking when I was responding to Josephine, I'd just said whatever I thought would make her leave me alone. But maybe I did understand what she meant. She said I wouldn't survive out there, out in Saint Juniper. As I peered at the front door through the darkness, I had the horrible, sickening feeling that she might be right.

CHAPTER 19
THEO

"YOU'VE GOT TO BE kidding me," Taylor groaned, pocketing the skeleton key I'd found and whirling back to the mess we had made of the closet. "We need to get out of here. Like, now."

"I thought you said your dad would be out most of the night," I replied, voice low and heart in my throat. We scrambled to put everything back where we'd found it and rushed out of the room in record time.

"He was supposed to be." Taylor tucked her mom's grimoire under her arm as she propelled me down the hallway. "If we hurry, I can sneak you out through the storeroom."

We got all the way to the bottom of the stairs, almost in the clear, when the lights flickered on in the shop. But the person standing in the warm flood of light wasn't Taylor's dad after all, and the girl behind the counter looked nearly as surprised to see us as we were to see her.

"So this is why you canceled on me tonight?" the psychic asked, scooping her keys and a white envelope off the counter.

"God damn, Anna," Taylor wheezed, one hand pressed to her chest. "You just took five years off my life. What are you doing here?"

"I forgot my paycheck. What's *he* doing here?" She pointed a finger at me.

"H-hi," I faltered as she came around the counter. "We met the other day."

"Oh, I know," she replied coldly, then turned her attention back to Taylor. She nodded at the book in Taylor's hands. "Elias is going to kill you if he finds out about this."

Taylor gripped it a little tighter. "You're the one who told me I should take matters into my own hands."

"I told you to talk to your dad, not steal from him," Anna shot back. "Especially not for whatever this guy has roped you into."

Before I had the chance to be offended, my phone buzzed in my back pocket. Not once, but over and over without stopping. When I pulled it out, a flood of notifications lit up the screen.

Taylor and Anna kept arguing, but I wasn't listening anymore. The second I read *someone found the house*, everything other than the sea of missed texts and calls from Jaime faded into the background.

"What happened?" Taylor asked, finally sensing something was amiss.

"It's Jaime," I said, turning my screen to show her the notifications. I was vaguely aware of Anna saying something else as Taylor's eyes scanned the texts, but I didn't hear the words. "I need to leave, I need to—"

"Go," Taylor said, pushing my phone back into my hands. "If I come I'll just slow you down."

Leaving the shop and getting into my car was a blur. Every possible scenario screamed inside my head as I flew down the road to the folly, running every stop sign and praying I wouldn't get pulled over. I tried to call Jaime, my pulse racing faster with every ring. He didn't pick up the first time, or the second, and by the third, I was sure something had gone terribly wrong.

I ran as fast as my legs could take me through the woods, my breath searing the inside of my throat as my feet thumped against the rain-soaked ground. When I broke through the trees and stumbled into the meadow, I almost ran up to pound on the front door, but thought better of it in case the intruders were still on the property. Instead, I raced along the length of the porch, looking in through the windows for any hint Jaime was okay.

I stopped when I reached the greenhouse entrance at the back of the house, but still couldn't see any movement through the tangle of vines. As I dipped my head to try to get a better vantage point, I reached out to steady myself without thinking. But where my hand should have connected with the barrier, it clipped through the space like the invisible wall had never been there in the first place.

A knot of unhelpful theories bombarded my mind as I fell to the ground, but I didn't give myself time to investigate them. I scrambled to my feet and into the house, adrenaline surging. The layout of the ground floor wasn't at all what I'd expected, so I was briefly disoriented until I skidded to a stop in front of the staircase. I took the steps three at a time, barely able to see through the haze of panicked tears welling in my eyes. And that was how I ended up running smack into Jaime, hard enough to knock us both on our asses. We tumbled onto the landing in a tangle of limbs.

"Jesus," he wheezed under me, eyes squeezed shut in pain, shock, or a combination of the two. "Are you trying to kill me?"

"Oh god, no, I'm sorry," I said, hands flitting nervously over his chest. "I just got your messages and rushed over. Are you all right?"

Jaime groaned. "Well, my stupid phone took its sweet time sending them. Everyone is gone now."

I let out a sigh of relief, but it was lost in a string of shallow breaths due to my breakneck run through the valley. Jaime was looking up at me, hair tossed messily across his forehead, and it wasn't until that moment I realized I had my knees planted firmly on either side of his hips. By the look of it, he realized what position we were in at the exact same time. I willed my brain to think of something, anything logical to say, but he beat me to it.

"How did you get in here?" he asked, sounding dazed.

Deadpan, I replied, "The back door was open."

We looked at each other, winded and bewildered, then burst out laughing so hard we lost our breath all over again. The whole thing was so ridiculous that some floodgate burst and we both completely went off the deep end. I rolled off Jaime onto the landing and watched him as he jammed the heels of his hands into his eyes. He laughed and laughed until he was practically hyperventilating.

"This is insane," I said once we managed to get a grip again.

"I can't believe you're here," he said. Then he sat up so fast I jumped. "Oh shit, you're *here*."

"Uh, yeah." I pushed up onto my elbows. "Hi, hello, nice to meet you. What are you—?"

"You have to get out," he said.

I only had the chance to feel insulted for half a second before he grabbed my wrist and started dragging me back down the stairs. "Jaime, hold up. What's wrong?"

"What if you're stuck now?" He wheeled on me once we got to the foyer. "Did you even think about that before you came barging in here?"

"You were in danger. I didn't have time to think. Why are you so mad?"

"I saw Josephine after those assholes broke in here. I tried to leave again, and she flipped out. I thought she was gonna kill me. What if she shows up again? Or worse, what if—"

"Okay, slow down," I said as evenly as I could. Anxiety spiked in my chest, but I'd never seen Jaime so frazzled, and I didn't want to make things worse. "All we can do right now is see if I can leave."

Jaime shifted nervously next to me as I unlocked the front door, glancing around the dark shadows of the foyer. But if Josephine was watching us, she didn't make her presence known. I paused at the threshold of the door for a moment, sucked in a huge breath, and took a step forward.

The second my foot connected with the porch, relief flooded through me. Behind me, Jaime let out a huff of air that told me he had been holding his breath too. But when I turned to look at him, he still seemed tense.

"Jaime, this is *huge*. Maybe the barrier really is down. What if you tried one more time?"

"I can't," he said quickly, shrinking back from the door. "It's not going to work. She said I couldn't leave."

"Just try it." I held out my hand. "Please, for me."

Jaime looked so terrified I almost thought he'd refuse again. But after a pause, he took a step forward and lifted his hand up to the threshold. His brows drew together as his fingers hovered inches from mine. They reached out slowly, slowly, then connected with the barrier just as they always had.

"It's okay," he said, pulling his hand back quickly, but something in my chest twisted at how hollow his voice sounded. "It's probably for the best anyway."

"What do you mean?"

Jaime opened his mouth to reply, but all at once, the weight of what happened crashed down on him right before my eyes. He tried to turn and hide the pain on his face, but I still saw his expression crumple in profile, flooded with emotion in a way I'd never seen before.

In a fraction of a second, I crossed the threshold again and pulled him into my arms. He went still at first, probably stunned by the closeness. I was too—besides our collision upstairs, which I'd barely had time to appreciate, we had never touched. And maybe that was why, with my hands on his back and his chin resting against my shoulder, he finally cracked.

"I was so scared," he said in between gasping breaths. "With Josephine, with the people who broke in. I feel like I'm losing it, Theo. This place is fucking with my head."

"I know, but I'm here. You're safe now," I murmured, rubbing a hand along his back. "What even happened to the people who found you? How did you get them to leave?"

"I pretended to be a ghost," he said miserably.

His response was so unexpected it pulled me out of my somberness. I tried not to laugh, but I could feel his shoulders shaking in silent laughter too. It felt a little unreal that just a few hours earlier, I'd been looking for an excuse to avoid him.

I felt a rush of disappointment as Jaime pulled back to look me in the eye. He was beautiful even with tears staining his cheeks. It was the type of thought that might have sent me into a panic any other time, but right then, I couldn't bring myself to care. Not when his hands were on my shoulders and he was closer than he had ever been.

"So," he said with a sad smile I couldn't refuse in a thousand lifetimes, "do you want a tour?"

CHAPTER 20
TAYLOR

THE SUN WAS JUST starting to crest the mountains as Jaime, Theo, and I ventured up to the third floor of Blackwood. We had met at dawn, all of us too twitchy from the night before to get any sleep. When Theo and I realized we could both come and go from the house without issue, we were eager to test the locked mystery door. But once we got up there, the three of us stood shoulder to shoulder, none of us willing to make a move. The skeleton key we'd found in Elias's closet was clutched in Theo's hand.

"Are we sure this is a good idea?" Theo asked, eyeing the door warily. "What if trying to get in makes *you know who* mad?"

Jaime shrugged. He would've been the picture of indifference if he hadn't been shrinking back, arms crossed tightly over his chest. "I think if she wanted to stop us, she would've done it already. She's pretty proactive."

"Okay, so do you want to do the honors?" Theo asked, extending the key to Jaime.

"Absolutely not," he replied quickly. "It has to be locked for a reason, right? What if there's, like, a dead body in there?"

Theo paled. "Do you really think there will be?"

"We're not going to get answers just standing around." I sighed, and the boys turned to me expectantly. I didn't love the idea of barging in there either, not when I could feel Josephine's uneasy presence more clearly than ever. But there was no way Elias's having something from Blackwood in his office closet was a coincidence, and my curiosity won out over my anxiety. With a sigh, I swiped the key from Theo. "Fine, I'll do it."

I squared my shoulders, trying to give off the vibe I was confident and in control, but it took both of my shaking hands to fit the key into the lock. I turned it slowly, slowly, and when it finally clicked open, all three of us jumped.

When the door swung open, a blast of musty air hit us in the face. Through the dust motes churning in the morning sun, a small library with dark wooden shelves lining every wall took shape. Books overflowed into little piles on the damask maroon rug at the center of the room. A leather armchair in the corner and a blue velvet sofa were littered with volumes.

"No dead bodies, right?" Theo asked anxiously behind me.

"None that I can see," I said, moving tentatively into the room. There was a lot to take in, but the scent was what distracted me most. "Do you guys smell that?"

"The hundred years of dust? Yeah, can't get enough," Jaime deadpanned, walking to the bay window at the far end of the room that looked out on the valley. When he cracked it open, a gust of fresh air stirred the dust up even more. But underneath it all, I swore the familiar scent of sage and rosemary was clinging to the furniture. "I don't know what I was expecting, but this wasn't it."

"Why would a library be the only locked room in the entire house?" Theo asked, finally venturing in.

I glanced around the cluttered space. "I guess there's only one way to find out."

On the surface, the library did seem pretty innocuous. But after combing through the volumes for the better part of the morning, we finally started to put the pieces together. Nestled between copies by Dickens and the Brontë sisters were dozens of books about folk medicine, herbology, and spiritualism.

"In the article about Josephine's death, I think it said 'unnatural demise' or something," Jaime pointed out, settling onto the couch with a small leather-bound book on tinctures. "I thought it was just a polite, old-timey way to say murder, but do you think this is what they meant by unnatural? Like, *supernatural?*"

"Maybe. Whoever lived here definitely practiced witchcraft, or at least knew a hell of a lot about it," I said, leaning against one of the shelves. "There's obviously more to Josephine's story, more to all of this, that we don't know yet. We just have to keep looking."

After Jaime explained more about his most recent Josephine sighting, I was pretty confident that her aggression wasn't about keeping the house pristine like we'd thought. So with an abundance of caution and a boatload of curiosity, we decided to search the house top to bottom.

Blackwood was even stranger and more unnerving on the inside than I expected. None of the glimpses I'd gotten from the front door could have prepared me for the whimsical furniture, ornately framed oil paintings, and dizzying patterns that crowded my vision no matter where I looked. Tapestries hung in every hall, and each cloth napkin around the dining room table was monogrammed with a looping 'B' for 'Blackwood.' All of it was definitely bizarre, but none of it seemed like a crime scene.

The boys stuck together as they rifled through cabinets and poked around the plants in the greenhouse. Theo was terrified of being left alone anywhere in the house, and though Jaime tried to hide it, he was jumpy after his latest run-in with Josephine too. After three days of searching without incident, I started to think they were using her as a thinly veiled excuse to spend more time together.

I was happy to give them space, for that and for my own reasons. The smell that had wafted over me when I entered the library was still on my mind. Rosemary and sage were both heavy hitters for cleansing negative spiritual energy, and I didn't think I'd be able to smell them if someone hadn't used those herbs within the last couple of months. Someone like my mom.

So one overcast afternoon, when the boys were rummaging through the pantry, I climbed up the stairs and did another sweep of the library. In the dim light, I ran my fingers over the spines of the books, scrutinizing every nook and cranny of the room. I even got down on all fours, the roughness of the rug prickling my knees, to peek under the couch. No luck. I was almost ready to give up when the sun emerged from behind a cloud. And if it hadn't been for that one brief ray of light illuminating the room, I would never have seen the blood.

The color was nearly indistinguishable from the burgundy of the worn carpet, but there were unmistakable droplets at one corner. I squinted as the sunlight shifted again, and though the stain was camouflaged by the intricate design of the rug, there were streaks of blood marring the pattern, like someone had tried to scrub it clean.

I quickly moved to the edge of the rug, pushing the couch out of the way so I could see it more clearly. But in the process, I nudged the rug out of place. And there, drawn on the floorboards in white chalk, was the edge of a sigil. It was a little smudged, but I instantly recognized it as the kind of thing my mom used in her spellwork all the time. But as I pulled back the rug, I could see this one was massive and far more detailed than any I'd seen before.

The staircase creaked behind me, and I quickly dropped the rug over the sigil. I'd only just managed to pull the couch back into place when Theo burst into the room.

"Hey, do you think this a potion or really old absinthe?" he said, a little breathless, holding out an elaborately crafted glass bottle full of green liquid. I dipped my head and took a sniff, then wrinkled my nose.

"I'm gonna go with absinthe, but either way, don't drink it."

"Roger that," he replied cheerily. "There's some other weird stuff down there. Do you want to take a look?"

"Sure, why not," I said, trailing behind him.

As we padded down the stairs, I tried to commit the sigil to memory as best as I could. If my mom had drawn it, and if that blood was from a blood magic spell, did that mean she had tried to exorcise Josephine from the house and failed? I'd barely had the time to process the blood magic I'd found in my mom's grimoire, let alone figure out a way to explain it to Jaime and Theo, and this was just another complicated piece to add to the puzzle.

Theo must have interpreted my silence as gloominess, because he nudged me when we reached the second-story landing.

"You okay? Is Anna still giving you the cold shoulder?"

"The coldest shoulder ever." I sighed. "She hasn't answered any of my texts, and she switched shifts so we won't work together tomorrow."

"Do you know why she has such an issue with you helping us?" he asked. It was a good question, one I had been avoiding for too long. Anna must have seen my future that night the valley had called out to me, and her being dead set on keeping me away from Blackwood wasn't a good sign. But there was no point in telling Theo that, not yet. I just shook my head.

"I'm not sure. I mean, if I can get in the same room with her, maybe I'll find out. But it feels shitty to be losing my last real friend in Wolf's Head."

"I'm really sorry this is getting between you two," Theo said as we reached the ground floor, looking back at me with a sad smile. "Kind of goes without saying, but Jaime and I have your back. At least you have us, right?"

"Right," I said, guilt twisting in my gut like a knife as Jaime poked his head out of the pantry.

"What's the verdict on the green shit?"

"It's probably absinthe."

Jaime grinned. "We could try—"

"*NO*," Theo and I said in unison.

Jaime hit Theo with his best attempt at puppy-dog eyes, Theo launched into a diatribe on underage drinking, and I leaned against the counter to watch them fight or flirt or whatever combination of the two it was that particular day.

This delicate equilibrium we had reached with each other was exactly why I didn't want to tell them about the blood magic, or what Anna might have seen. It was also why I hadn't mentioned that the longer I spent in the house, the less Josephine's haunting of Jaime added up.

It didn't make sense that Theo and I could come and go whenever we wanted, and I was starting to form a hypothesis: Jaime himself was more of a factor in this than any of us had originally thought. But I had no idea how to broach the subject without freaking the boys out. Especially Jaime.

It didn't take long for me to see he didn't like being in the house alone, so I was always at Blackwood on the days Theo was working some of his final shifts at the library for the summer. We didn't always feel the need to fill the silence, but when we did talk, I was surprised by how much I liked his quiet sort of intensity. When he wasn't being a smartass, he could be surprisingly thoughtful. He asked what it was like working at the apothecary, and I told him all about the early morning deliveries and late-night stocking I'd gotten used to since I was thirteen. And even though we had drastically different upbringings, we found common ground when

I talked about my move from Boston and how hard it was to start over somewhere new where so few people looked like me.

Jaime's memories of his childhood were spotty by his own admission, and I could tell he didn't like digging into his past. Every time he referenced foster care or his first time living in Saint Juniper, it felt kind of monumental. That's why I was a little touched that, after I'd mentioned video calls with my extended family back on the island, Jaime admitted he was bothered he hadn't learned any Spanish as a kid.

"It wasn't really up to me, but I still feel kind of embarrassed about it," Jaime said, leaning against the game room wall. Theo was at work, and we had wandered in to play some pool. With a breeze drifting in through the greenhouse, the space smelled like summertime and fresh soil. "I picked up some slang from foster siblings I've had over the years, but it's mostly swear words."

"I wish you didn't feel that way, tons of second-gen kids don't know Spanish," I replied gently. "But if you want to learn, I can try to teach you."

Jaime's brows drew together. "Really?"

"For sure. I mean, Puerto Rican Spanish and Mexican Spanish are pretty different, but it could be fun," I said, ducking under the moose head and making my way to the cue ball. "We could do weekly study sessions. There's a coffee shop in Wolf's Head that I think you'd love."

"Oh," Jaime said haltingly, frowning a little. "I dunno."

"I won't make you do homework or anything, if that's what you're worried about," I teased, and Jaime shook his head.

"No, it's not that. I want to learn. I guess it's just hard for me to imagine my life outside of Blackwood right now."

"What do you mean? Aren't you excited to get back to real life after all this is over?" I asked as I leaned down to figure out my next play.

Jaime shrugged. "Yeah, I guess so."

"Very convincing," I replied, peeking up at him. Jaime shared the same glib expression as the wild boar head mounted on the opposite wall. "If I make this shot, you have to tell me how you really feel."

I shut my right eye, held my breath, and knocked the six ball cleanly into one of the far pockets. Jaime rolled his eyes, moving to the opposite end of the table.

"You're gonna think I'm crazy," he said.

"I'm really not."

Jaime lined up his shot. "I know I can't stay here, but part of me doesn't want to go back. At least not to the Saint Juniper I think is waiting for me on the other side."

"It won't be as bad as you're imagining," I said, watching him sink the ball. When he looked up at me, I could see the worry splashed plainly across his face. "You know me, you know Theo. You're not alone."

"I guess," he said, and his hesitancy made something click inside my head.

I remembered what he had told me about his dreams of Josephine, about how she was pressuring him not to leave and playing on his fears. I thought back to how he'd said the valley, or this house, was calling out to him. Maybe him admitting he didn't actually want to leave wasn't a coincidence.

"I promise we won't let you suffocate out there," I said simply, my mind still reeling.

"I hope that's true. But it feels like every time I want something bad enough, it ends up falling apart." Jaime turned his face away from me then, picking at his fingernail. He paused, then, painfully quiet, added, "I don't want this to fall apart too."

I already knew the web I was weaving wouldn't easily be untangled, but comments like that made it all feel even more impossible to manage. I didn't want things to fall apart either, not for me or Jaime or any of us. But I knew if I wasn't careful, I might not have a choice.

CHAPTER 21
THEO

"FASHION WAS WILD BACK then," Taylor said, flipping through a leaflet on 1890s style. Like most days since the break-in, we were holed up in the library. "You should recreate some of these looks. If you ignore the muttonchops, they have real potential."

"I actually think muttonchops are what's missing from modern men's fashion," Jaime said, holding out a hand.

"You're a visionary," Taylor said dryly, passing the brochure to Jaime.

I peeked up from the book in my own hands, watching as Jaime squinted at the pictures. It was oddly endearing. I wanted to press my finger against the little furrow between his brows and smooth it out. I could, now that I was sitting closer to him than I ever had. All I had to do was reach out and—

"You might be on to something here. Assless chaps are still cool," Jaime said, then turned to me. "Do you think I could pull them off?"

"You could probably pull anything off," I replied, too dazed to be anything but honest.

Jaime burst out laughing, a crooked smile spreading across his face, and it was one of those rare displays of happiness that felt like the sun coming out from behind a cloud. He moved to the other end of the library, scooping up the rest of the smaller magazines we'd set aside, and I stared after him. I didn't realize until a good five seconds later that Taylor was watching me watch him. She arched a dark brow in my direction.

"What?" I asked.

"Nothing," she replied with a knowing smile, turning back to her stack of books.

Okay, so I was a little distracted. It wasn't my fault, though. I had spent weeks getting to know Jaime from five feet away on the opposite side of a door. It was hard not to get preoccupied with all the things I hadn't noticed until he was so . . . close.

I was taller than him, for one. Maybe only by an inch or two, and he looked like he wanted to strangle me to death when I pointed it out, but it was the kind of thing I could have never noticed until we had the chance to stand side by side. He would touch his face when he was reading, rubbing his thumb along his lower lip in a way that was far more attractive than I wanted to admit. Sometimes he would tuck his hair behind his ear on one side, and I was obsessed with the way it left a bend when it came free so the lock closest to his face curled gently against his cheek.

And then there was the closeness, or the potential for it. Since our collision on the stairs and our hug in the foyer, I actually noticed with searing, painful precision when we touched and when we didn't. Every time he came within a two-foot radius of me, I could feel a kind of electricity in the air, a silent pull that made me think my legs would turn to jelly if he so much as breathed in my direction. It was positively Austenian in its ridiculousness. He would pass me a book, and our hands wouldn't quite touch, but the thought of them brushing was enough to make me feel a bit unhinged.

Five days after the break-in, Jaime was the one who broke the tension. Taylor was at work, and we were checking the armoires in the sitting room when he suddenly grabbed my arm.

"Theo, *look*," he whispered.

My brain leapt to the worst-case scenario, and I whipped my head toward the window to see a tiny fawn, maybe only a few weeks old, grazing in the clearing. *This boy*, I thought, *is actually going to kill me one day.*

Then I realized Jaime's hand, warm and calloused, was still very much on my arm. I looked at it, he looked at it, and then we looked at each other.

"Sorry, is this—?"

"No, it's not—"

"No?" He retracted his hand.

"No, I didn't mean no! It's just, I'm just—" *Am I having a stroke? Oh my god.* "It's fine, we're fine."

Jaime grinned at me, all soft lips and softer eyes. "Okay."

After that, any concept of personal space kind of went out the window. Still, every time he jostled my hip playfully as we walked up the stairs or balanced his chin on my shoulder to read the book I was poring over, it made me want to combust.

But as distracting as Jaime could be, it didn't keep me from worrying about our lack of progress. On the days I was stuck working, I used the library's intranet and town hall databases to search for information about Josephine. I figured if I could find any details about her life, I might be able to follow them to living ancestors or something at the historical society that would shed light on what had happened to her. But Josephine's only son passed away during a smallpox outbreak the year before she died, and her family tree seemed to stop there. I found her home address in the town census, but when I pulled up a street view on my phone, it seemed like the house had been demolished and the lot had become part of a public park. I couldn't find any mention of an investigation into Blackwood for Josephine's death either.

Our search of the estate wasn't yielding much better results. We had combed almost every room in the house except the attic and two of the more vacant bedrooms on the third floor, but couldn't find a single family photo, journal, or anything truly personal to whoever had originally lived there. Taylor and I had gotten so desperate that we'd resorted to pulling all the books off the shelves in the library, shaking them to see if some letter or postcard was wedged between the pages.

"I feel like we have to be missing something," I said, sighing as I placed another book in my teetering reject pile. Taylor tried to hold the stack steady, though with a few more volumes, it would almost be as tall as her. "We've been looking all week with no luck. Doesn't that seem kind of suspicious?"

"How so?" she asked, and Jaime popped his head up from where he had been drifting in and out of sleep on the couch.

"I'm starting to think someone wiped this place clean," I said, turning to Taylor. "And I can think of one person we know who would be the prime culprit."

"You think it was Elias," she supplied.

"That would make a lot of sense," Jaime chimed in, stretching a little so the hem of his shirt rose to reveal a sliver of skin that— *Stop it, Theo. Focus.* "We might not know a lot about who lived here, but they were definitely into some spooky stuff. If Elias had this key in his office, is it that much of a leap to think he sanitized the place?"

"As much as Elias hates witchcraft, I don't understand why he would go to that much trouble," Taylor replied, frowning a little.

"Do you think you could talk to him about it?" I asked. "Or maybe get into his office again? If he did take stuff from Blackwood, I bet it would be in that closet."

Jaime and I looked at her expectantly, but she seemed torn.

"I'll think about it," she said finally, turning away to pull another stack of books off the shelves.

I knew Taylor's relationship with her dad was a minefield of unresolved issues, and I didn't want to push her when it seemed like her personal life was fracturing even more than it had been before we met. I just hoped that when push came to shove, she would do what had to be done to help Jaime.

———

Jaime was running low on food, so later that afternoon, I left him and Taylor at Blackwood and headed into town. The sky was just starting to go lavender around the edges when I pulled into a spot on Main Street.

The corner store was as busy as it ever got, which was to say it wasn't busy at all, so there were only a few other people milling around as I grabbed snacks. My mind ran over the theory about Elias again, and I was so lost in thought I almost tuned out the conversation happening one aisle over.

"I'm surprised they're actually going to do something about it," a woman said. "I didn't think anyone even cared. Kids break in there every year."

My hand froze on a can of veggies. There was no way they were talking about Blackwood, right?

"Just between me and you, one of the kids who got spooked was the mayor's daughter," a man replied. "If she'd gotten hurt out here, he'd have our heads."

"Go figure," she marveled, and the man let out a huff of laughter.

Without drawing attention to myself, I sidled to the end of the aisle and peeked around the corner. The man was in a police uniform, one hand resting on his belt.

"The sheriff already green-lit the whole thing to keep him quiet," he said. "The demo crew is coming out two weeks from tomorrow."

No, nonono. I took an unsteady step back, head spinning. The DCF visit was already too soon, too daunting. There was no way we could get Jaime out of the house in two weeks.

"Hey, Theo, you finding everything okay?" one of the shop employees asked behind me, and I nearly jumped out of my skin.

"I j-just remembered I have somewhere to be," I stuttered, putting the food I had collected back onto the shelf. The employee stared after me as I hurried out of the store, but I didn't care. Nothing mattered except the dread that had settled in my chest as I started my engine and turned to drive back into the valley.

CHAPTER 22
JAIME

THE LATE-AFTERNOON SUN was fading from the library, but there was still enough light to cast soft beams across the stacks of books we'd pulled off the shelves. Between the dust motes churning in the orange glow and the pleasant smell of time-worn wood, the space felt like a hushed oasis. Taylor was curled up next to me chatting about the inaccuracy of some show about teen witches on The CW. I was so comfortable I was having a hard time not nodding off.

Josephine had been keeping me awake most nights, shifting in the shadows of the house or taunting me in my dreams. Nothing she said was new, but that didn't make it any less terrifying. She just kept on telling me I couldn't leave, and I didn't want to admit it, but I was starting to believe her.

I had already told Taylor as much, but I didn't want to let Theo know I was struggling. I knew the look he would give me if I did. It was the worst one he had in his repertoire, the one where he looked at me like I was a problem he wanted to solve. I far preferred it when he was looking at me like he normally did, holding me captive by his attention in a way that made me feel both safe and jittery enough to jump out of my skin at the same time.

Sometimes he looked at me like he was trying to remember something he had lost. His brows would knit together, and he would think so hard that I could have sworn I heard gears turning in his head. Other times, he looked at me like he was trying to memorize my features. His eyes would search my face like it held all the secrets of the universe, like I was actually worth remembering.

If I caught him staring like that, I would say something, anything, to break his focus and make him look away. Those looks were too intense for how fragile my feelings for him were. Other times, when the pressure wasn't so high or I was feeling particularly daring, I would let him stare, basking in the attention for longer than I cared to admit. But sometimes, during rare moments that felt like they would be etched in time forever, I would actually hold his gaze, and we would just look at each other for a beat or two or ten. I'd let my eyes linger, tracking the freckles that dusted the bridge of his nose and his eyelids. I wanted to count them all, or kiss them.

I think deep down I knew what they meant—the glances we shared that were so heavy they almost felt like a physical touch, and the touches that made my mind go blank. But none of it added up. The logical part of my brain couldn't make sense of why a boy like Theo would want any part of me. The illogical part of my brain—well, I'd never really had the luxury of being illogical before. I'd never thought I was the type of person someone would want.

"What's with that face?" Taylor said, waving her hand in front of me. "Did you hear anything I just said?"

I blinked at her. "Would you kill me if I said no?"

She picked up the pen she'd been writing with and lobbed it at me, but I caught it before it smacked me in the face. There was a rustle in the clearing, and we both turned to watch Theo emerge from the swaying ferns below. I could tell his face was doing that thing I hated, his brows bunched together in worry. But it wasn't until he burst through the library door that I saw his eyes were wild too, and his face was flushed.

"The sheriff knows about Blackwood," he said, and all the warmth left the room in an instant. "They're going to tear the place down."

"Whoa, back up," Taylor said. "Did you talk to him? What did he say?"

"I overheard an officer talking about it at the corner store. They said the demolition is scheduled for two weeks from now," Theo rattled off, and my gut twisted painfully when he turned to me. "What if they find you? What about the DCF?"

"The DCF would be the least of my problems," I replied stonily. "If they find me stuck in a real-life haunted house, they're gonna call the fucking CIA."

"Shit," Taylor said simply, which was much milder than the string of words filling my head. This was bad. Really bad.

"What the hell are we supposed to do?" Theo asked, starting to pace back and forth. His shoulders were impossibly tense. "We still haven't found out anything new about Josephine."

Taylor chewed her lip. "I'm starting to think that shouldn't be our main focus after all."

"What do you mean?"

"Maybe we're looking at this from the wrong perspective," Taylor said, turning to me. "Haven't you wondered why Theo and I can leave but you can't?"

My stomach flipped. "I thought it had something to do with that window I broke. She's just angry with me, right?" Taylor took a deep breath, and I knew I wouldn't like what she was about to say next. "This might sound like a stretch, but hear me out: What if you're the one who trapped yourself here?"

"*What?*" Theo and I said in unison, but with two completely different tones. He was intrigued; I was horrified.

"Think of it like a science experiment," she said. "Before, there were too many variables up in the air. But since the break-in, all the variables have changed except one: you. I've read about this type of thing happening before to people who are born with special abilities like mine, only they don't realize it. If you've never learned how to control yourself, you could end up in all sorts of nasty situations."

"That's impossible," I said firmly. "Don't you think I would have noticed if I had powers?"

"Jaime, you barely remember your childhood," she said, and I felt the blood drain from my face. "It's not that uncommon for someone to grow up with them and not know it, especially if they had a really stressful upbringing."

"I didn't tell you about my family so you could throw it back in my face," I said, getting up from the sofa and pushing past Theo, who at some point had stopped pacing and was now rooted in place.

"Crap, I didn't mean it that way. Jaime, hold up," Taylor said, moving between me and the door. "You were stressed when you first got to town. You needed to get away, and you said you felt this place calling to you. Do you really think it's a coincidence that you're still here when everyone else can walk in and out whenever they want?"

"What, so it's my fault now?"

"It's not, but you admitted the other day you don't really want to leave."

Theo's eyes met mine, and I wasn't prepared for how betrayed he looked. "You really said that?"

"I didn't mean it," I lied, but the hurt on his face didn't budge. Anxiety and exhaustion were battling for my attention, and I couldn't think straight. I turned back to Taylor. "Are you just gonna keep throwing me under the bus, or are you planning to share a solution to all this? Even if everything you said is true, I obviously can't control it."

"We don't know that," Taylor said, her voice on the edge of pleading. "You can try. We can figure it out together."

Theo nodded, and even though I knew it was illogical, I felt like they were ganging up on me. I didn't need another thing that counted against me being whole. I barely had the energy to carry everything that was wrong with me as it was.

"This is a waste of time, don't you get it? Just let it go and stop trying to fix me."

I turned to go, not entirely sure where, but I could hear Theo following me down the narrow staircase to the second floor.

"I'm not trying to fix you," he said, "I'm just—"

"Yes, you are," I fumed. "I don't want to be your little project anymore. I'm sick of it."

"Jaime, wait." When I didn't, he grabbed my shoulder until I looked him in the eye. "That's not what you are to me and you know it."

"Then what am I to you, Theo?" I asked, my heart lurching painfully as we stood face-to-face in the second-story hallway. I knew I was asking too much, that it wasn't right to put him on the spot in the middle of an argument, but I felt like I had to. When he didn't respond for a few tense moments, I knew I wasn't going to get an answer I liked.

"That's what I thought," I said bitterly. The words tumbled out of my mouth before I had the sense to rein them in. "You're always helping even though I never asked you to. Maybe if you had anything at all going on for yourself, then you'd have something else to fixate on. I'm not some puzzle you can solve just to ignore your own shitty life."

"Don't be an asshole," he snapped back, his face twisted with an anger I'd never seen before. "Maybe if you weren't so closed off, then we wouldn't be the only ones trying to help you."

I recoiled, his words a punch in the gut that knocked the wind out of me. It was one thing for me to feel that way about myself, but something else entirely to hear it coming from him.

"Sorry to break it to you, but I am an asshole, Theo!" I shouted, spitting his name out like it was coated in venom. My palms were itching, and the walls felt like they were closing in. "Get the fuck out. I don't want to look at you."

Taylor emerged from the second-story landing, worry etched across her face. All I wanted to do was hide, to put some distance between me and this entire conversation. My head was spinning, and an image of my parents glaring at me with the same disgust Josephine wore in my dreams flashed in my mind.

I took a step back, and when Theo instinctively made a move to follow, he ran right into a barrier on the second floor where one had never been before.

I watched numbly as he stumbled back into Taylor, and when he lifted his hand to his nose, it came away slick with blood. None of it felt real, not the conversation or what had just happened. I tried to think of something to say, of a way to take it all back, but came up blank.

"Fine," Theo finally said, wiping the blood off his face with the back of his hand. "If you want us gone, then we're leaving."

CHAPTER 23
TAYLOR

THE BELL ON THE shop door jingled as another customer left with their purchase, but the silence that lingered in their wake put me on edge. Even though I had overloaded my schedule, no amount of work could seem to get my mind off the fight.

I'd known that my theory about Jaime would rock the boat, but I'd had no idea it would upset him so much, let alone send the conversation into chaos. It felt like I'd said all the wrong things, and my words played on a loop inside my head until I wanted to crawl out of my own skin.

As I'd left the meadow that night, I'd turned to look back at the house one last time. I could see Jaime standing tall and spectral in one of the second-story windows, though I couldn't tell if he was looking back at me or just standing there all alone, his impenetrable fortress wrapped around him like a cloak in the night. I still couldn't get that image of him out of my head.

When I wasn't in a shame spiral, I was poring over my mom's grimoire. This new information about Jaime meant I had to switch gears. I knew I'd have a better shot of getting him out of Blackwood if I could find a spell that might neutralize his powers, but I hadn't found one that fit the bill.

What I did find was a blood magic spell matching the evidence I'd found in the library, a lengthy and powerful exorcism spell meant for particularly vicious spirits. It called for sage and rosemary, just like I thought, and the sigil she'd drawn in her grimoire looked just like the one I'd seen under the carpet in the library. Which meant my mom must have been to Blackwood and tried to exorcise Josephine like I thought.

I'd suspected for a while that she'd been involved, but it still felt like a punch in the gut to realize there was so much I didn't know about her. My mom had always made me feel like the two of us were in cahoots, sharing secrets and inside jokes that Elias could never understand. But how close had we really been if she'd never told me about her blood magic or Blackwood?

Even though I felt betrayed that she had kept things from me, that betrayal was eclipsed by heartache. It didn't matter if I was mad at her, because she wasn't there to be on the receiving end of my disappointment, and she never would be. Every time I pulled out the grimoire, it just reminded me that she was gone. I couldn't bring myself to add my own annotations to the pages, so I'd started taking notes in a separate notebook, copying down the elements of the exorcism spell that might help me make sense of all her secrets.

It wasn't until later, two days after the fight with Jaime, that I noticed that one of the most crucial elements of the spell was obtaining a personal item from the spirit you were trying to exorcise. I thought back to Theo's suggestion that Elias might have taken any evidence of Josephine from Blackwood himself, and something finally clicked into place: If my mom really had tried to exorcise Josephine, had Elias cleaned the house to stop me from doing the same?

I hadn't been brave enough to try any of the blood magic spells myself, but with my frustration with my dad and anxiety about the demolition growing by the second, I couldn't sit still anymore. Elias and Anna were closing the shop for the evening, so I knew I had some privacy for a little while longer. I flipped through the other spells at the back of the book, each page littered with drawings identical to the kinds I would find on sticky pads next to our landline in the shop after Mom took a call.

I traced a featherlight drawing of a storm cloud, and my heart ached. I longed to feel connected to my mom again, to feel like I had some handle on anything that was happening. Maybe I could try a spell from the back without using blood, just for practice. Without its key element, the spell probably wouldn't hold up, but there was no way to be sure unless I tried.

Flipping through the pages, I landed on the spell titled Forget Me Not. I had already looked it over, and as far as I could tell, it was a simple spell that summoned an object beloved by someone who had recently passed.

I quickly grabbed candles, a bundle of wild spearmint, and a few witch hazel twigs from my stash. With the grimoire splayed out in front of me, I lit my candles one by one, casting a circle like I would before any spell. Reading over the text one more time,

I tried to set my intentions and imagine the feeling of the words against my tongue. Then, with one last deep breath, I started.

It was painfully clumsy at first, to the point where I almost stopped altogether. I stumbled over the words and messed up the cadence, so it felt stilted and unassertive. But I pressed on, and eventually the energy surrounding me shifted. It tingled up and down my limbs, like electricity was zapping each of my nerve endings. My self-doubt melted away and was replaced with a sense of power that I'd never experienced before. I felt invincible, and it was almost addicting.

Once I had finished, I took my time doing a slow sweep around my room, scrutinizing every crack and corner for some kind of sign. But just as I had suspected, the spell didn't seem to have worked. I closed my protective circle, but just as I began to snuff my candles, I heard something shatter downstairs.

"TAYLOR!" my dad bellowed. "¿QUÉ DEMONIOS HAS HECHO?"

Shit. Shitshitshit.

"UH, NOTHING, WHY?" I shouted back, half shoving the grimoire under my bed and snuffing the rest of my candles in record time. It hit me that I might have performed the spell wrong, that it might have done something to him by accident. I scrambled out of my room and down the stairs in a panic, but Elias was waiting for me at the bottom in one piece. Livid, but in one piece.

"Come outside and see for yourself," he said, voice strained with barely concealed anger.

My heart hammered in my ears as I followed him through the shop. There was a jar of tiger eye crystals shattered on the floor, and light was fading from the windows at an alarming speed. I realized a storm was rolling in as Elias pulled the shop door open. I was already feeling nauseated by dread, and when I joined him in the doorway, it took everything in me not to gag.

There under the darkening sky lay a perfect half circle of glassy-eyed birds, wings spread wide, as if they had fallen out of the sky midflight. They were all different shapes and sizes, but what they had in common made my breath catch in my chest: they were all soaked in blood, and they each had a single lily clutched in their feet.

I remembered exactly how our kitchen counter looked the week after my mom passed, lined with dozens of bouquets of her favorite flower. I couldn't get the smell of lilies out of my nose for weeks. Forget Me Not had definitely worked, and it had claimed its blood price whether I wanted it or not.

"So this is what you're doing now?" Elias said, quieter than I expected. There was some emotion simmering just below the surface, but I couldn't tell if it was anger or disappointment. "When Anna told me you'd taken your mom's grimoire, I thought she was lying. I said, 'My daughter would never do something like that.'"

Despite myself, I laughed. It was an ugly, horrible sound, swathed in grief and rotting in the middle. "Wow, it really must be the end of the world if you're taking her side over mine."

"She was worried, and so am I. This"—he pointed at the carcasses—"is not something that you can play with."

Elias pushed past me into the shop, and I trailed behind him as he stomped up the stairs. "Where are you going?"

"I'm taking the grimoire back. It's obvious you can't be trusted with it."

"You can't do that," I said, but Elias barged into my room anyway, grabbing the grimoire from where it was sticking out from under my bed. I was afraid he'd look under my mattress and find my notebook and the rest of my witchy contraband, but thankfully he didn't stop to check. "It's as much mine as it is yours. Mom would have wanted me to have it."

"No, she wouldn't. She didn't want you to know about any of this."

"So, what?" I followed him out of my room, wishing he would stop and look at me for half a second. "You two were in on this together, lying about Blackwood? I know all about it, by the way. You were the one who cleared the place out, weren't you? Or was that her idea?"

"Taylor, that's enough," he ground out, but I couldn't stop.

"How long were you planning on hiding all this from me? Why didn't you tell me that Mom used blood magic?"

"Because I didn't know until it was too late!" he shouted back, and I froze. My understanding of my mom's death finally clicked into place—the way she got worse the more spells she cast, and the way it drove a wedge between my parents in those final weeks. "Now you can see why I don't want this life for you. I can't have you turning out like her, putting your life in danger just to test your power."

I wanted to tell him it wasn't his say how I turned out, and that it hurt when he talked about Mom like that, but I didn't have the energy. Not when I felt like I could burst into tears any minute. "I just need more practice."

"You can't practice with life. How do you not see how dangerous this is? You're going to get yourself—or someone else—killed."

"Then help me," I pleaded in a last-ditch effort, barely recognizing the desperation in my own voice.

"The only person who could have helped you is long gone, lilies or not," he said, turning away. "Close the windows, mija. A storm is coming."

Elias's office door slammed shut behind him, and I was left stunned in the hallway with nothing but hot tears of frustration welling up in my eyes. I needed to get out of our apartment, get some fresh air or scream or *something*. The stairs were a blur beneath me as my tears threatened to overflow, and just when I got downstairs, Anna emerged from the storeroom. I tried to blow past her, but she grabbed my arm to stop me.

"Hey, wait up—"

"I can't believe you sold me out," I said, pulling my arm free and wheeling to look at her. "I thought we were friends."

"I'm just trying to look out for you, okay?" Her wide brown eyes were filled with concern, or pity. "Why can't you see that I'm trying to protect you?"

"Protect me? From what?"

"From yourself," she said. "When I did that reading for the boy with the freckles, I saw some awful things. There was so much blood. I think you're going to hurt someone, Taylor. That, or you're going to hurt yourself."

I shook my head. No way that was going to happen. I wouldn't let it. "If keeping me from the truth is your idea of help, then I don't want it."

"You're pushing away the people who really care about you," she said, shaking her head. I started to leave, but she spoke up one last time. "I hope you understand before it's too late."

CHAPTER 24
JAIME

WHEN I SLEPT, I didn't dream, but I wouldn't call what I had nightmares either. They were layers of memories, sharp around the edges but soft and slow in the middle, overlapping at times so one started before another had the chance to end. The one thing they all had in common was the guilt. It colored the margins of my dreamscapes with a slippery, sinking feeling, a bitterness that told me I had hurt so many people and I didn't deserve to rest.

I saw my mom crying, screaming, mourning more times than I could count. I saw her plead with me to just be normal, placing her hands on either side of my face and begging me to stop—but stop what, I wasn't sure. I just remember feeling broken, feeling fear and sorrow that were too big for someone my age.

Josephine was there too, slipping between the memories until I wasn't sure what was real and what wasn't. I saw her standing by the bedroom window once, looking out at the valley. Her hair was loose around her, a cloud of russet waves framing her face like a phantasmal halo, and I wasn't sure if I was asleep or awake.

"Why are you crying?" she asked once, her expression stony. I pressed my fingers numbly to my cheek, and they came away wet with blood. "People always hate what they don't understand. You should know that by now. That's why it's not safe out there."

For the first time in what felt like ages, I found enough of my voice to do something other than sob. "I'm not safe here either."

"I'm not trying to hurt you, I'm trying to save you." It wasn't said with any degree of softness. She said it like she was tired of waiting for me to understand. "You still don't remember how it all started. You and I, we're really not all that different. This is your boulder, Sisyphus. Figure it out."

The burn of her voice sounded oddly familiar. I grasped helplessly at a thought from another life, but then it was gone, and she was gone too.

I dreamed of my childhood home again, but the walls were red, then blue, then red, flashing impossibly until I remembered it was just emergency lights splashing messily across everything in sight. I tried to dissect what it meant, but I was too tired to care. I was so exhausted I was tired even as I slept.

When I finally woke up, I could still see the burn of lights against the backs of my eyes. I hadn't seen Theo or Taylor in three days, and I felt even more raw and emotionally hungover than I had the day before. I had never actually been hungover, but I had to assume feeling like absolute shit came close.

I knew I had acted like a monster with Theo and Taylor, so much so that I barely recognized myself when I thought about it in retrospect. I still couldn't wrap my mind around what had happened with the barrier. It was like I blacked out and when I came to, Theo was on the ground with blood running down his chin.

I rubbed the sleep and that horrible image from my eyes with the heels of my hands and, having maxed out my capacity for wallowing, headed downstairs. I had just started to mentally catalog what canned goods were left in the pantry when I saw a note that had been slipped under the front door. Knowing right away it was from Theo, I rushed to pick it up.

Brought more food, whether you want it or not.

—T

I unlocked the deadbolt, and when the front door swung in, a bag of groceries hanging on the doorknob swung with it. That smart little bastard. I wasn't sure if I wanted to laugh or cry at the food, the passive-aggressive note, and the fact that he wasn't mad enough to let me starve.

As I grabbed the bag and made my way to the kitchen, another wave of guilt threatened to yank my mood into deeper, darker waters again. In one fell swoop, it felt like I had flung myself all the way back to square one with Theo. I thought I'd changed since then. I didn't want to be the same person who'd nearly bitten his head off those first few times we talked—the same person who was so busy lighting our relationship on fire for warmth I never noticed he was asking me to sit in the sun with him. And if I had any brains at all, I wouldn't have made the same mistake twice.

Maybe that was what had set me off in the conversation with Taylor. I knew how much Theo cared about me, and that was exactly why I was so terrified of being a burden to him. If I was the one who had trapped myself in the house, then all the time and effort Theo had invested in helping me was a waste.

But the way Taylor had talked reminded me of the way my parents used to talk to me too. Between that and the dreams and conversations with Josephine, I felt like there was something missing. Some itch I needed to scratch that was just out of reach.

So for the first time since Theo spent the night at Blackwood, I let myself really think about my parents. Not the surface-level glossy memories that sometimes flitted into my head uninvited, but real, gritty memories from the first few years of my life. The ones I'd worked so hard to forget I wasn't even sure they existed anymore.

Thinking that far back was like wading through mud, thoughts made infinitely heavier when colored by anger and grief. Even though I couldn't picture my dad's face very clearly, I did remember he was tall. Then again, maybe I only thought he was tall because I was so small back then. He was strong, sturdy, a decent man by traditional Latino standards. He didn't make an effort to hide how disappointed he was at having a soft, sensitive, overthinking son like me who cried over stray cats and struggling bugs on the sidewalk.

As I unloaded the groceries into the pantry, I wondered if he'd be happy that foster care had forced me to trade in my emotional side for a thin veneer of acidity to survive. A "don't mess with me, don't even look at me" attitude was the only thing standing between me and a black eye or a broken nose, so I didn't really have a choice.

But no matter how much I changed, I was still the scared little boy who knew that his dad only ever saw him as an accident. I recognized the regret on his face every time he looked at me, and I recognized it the last time I ever saw him.

I must have been about six or seven years old, sitting on the couch as my parents huddled in the front hall. Their faces were stony, illuminated by flashing red and white lights as a fire engine peeled away from the curb outside our house. Then my dad stared over his shoulder at me like you might look at a piece of trash on the sidewalk.

"He never should've been born," he said. "We should have gotten rid of him when we had the chance."

But instead of getting rid of me, he was the one who was gone the next day.

My mom was a different story, but not by much. She hid it better than he did, but it was just the same shade of hostility in a different hue. For every memory I had of us making pancakes on a cornflower-blue Sunday morning, I had another of her with tears of frustration pouring down her face, asking me why I couldn't just stay out of trouble for once in my "short, insignificant life."

Strangely enough, those flashing police and fire engine lights colored nearly every painful memory I had of my parents and of Saint Juniper. I never questioned it as a kid, and when I asked my foster siblings, they told me they had grown up around the same kind of thing. But as I racked my brain, I couldn't figure out why they were always there. My parents' fights weren't violent enough to warrant a police visit, so what else could it have been?

I gave up on trying to organize the pantry and headed back to the foyer to lock the front door, a new habit I had formed after the break-in. My hand was almost to the deadbolt when I froze, a memory coming back so suddenly it momentarily stunned me.

It was flashes of my mom at a home improvement store, my arm in her iron grip as she pleaded for the sales guy to find her doors that didn't jam shut.

"He locks himself in every room in the house," she said. "I don't understand how, but it's driving me crazy. I just don't get it."

I remember thinking it was funny because that wasn't what I was doing at all. Hiding like that was sort of a game to me. Even if I couldn't be safe, at least I could be alone. I would find an empty room or closet and hunker down until my parents found me. They would beg and plead for me to come out, but I never would. I would only come out later, when there was a stranger on the other side of the door who talked to me softly.

My hand dropped away from the lock as my mind reeled, and I stepped back until I bumped into one of the staircase banisters. Had my parents really called the sheriff and the fire department all those times because they couldn't figure out how to unstick or unlock a door?

But then, as I gazed across the entryway at the deadbolt on the heavy wooden door, everything shifted into focus. Not every place I'd hidden in that tiny old house had a lock. Even when there was one, I never used it. It was just me, climbing into a linen closet or a pantry and sealing myself inside without having to touch anything.

I thought back to the dreams that had been haunting me for weeks, about all the bizarre things Josephine had been telling me since I had come to Blackwood. And like a cascade, moments from my childhood that had never made sense started snapping into place: The way the neighbors used to stare at us every time we left the house. The way my parents seemed terrified of me for no good reason. The way my mom leaned down the day she left me in that shopping mall and said, "I'm sorry, I can't do this anymore."

The last thing she ever said to me wasn't about her being a parent, it was about *me*. Anguish welled up so fast I thought it would choke me. I reached for the handrail and missed, my vision blurred with unshed tears. I sank to my knees on the stairs and tried to hold myself together as my breath became ragged.

I had always blamed my parents for leaving me, for throwing me away like I was trash. But as the hot tears of frustration finally started to roll down my cheeks and my mind darted back to Theo and Taylor, I feared that what my parents had known years ago was right all along. I was broken, and that was why I deserved to be alone.

CHAPTER 25
THEO

THERE WAS A NEW voice mail from my sister and a growing collection of texts from Taylor waiting for me when I woke up.

The sun hadn't managed to break through the clouds that morning, and without it as my alarm, I could tell I'd slept in. Still, I was surprised to see it was nearing eleven a.m. when I finally checked the clock on my bedside table. I couldn't remember the last time I'd slept so late, even when school was out.

Grace didn't call often, let alone leave voice mails, so I worked up the nerve to check out her message first. But when I pressed play, I instantly regretted it.

"Theodore, this is an intervention," she said curtly. The muffled din of coffee shop chatter echoed in the background. "Mom and Dad are worried, and instead of talking to you directly, they made the healthy and uncomplicated request that I do it for them. Dad thinks you're on drugs, which I told him was absurd. I mean, you don't even take a Tylenol when you get a headache."

I almost moved the phone away from my ear to stop the message, but paused as I heard her chair scrape back. The sounds of the coffee shop receded, and she sighed.

"If there's something going on, I'm just a phone call away, all right? They might not see you, like, really see you, but I do. And if you think I don't, I'd like to try." The pit in my stomach stayed lodged there long after the line went silent and my phone screen blinked to black.

Three days had passed since I'd last spoken to Jaime. It didn't seem like much, but it was the longest we had spent apart since we met. I guess I wasn't handling the space as well as I thought, especially if my parents had noticed I was sulking.

But even if I did call Grace back, I wasn't sure what I would say to her. I wasn't sure I could put into words how devastating the fight with Jaime had been, how the place in my chest that had felt unbearably full since we started spending time together was hollow now. There was only one person I could think of who might understand how I felt, but I hadn't worked up the nerve to text her back.

When I pulled up my text conversation with Taylor, another wave of guilt hit as my eyes scanned a string of missed messages. At the bottom, her latest message read, *I know things are weird, but we need to talk.*

After the fight, I'd walked Taylor back through the forest and driven her home in silence. When I collapsed into bed later that night, I didn't have it in me to check my phone. I didn't have it in me the next day either. I wasn't mad at her—far from it, actually. I was paralyzed with fear, hyperaware that we were running out of time and ashamed I didn't have a plan to patch things up. I was the one who'd brought us all together, but now I wasn't sure if I could do it again.

Before I lost my nerve, I typed out a reply and hit send. *Do you want to go for a drive?*

A few texts and hours later, Taylor was in my passenger seat and we were heading west, toward Jay State Forest. Normally when I wanted to clear my head, I would drive through the valley. But since the fight, I had only ventured out there once to drop off food. Going into the woods, even without any contact with Jaime, had made my heart constrict so painfully I couldn't bear the thought of going back. Not until I had a plan.

Taylor was silent as we left town limits. The roads were relatively empty, and the day was perfect for a road trip, gray and hazy and soft around the edges. Long drives were usually a religious experience for me. I loved my ugly old Subaru, which was probably five years past its deathbed. I loved passing through towns like Saint Juniper and wondering if there was someone like me out there, someone confused and unhappy even though they didn't think they had the right to be. I loved getting all the daydreaming out of my system so when I went back to my real life, I could keep my focus where it mattered. But this drive wouldn't be one where I could file all my thoughts away into neat little piles.

It wasn't until we started winding through fields and speeding past isolated farmhouses that Taylor finally spoke up.

"I wanted to apologize," she started. I should have realized sooner that her silence was terribly out of character, but it wasn't until she started speaking that it hit me how nervous she was. "I shouldn't have put Jaime on the spot like I did, and I'm sorry for setting that argument in motion."

"I think you did the best you could," I replied after a pause. "I was the one who made things worse. I shouldn't have pushed him. I should have let him think or listened to him or *something*."

A little of Taylor's nervous energy seemed to dissipate, and I saw her shake her head out of the corner of my eye. "We were all stressed. I don't think any of us expected it to turn out the way it did."

I nodded, but the tightness in my chest wouldn't unfurl. The cold, unreadable expression on Jaime's face when he'd kicked us out of the house was still fresh in my mind. When I'd looked up at him from where I had fallen to the ground, I couldn't tell where the shadows that swallowed up the edges of the hallway ended and where he began. He was as imperious and grim as the night that was descending on us, and for a split second, I was genuinely afraid of him. I was ashamed of myself for thinking that now, and the longer I sat on it, the more it felt like it was eating me from the inside out.

"Well, now we have our missing piece," I sighed, pulling into a gravel overlook and putting the car in park. "I wish we hadn't learned it the hard way, but you were right."

"I kind of wish I wasn't. Things just got a lot more complicated for him. For all of us," she murmured. It had started drizzling, a steady mist that quickly blanketed the windshield, and

I watched as the drops began to pool together. "Elias took the grimoire."

"I'm sorry, *what?*"

"I wrote down some notes before he swiped it, and I think I have a plan," she added quickly. "But if we want to pull it off, we need to talk to Jaime and get to work. We can't afford to lose any more time."

"I know that," I said, and it came out far terser than I meant for it to sound. I took a breath and tried again. "I'm just not sure if I can fix things."

"I understand if you're mad at him, but—"

"It's not that."

"Then what is it?" she asked, turning in her seat so she was facing me fully. "I need you, and Jaime needs you too. But it seems a little like you just stopped caring."

I probably would've laughed at how far off she was if we weren't in such dire straits. I opened my mouth to try and vocalize the tangle of thoughts inside my head, but they caught in my throat before I could force them out. I only spoke again when I was sure my voice wouldn't break.

"I care so much it scares me," I said quietly, looking straight ahead out the windshield so I wouldn't have to see her react. "And I hate myself for hurting him, and I can't imagine what I'll do if we don't get him out of there in one piece. If I think about it too much, or if I think about him too much, I feel like I can't breathe. He's more than just a friend to me. So please, *please* don't say I stopped caring. I couldn't stop even if I tried."

"Oh," she said. Then my meaning finally hit her. "*Oh.* Shit, Theo. I feel like an ass. This was not what I expected to talk about today."

"Yeah," I breathed, leaning back against the headrest. "I didn't expect this either. I kept trying to tell myself that how I felt wasn't a big deal, but I don't think I can ignore it anymore."

"Does it have to be a bad thing?" she ventured.

"It doesn't have to be, but it is for me. I'm turning eighteen next week. I'm supposed to have my life together. I know what my parents expect of me, what my friends expect, and liking boys is not on the agenda," I said. My eyes followed the rivulets of rain that wound down the windshield. "I've spent so much time trying to be the type of person who makes everyone proud, and I've made it this far without messing things up for myself. Throwing all that out the window feels . . . I don't know. It feels selfish."

Taylor didn't respond right away, but when she did, she spoke with a gentleness I wasn't sure I deserved. "For the record, I think you could stand to be a little more selfish. You're going to run yourself ragged trying to be perfect all the time."

"I don't know who I'd be if I wasn't trying to be perfect," I replied, but I knew she was right. Then, quieter, I added, "If I feel this way about him, then what does that make me?"

"Theo, look at me," she said firmly, placing a warm hand on my shoulder. "It makes you the same person you've always been."

And just like that, I felt a rush of relief that knocked the wind out of me. She'd somehow managed to say the one thing I needed to hear most, and it was like all the tension from the past few weeks eased up just enough for me to breathe again.

"I still don't know how to fix this with Jaime," I said. "I'm afraid I ruined things between us. Between all of us."

"I don't think that's possible," she said gently. "I'd go and apologize to him myself, but I think he'd want to talk to you first. All I know is we have to try to patch things up."

"And what if he doesn't want to talk to me?"

Taylor sat back in the passenger seat. "I seriously doubt that. But there's only one way to know for sure."

———

By the time I dropped Taylor off, the rooftops and telephone poles lining her street were nothing more than abstract shapes crowding the painting of the late-afternoon sky. We'd talked all the way back into town, passing the endless stream of tiny shops, humble houses, and crimson barns with flaking paint dotting the countryside. And the longer we talked, the more I wanted to see Jaime.

So when I stopped at the fork in the road that could either take me straight back to Saint Juniper or down into the valley, it didn't seem like the worst idea to take the scenic route. And when I reached the bend in the road where I usually parked my car, pulling off to the side didn't feel that bad either.

I thought long and hard about what I wanted to say on the walk to the house. I felt ready all the way up until I was standing on the porch, but all the words I was going to say died on my lips the second I saw him open the front door. It wasn't just because a surge of emotion passed across his face, half elated and half annoyed. That I was expecting. It was because I had missed him even more than I realized, and seeing him again solidified all the feelings I had spent the last few weeks running from.

Jaime stepped aside so there was room for me to walk through the doorway. "Do you want to come in?"

"Can I?" I asked, then realized a half second too late that it could've come off as combative. But if Jaime interpreted it that way, he didn't let on.

"I think so."

I hesitated a bit before I made my move, but when I stepped over the threshold, I was able to walk right in. Jaime and I paused in the foyer. I tried to think of where to start with my apology, but there were too many things I wanted to say and not enough words to express them. When the silence stretched on a little too long, Jaime let out a huff of air.

"God, this is so weird," he said, running a hand through his hair. "It is weird, right?"

"It's very weird," I said. "I'm sorry for the other day, for all of it. Taylor and I shouldn't have pushed you like that. It was selfish, and you had every right to be frustrated with me. I was in problem-solving mode, and I wasn't thinking about your feelings at all."

Jaime considered me for a moment. Maybe I'd said too much, or hadn't said enough. Would it be overstepping to tell him I'd missed him? I wondered if it would be ridiculous to tell him that no matter how badly he wanted me to leave him alone, I wouldn't give up on him.

"You wouldn't be my favorite steamroller if you had been," he said with a sigh, and I wasn't sure whether to feel happy or offended. He nodded toward the stairs. "Can we go up? I hate that we're standing here like strangers."

I was so stunned that he was halfway up the first flight of steps before I moved to follow him. "Wait, really? Aren't you mad at me?"

"I definitely was," he said as we walked. "I'm not gonna pretend I wasn't, but it'd be kind of hypocritical if I iced you out. I mean, I said some awful shit to you too."

"I kind of deserved it," I mumbled, and Jaime gave me a skeptical look as we reached the third floor.

"No, you really didn't," he said, heading into the library and sinking onto the couch. "I was upset and exhausted, but that's no excuse. I'm sorry too."

I nodded, hovering in the doorframe until Jaime looked at me expectantly, and I finally joined him on the couch. "No offense, but I didn't expect this conversation to go very smoothly."

"I don't blame you. Honestly, it helps that you guys were right," he said. "Taylor's theory, I mean. About me and the house, about everything."

It took a while for Jaime to recount his lost childhood, how so many things that could explain his powers were lost in memories moth-eaten by trauma. He told me how he'd been too young to realize the strain this power of his had put on his parents' already rocky relationship, how that probably was why his dad had left and his mom had given him up.

I watched his face closely the entire time he talked. He'd clearly given this a lot of thought in the days we'd spent apart. Part of me was sorry I hadn't been there for him, but another part thought maybe the solitude had been what he needed to finally start working through everything. There was still a kind of detached sadness tinging the edges of his stories about his parents, and his voice sounded especially raw when he spoke about his mom. But more than anything, it seemed like a weight was lifting off him the more he spoke.

"This explains a lot," he said once he had finished. "But it still doesn't explain everything. I guess I have to deal with it whether I like it or not."

"I mean, other than the fact you're stuck, don't you think this is kind of cool?" I offered, and Jaime snorted. "I'm serious. You and Taylor, you're kind of like superheroes."

"My superpower is pushing people away, literally. My life is a joke."

Nothing I could say would properly express how wrong he was for thinking that way. I understood now that he'd had so many doors slammed in his face when people got tired of looking at him, he probably just wanted to slam the door in someone else's face first. He wasn't a monster, he was just a boy with a destiny so big he had to break off pieces of himself to survive. In a funny way, I think we were both learning that hiding never works out the way you think it will.

"You were just protecting yourself," I said eventually. "You still are."

"Maybe," he conceded. The last rays of afternoon sun emerged from behind a thick haze of clouds and cast a soft glow around the room. "I just can't believe I kept all this repressed for so long. I mean, I don't do that. I'm not you."

"Um, ouch?" I shoved Jaime away from me as he cackled at his own stupid joke. I couldn't stop staring at the way the light bounced off his hair and how his eyes crinkled at the corners when he smiled. God, I'd missed him.

"I just needed to get that one dig out of my system. I'm good now," he said, sporting the genuine sort of smile I loved most on him. I couldn't not smile back.

I knew it'd take more than a simple apology to patch things up. Being with him still felt fragile. But not so fragile that our relationship would break after being dropped once. It felt good to know that now.

"I'll let it slide. No more fighting?"

I held out my pinky, and he stared at it for a moment before sighing and reaching out to meet me in the middle. When he looped his pinky around mine, it sent a pleasant shock down my spine.

"No more fighting."

CHAPTER 26
TAYLOR

MY FIRST ORDER OF business after Theo made up with Jaime was to apologize myself, but when we met up at Blackwood the next morning, Jaime wouldn't hear it.

"I'm really sorry about the other day. I didn't mean to—" I started, but he just waved me off.

"Don't worry. It was a group effort."

"I know, but I'm still sorry."

Jaime paused, and a little quieter, added, "I am too, for being an ass. But we're good, I promise."

Pretty soon, we were all curled up in three comically different armchairs in a sitting room on the ground floor. Jaime filled us in on his latest run-ins with Josephine and explained all the pertinent details from his big anxiety-induced revelation.

"I think I finally understand why those people were able to break in," Jaime said once he had gone over everything. "I thought it was you two coming through the woods, so the barrier must have lifted. They got in before I shut down again."

"So it's just a mental thing, then?" Theo said, as if it were the easiest thing in the world to fix. "Can't we just, you know, trick you into leaving?"

"I don't think it's that straightforward," Jaime replied with a little laugh.

"You're right." I shifted in my chair, pulling my knees to my chest. "Even if you think you want to leave on the surface, deep down there's something that's tethering your spirit to this house. There could have been moments where the barrier dropped for a second when you felt comfortable, probably more times than we even realized. But the only way you can leave is if you learn how to control your power, and if you really want to leave deep down."

"Uh, bold statement here, but I don't think I have time to unpack all my childhood trauma in a week and a half," Jaime said uneasily. "And Josephine is in my head telling me I'll die if I leave. I'd be lying if I said she wasn't making it worse."

"I know, but that's where I think I can help," I replied. "There's an exorcism spell in my mom's grimoire that I think she tried to perform here, to untangle Josephine's spirit from the house and help her pass to the other side. I think it might help detach your spirit from the house too."

Theo and Jaime exchanged a nervous look, the type that told me explaining how volatile and dangerous blood magic could be might make them panic. And if they did, if they vetoed the exorcism spell and all the risks that came with it, I wasn't sure we'd be able to get Jaime free before the demolition. So even though it was eating me up inside, I kept my mouth shut.

"Are you sure this is the right spell to get the job done?" Theo asked, and I knew he didn't mean it unkindly.

"It's the only one I took notes on before Elias took the grimoire back," I replied quietly, hugging my knees closer to my chest. "Right now, it's our only option."

Theo nodded tightly. I didn't need to remind him that we were running out of time. After a beat, Jaime broke the silence.

"If this is our only chance, we have to take it."

So we made a game plan. Jaime would train to control his powers, I would focus on recreating my mom's spell, and Theo would keep us both sane in the process. We had ten days to nail it all down, and the pressure was on.

My first order of business was rolling the rug up in the library and copying down the sigil. I drew it alongside the list of materials I remembered reading in the grimoire: rosemary oil, sage, angelica, yarrow, peridot. I also grabbed the personal item I needed from Jaime, one of his well-worn black T-shirts.

Thankfully, since the spell would be directed toward Jaime, I didn't think I needed a personal item from Josephine to make it work. I desperately wanted to keep digging into her past, into what about her had made my mom so obsessed with helping her pass to the other side. But if I kept pushing Elias about Blackwood, or tried to go through my mom's things again, I had no idea how he would react. I wasn't willing to take that risk, not with the demolition hanging over our heads and Jaime's future on the line.

I spent most of my time at Blackwood as I worked on the spell, and the one shift I had at the shop that week was positively frigid. Elias didn't talk to me unless we were in front of customers, and when he did, he looked through me instead of looking at me. I figured our relationship had already been damaged enough that my pursuit of the truth wouldn't make much of a dent. Clearly, I was wrong, and the freeze-out hurt me in a way I hadn't expected.

It didn't help that I'd barely processed our fight in the first place, especially what he'd implied about my mom's death. I couldn't believe she had kept such a massive secret from me for so long. I tried to imagine a world where I kept a secret like that from the people I loved. I pushed down the part of me that said I was doing the same to Jaime and Theo.

The only thing that quieted that guilt was helping Jaime train. We spent a few days focusing on how he could center himself and get in touch with his internal defenses, which of course he hated. When we moved on to trying to shift the edges of the barrier, things started going a bit better. But the few times he was able to nudge it an inch or two, it would slip through his fingers right after he noticed a change.

"You've got to stop thinking so hard," I told him for the fourth time in fifteen minutes.

Jaime was standing in front of the open front door, hands out in front of him and palms flattened against the barrier. "I didn't even say anything."

"I can hear you thinking," I replied, ignoring him as he started to protest. "Being a smart-ass also counts as thinking. Just try to clear your mind, okay?"

"I haven't had a clear mind since the day I was born," he huffed, slumping against the barrier. "I've decided magic isn't real. This is all a prank to make me look stupid."

"Technically, for you, it isn't magic," Theo said from the porch. I had put him out there hoping it would motivate Jaime, but I wasn't sure it was working. "I think it would qualify as psychokinesis."

"Booooo," I called through cupped hands. "We don't want your logic, science man."

Jaime laughed, pushing himself away from the door and moving down the hall to the kitchen. "No matter what you call it, it's still impossible."

"You're not going to get anywhere if you keep talking like that," I said, trailing behind him. "You'll get a feel for it eventually."

"Well, of course you'd say that. All this is second nature to you," he said as he picked through the pantry. "It's new to me."

"It might be second nature, but everything I'm working on right now is new to me too," I said. "We're really not all that different."

Jaime poked his head out of the pantry. "That sounds familiar—did you get that from a book or something?"

"I don't think so. Déjà vu?"

"Something like that," he said, tossing me a granola bar and nabbing one for himself.

"For you, it has less to do with effort and more to do with conviction," I said as he took a bite. "You have to want to leave, deep down. You have to believe that you'll be safe out there, that things will be better once you're free."

Jaime chewed for a bit, worry seeping into his expression. "What if I'm just a coward? I thought foster care had changed me, but maybe I'm just the same scared little kid I've always been."

"You're not a coward," I said, but Jaime was already shaking his head.

"Okay, and what if I can't pull this off?" he asked. "What if this thing I hate about myself is all I've got? What then?"

"That's why I'm here. That's what the spell is for."

"Level with me for a second, okay?" Jaime said, his voice dropping to a whisper. "I can tell you're anxious. How dangerous is this going to be?"

I swallowed, my mouth suddenly dry. "I—It's pretty dangerous. But I don't want you to get hurt."

Jaime's gaze raked over my face. When he spoke again, his voice was quiet but firm. "I don't want to know what the police would do if they found me stuck here. If it's a choice between leaving me in here and getting me out no matter what, I want you to get me out."

My stomach lurched.

Then Theo called out from the porch, and Jaime pushed himself away from the counter. "Don't mention I said anything to Theo, okay? His birthday is coming up and I don't want him to be stressed."

I nodded, but as Jaime went off to see what Theo needed, the weight of yet another secret settling on me didn't feel like a good omen. Still, Jaime and Theo were counting on me, and it was up to me to not tear them apart.

CHAPTER 27
THEO

IT WAS THE LAST week of August—there were only a few scorching days left before summer burned through its fuse, and we had six days before Blackwood was set to be demolished. Admittedly, I was a little bit of a wreck.

Jaime was training to control his powers around the clock, and Taylor was busy gathering the herbs and crystals she needed for the spell. They were both making good progress in their own ways, which was great, but I wished I could help in a more tangible way. Instead, it just felt like we were running out of time, and I was letting the days hurtle by at double speed.

Downtown Saint Juniper was busier than usual. Our Summer's End Festival was two days away, and the town was buzzing with preparations. Forest-green pennants hung from nearly every lamppost, and a few tents were already pitched in the town square. Normally, it was one of my favorite times of year.

Under the current circumstances, it felt a bit like a ticking time bomb being shoved in my face. *The school year is just around the corner,* it said. *Better hurry.*

Yet despite all my panicking and my best attempts to stay pragmatic, every once in a while, I did let myself daydream about what life might be like if Jaime was set free. If we pulled everything off, we would be taking the same classes together in a matter of weeks. But I also knew I'd have to think about college again, about everything I had been avoiding for the bulk of the summer, and I wasn't sure where that left me. One afternoon, I decided to bring it up with him while I was perched on the kitchen counter.

"Are you nervous for senior year?" I asked, watching Jaime take stock of the food in the pantry.

"Not really. I guess I haven't thought about it much."

"How is that possible?"

"Dude, you are such a Virgo. Not everyone was born nervous like you," he said with a laugh, moving into the sunlit kitchen. "Don't try to deny it—I can see the existential dread in your eyes as we speak."

"Well, how else am I supposed to feel? It's our last year of high school," I replied. "I should have everything figured out."

"Says who?"

I considered it for a moment. "The universe."

"You put way too much pressure on yourself," he said, then cut me off when I started to protest. "Don't argue, you're not helping your case. You're so tightly wound, one of these days you're gonna snap."

"That's absurd."

"Sounds like something you'd say if you were on the verge of snapping."

"I just want everything to be good," I sighed, ignoring his teasing. "I *need* it to be good. I don't want to start college feeling all mixed up."

"That," he said, his hand landing on my shoulder with a soft thump, "is going to require you to remove the massive stick that's up your butt."

"Hilarious," I deadpanned as Jaime dropped his hand and hopped up onto the counter next to me, his shoulder pressed firmly against mine. "But don't you ever feel that way too? Like you're running out of time?"

"Theo, we're seventeen."

"I'll be eighteen tomorrow. That's ancient."

"Theo."

"I know, I know. But it's like, I can so easily see a version of myself where I stay in Saint Juniper forever and do exactly what everyone wants me to do," I said quietly. "I'm so scared life might pass me by, and I don't want to wake up one day and realize I've been faking everything so long I never actually figured out how to live for real."

"You're the realest thing about this whole place," Jaime said after a pause. When I didn't respond, he bumped his shoulder softly against mine. "I'm serious, okay? Life is not just going to happen to you. You're gonna find your way, I promise."

I turned to look at him then, my eyes tracing the elegant slope of his nose and the curve of his lashes. "What makes you so sure?"

"Because you're special," he said simply, locking eyes with me. "Someone like you has to make it."

Jaime was always saying things that lit a fire in my bones and turned my entire world on its side. In moments like that, I wanted to tell him I couldn't believe we'd gone from strangers to whatever we were so fast I'd almost missed it. I wanted to tell him everything. But then a bird warbled at us from outside the kitchen window, and the moment slid to a quiet stop as Jaime hopped off the counter. I wasn't sure where the conversation left us, but I felt a little bit different than I had before.

A part of me wanted to exist forever in this strange reality we had created, suspended in our private little pocket of time. I wanted to remember in perfect detail how incredible it was to piece this picture of him together, because as I unraveled him thread by thread, I also was unraveling my feelings for him. I knew I had to tell him how I felt eventually, and every day that passed, I got a little bit closer to actually wanting to.

When I parked my car in the valley the next day, the sun had already begun to set, the sky a pretty cotton-candy mix of pink and baby blue. Jaime had specifically asked me to come over after my shift at the library, one of the last ones I had on the schedule before school started. The request struck me as a bit odd, since I always came by Blackwood after work, but I hadn't pointed it out.

I had been dreading my birthday for weeks, panicked by the idea of turning another year older with no real wisdom or self-possession to show for it, but maybe it wouldn't be so bad after all. With the wind at my back and birds performing their evening chorus in the branches above my head, I couldn't help but feel a little giddy.

When I approached the house, the remnants of the sunset reflected in its warped windowpanes, my suspicions were confirmed. The impish look on Jaime's face when he met me at the front door definitely meant something was up.

"All right, what did you do?"

"Theo, you wound me," he gasped, pressing a hand to his heart. "When have I ever led you astray?"

"Pretty much every day since I met you," I replied lightly, but he ignored me, turning to practically jog up the stairs. "You're really not going to tell me what you're up to?"

"If I did, it wouldn't be a surprise," he called back. The excitement in his voice made it impossible for me not to smile.

I followed Jaime up the stairs, expecting us to head to the library, but he led me right past the door and only stopped once we were at the end of the hall. He pulled down the access ladder to what I could only assume was the attic, and I raised an eyebrow at him in disbelief.

"Are you going to murder me in the attic? Is that my gift?"

"After you," he said with a shit-eating grin, but he put a hand on my arm as I reached for the ladder. "Close your eyes before you get to the top. I don't want you to see anything until I say so."

I hummed in agreement and I did as he said, clambering up the last rungs of the ladder by touch alone. The air up there smelled surprisingly clean, nothing like the mustiness I'd expected. I heard Jaime climb up behind me, then shuffle around doing god knows what. I waited patiently until he spoke.

"Okay, open your eyes," he said, and I did just in time to see Jaime moving a large tarp to reveal a gaping hole where the ceiling and a good chunk of the wall should have been.

"There is a hole," I said, "in the roof. My birthday present is a hole in the roof."

"No, your birthday present is dinner and a show," he said. I realized belatedly that I was standing on something soft, and I looked down to see the blankets I had given him laid out on the ground. Jaime had set up a whole picnic for us in the attic, complete with a spread of the best nonperishable food I had brought him in the last few weeks. "Cards on the table here: a branch fell through the roof last week. But I'm gonna need you to pretend it was part of a larger, well-orchestrated plan."

"You're insane," I laughed, looking over the little bags of freeze-dried fruit and chocolate-covered pretzels. "What is all this?"

"I've been asking for all your favorites for weeks and stockpiling them."

"Wait, that's why you were asking for all this stuff?" I stared at him, impressed. I was surprised he'd even remembered my favorite foods from our passing conversations, let alone had the foresight to plan this out. "You realize you made me buy my own birthday dinner, right?"

"My options were limited, okay? Improvise, adapt, overcome, or whatever."

I peered at him. "If this is dinner, what's the show?"

"I'm so glad you asked," he said, coming up behind me and putting his hands on my shoulders. It sent a pleasant shiver down my spine as he steered me closer to the exposed ceiling. "I know you've been worried about my training with Taylor. Don't even try to argue—you have a terrible poker face. Either way, I thought you might like to see how things are going."

Jaime raised a hand to the spot where the ceiling should have been. His eyes fixed on some distant point up in the branches, and after a beat, I watched in disbelief as his hand inched farther and farther beyond the confines of the house.

"I can't believe it. This is amazing," I whispered, and Jaime's eyes met mine. "*You're* amazing."

Jaime opened his mouth to respond, and all of a sudden, his hand ricocheted off the edge of the jagged opening. "Clearly, I still have some practicing to do. Taylor says I get distracted too easily," he said, running a hand through his hair. "It's not much, but hopefully it'll be enough."

I hardly knew what to say. Not just because I was proud of him, but because he wanted to show me what he could do. To let me know that this rushed plan we had set in motion might actually turn out okay.

I was still collecting my thoughts when Jaime motioned for me to settle onto the blanket. "Come sit. If you look up, the view is really pretty. I think there's a full moon tonight."

He was right: the view was gorgeous. From where we sat together on the floor, the DIY skylight (his words, not mine) allowed a view of the early night sky that was so clear it looked like it belonged in a travel magazine. Out in the valley with so little light pollution, you could see more stars than you'd ever dreamed existed in the first place. They were usually shrouded in foliage, but the attic was up high enough that we cleared most of the pesky branches that might have obstructed the view. The sky was just a perfect shade of indigo as far as the eye could see, exactly the way I liked it.

I was actually floored by how well Jaime had managed to surprise me, especially as someone who prided myself on being unsurprisable. The attic, small as it was with its peaked roof and dark wood paneling, felt homey with the addition of a few pillar candles. It wasn't just that, though. It was how proud Jaime was that he'd managed to pull it off. For some reason, it kind of made me want to cry.

We sat shoulder to shoulder and laughed and talked and ate for hours, and it was already the best birthday I'd had in recent years, maybe ever. Jaime insisted that I tell him about which constellations we could spot from our vantage point. I pointed out Vega and Lyra and the edge of Cygnus where it peeked out from behind the branches of a fir tree. Before I knew it, we ended up reclining so far back that we were practically lying on the ground, side by side, gazing at the stars as we chatted away.

I shifted a few times, trying to be subtle, but Jaime picked up on it quickly. "What's wrong?"

"I'm not trying to sound ungrateful," I hedged, "but lying on the floor is kind of uncomfortable."

"You're just too boney. Here, lift your head up for a second," he said, shifting next to me. I did as he said, and before I could even process what he intended to do, he had already slung his arm around my shoulders. "Better?"

"Yep," I replied, immediately embarrassed at how breathy my voice sounded.

It wasn't that we'd never been that close before—between the casual touches we'd shared since I came into the house and the number of times we'd tangled our legs together on the sofa in the library, it should have felt normal. But everything felt different when we were wrapped in the blue glow of twilight.

The fabric of his shirt brushed my bare arm, making me shiver. I was hyperaware of where my shoulder connected with his, and how one of his knees was resting against my leg. I wanted to melt into his touch, but I also felt strangely rigid, like I had to hold my breath because if I moved even a fraction of an inch it would all fall apart.

"Do you ever think—" I started, hoping to break the tension but realizing it was still there even when I did speak up. "Do you ever think about how the forest won't remember us?"

"What do you mean?"

It took everything in me not to turn my head and look at him. I was afraid if I did, I might not be able to look away. I might set something into motion that I didn't know how to stop.

"Well, we're going to remember everything that happens here, but it doesn't mean much to this place," I said, rambling to make myself less nervous. "It's like, this valley has seen centuries pass and this moment is just a tiny blip in all that *stuff*. We're just animals, like everything else that lives here."

"Can I be honest?" he asked, and I automatically tensed. "That is straight up the most depressing thing you've ever said."

I let out all my breath in a huff and felt his shoulder shake next to mine in silent laughter. I almost wanted to elbow him, but I was too comfortable to move.

"Shut up," I replied lightly, realizing his joke had helped me settle into his touch a bit more. "I'm serious, though. I think it's kind of comforting, in a way. It's like anything we do here is just for us and no one else."

The second the words left my mouth, I wished I could take them back. Not because I didn't mean them—I'd often had that thought, I'd just never found the right time to vocalize it. I only got scared because I finally said something as weighty as the evening felt. It was an opening, and Jaime could either take the bait or let it slide.

"Just for us." He tested the words, seeing if they would bear weight. There was something impossibly soft in his voice that made my pulse quicken, and I worried that he would be able to feel it from where his arm was draped around my shoulders. "Yeah, I guess I do like the sound of that."

Then I did turn to look at him, just a little. His eyes were half closed, and the way the silver moonlight clung to the tips of his eyelashes didn't do anything to dull the sweet pang of longing in my chest. Sometimes when I looked at him, it felt like the ache in my rib cage would swallow me whole. It was terrifying, I thought, to let someone pull me apart like this. Even more terrifying was the realization that I wasn't actually terrified at all.

And then, just like that, I made up my mind. About him, about us, about everything. I didn't know exactly what I was going to do about it, I just knew I desperately wanted to say his name aloud.

I sucked in a deep breath.

"Hey, Jaime?"

CHAPTER 28
JAIME

I HUMMED IN ACKNOWLEDGMENT, half so comfortable I could hardly keep my eyes open and half so electrified by Theo's closeness I was practically vibrating out of my skin.

The night had gone exactly as I'd planned. The look on Theo's face when he saw the picnic definitely made me feel like I'd knocked it out of the park, his eyes shining with a genuine, unconcealed joy I wished I could see on him more often. I could tell he loved the picnic, the chance to just talk and be idiots for hours without having to pretend to be working.

What I hadn't bargained for was having his face so close to mine that I wanted to melt into the floor. When I slung my arm around his shoulder, I swear I meant it to be platonic. I wanted him to do things at his own pace, if he was going to do anything at all. It wasn't until I could feel his hair tickle my neck that I started to really panic. I was too aware of how close we were, how still Theo had gotten, and how perfect my arm felt around his shoulders.

Theo cleared his throat awkwardly. *So he's nervous too.* "Remember the conversation we had a while back?"

"We've had a lot of conversations," I said, trying to sound like my heart wasn't beating out of my chest. "You're gonna have to be more specific."

Normally he would have done a little snort at a comment like that, but this time he didn't laugh. "The conversation about how you knew you liked boys." Oh. *Oh.* Now I did crack an eye open, turning my head a bit to meet his gaze. He had the strangest look on his face. "You know, with the songs."

"Uh-huh?"

"It was . . . really helpful," Theo started haltingly. "So thank you for that."

"Um, you're welcome?"

Theo's eyes flitted away from mine, a crease forming between his brows. "I've been thinking about what you said. Well, not just that specific thing, but that's been a big part of it. And I've been thinking about other stuff, too. Like, in the same vein. Does that make sense? I feel like this isn't coming out right—"

"Jesus Christ," I interrupted, my impatience getting the better of me. "Theo, you're killing me here. Spit it out."

"Oh my *god*," he snapped, sitting up suddenly in a blur of flustered movement. He twisted around to look at me, half hovering over where I was still spread out on the ground. "Can you not ruin the moment for two seconds? God, you're such a dick sometimes.

I'm trying to say that I realized the songs make sense when I think about you."

For a few seconds, it felt like my brain was buffering. Had I actually just heard him right? I didn't think I had ever been speechless in my life up until that point—I thought it was just something people said to be dramatic—but with Theo so close and my pulse going a hundred miles a minute, I had no idea what to say.

"Theo—"

"Can I ask my question for the day?" he asked, completely undeterred by my confusion. Hell, he seemed more confident than he had been all night.

We hadn't played the question game in ages, but I could tell he was serious. I pushed myself up off the blanket a bit, leaning back on my elbows so I could look him in the eye.

"Yeah, you can."

I only had a fraction of a second to brace myself before he opened his mouth again. "Can I kiss you?" The words hung low in the inky darkness of the attic, hope clinging to every syllable like dewdrops on a spiderweb. I considered how easy it would be to pull him to me and kiss him first, but I could tell he wanted to do things his own way. And for once in my goddamn life, I let him. It took me two tries to get the word out, but when I did say yes, it barely came out as a whisper.

Theo reached for me, pressing his palm to the side of my neck with a gentleness I should have expected but had never dreamed of in a million years, and I leaned forward to meet him in the middle. His fingertips brushed my cheek, and in the millisecond before our lips met, I worried, stupidly, whether it was going to be a good kiss.

But our first kiss wasn't clumsy like first kisses could sometimes be. It was me wanting to kiss him so badly that I might explode, and it was Theo so determined to get it right that it was almost chaste in its tenderness. The way he kissed me was as weighty and devoted as his attention had always been, sweet and soft and fiercely intentional. It reminded me of how his voice sounded first thing in the morning, how his eyes looked in the sun, and it set me on fire from the inside out.

Our second kiss was an exploration. Theo dragged his fingers along my jaw, then across my collarbone in a way that made me shiver. We both moved to deepen the kiss at the same time, and it was so good it felt like the entire room had tilted on its axis. That kiss was everything Theo had ever made me feel, but amplified. It was walking into a ray of sunshine on a chilly afternoon. It was finally coming home after a long, tiring day out. It was opening a window and feeling a perfect summer breeze on my face. But really, it was finally feeling safe in someone's arms after a lifetime of being uprooted. It was kissing the boy I had been obsessed with since the second I'd seen his worried face in the woods on that gloomy morning in July.

Our third kiss was an entirely different beast. Theo shifted, pushing me down in a way that made my breath catch in my chest. He hovered over me for a beat or two, face framed by the electric blue of the fading night sky, mussed-up hair hanging into his eyes. He looked beautiful—he looked, I thought, exactly like what I wanted my future to be. When he dipped his head to kiss me again, I honest to god thought I might have died and gone to heaven. His lips were insistent, but so were mine. This kiss had a little bit of fight to it, just like every conversation we'd ever had. It was less of a true battle and more of a familiar rhythm, a safe haven disguised as a challenge.

I put a hand on the small of Theo's back and rolled over until he was pinned underneath me—I wanted to get a good look at his face in whatever ghostly light we had left. But when I tried to pull back, his mouth followed. Holy shit, he actually wanted me. Theo Miller wanted *me*. I moved to kiss him under his jaw, and that distinctly Theo scent of fresh air and rosemary and something else I couldn't get enough of intoxicated me beyond logical understanding.

Everything about that night, about Theo under my hands, felt expansively and overwhelmingly alive. I hadn't wanted something or someone that bad in so long, maybe ever. I still wasn't sure I deserved him, or if I ever would. But his lips were on mine and his fingers were in my hair. His palm was against my ribs, then my waist, then my hip, and for once I couldn't bring myself to care about what I deserved.

Under the burgeoning glow of the full moon, I shed the final atoms of myself that had existed before I met him, and I never wanted to go back.

CHAPTER 29
THEO

THE NIGHT STARTED AND ended with Jaime's lips against mine. We took turns pulling each other closer, but I found myself thinking that no matter how close he got, it wasn't close enough. I desperately wanted to hold every piece of him all at once, like I would run out of oxygen if I couldn't. It wasn't enough to press his shoulder blades against my chest or trace the calloused spots where his fingers connected with his palms. There was some ache in the deepest corners of my heart that told me I might be greedy for all of him forever.

I managed to stumble into the kind of feeling that people would kill and be killed for, and I hadn't even had the foresight to waste my time hoping for it, to stay awake at night and wish for it on the stars. I wanted to bask in it forever, or maybe drown in it. Whichever came first was fine by me.

But it wasn't long after he fell asleep in my arms, his dark hair pressed against my cheek and breath tickling my neck, that he started to toss and turn. The shallow rise and fall of his chest sped up, and he murmured pleas into the darkness that I couldn't piece together. I didn't want to wake him, so I held him tight instead, feeling his breathing slow until we were able to drift off to sleep together.

It was dawn when he managed to pull himself out of his fitful sleep, and his eyes found my face right away.

"Morning," I whispered.

"*Hngh*," he replied, mashing his face against my neck.

I chuckled a little, too tired and blissed out to laugh in earnest. Jaime elbowed me lazily, I elbowed back, and any hope of us falling asleep again went out the window.

We watched the sun rise from our cocoon of blankets, trading lazy kisses until my stomach loudly insisted we untangle ourselves and find something to eat. Jaime was reaching for his shirt, which was crumpled by the remains of our picnic, when I decided to bring up his restless sleep.

"Hey," I started, getting to my feet, "are you still having the same nightmares as before? The ones with Josephine?"

Jaime cast a sidelong glance at me, and I watched intently as he pulled his shirt over his head. *I can do this now*, I thought, a little in awe. *I can actually look all I want.*

"Yeah," he replied. "But I've gotten used to them."

"Are you sure? Because it didn't seem like you slept at all last night."

Jaime shot me a look that told me he knew I wasn't being subtle. I shot him one back that said I didn't care. He sighed, leaning in and planting a kiss on my forehead before I could even think to react.

"She's not gonna convince me to stay. You're gonna get wrinkles if you keep worrying so much," he said, as if it were the easiest thing in the world.

"I have to worry," I said dryly. "It's what friends do."

I meant for it to be lighthearted, a call back to one of our old jokes, but it came out sounding much more miserable than I had intended. I could tell Jaime noticed—he was pinning me down with that catlike stare of his. There was a wicked glint in his eye, so it didn't surprise me when he captured my face in his hands. What did surprise me was the way he kissed me.

It was nothing like the kisses from the night before, eager and feverish and volatile enough to be combustible. It was nothing like our kisses a few minutes before, featherlight and indulgent, like we had all the time in the world. This was something else entirely.

When I opened my eyes, I half expected him to look smug. Instead, he looked determined.

"We are *not* friends."

"You can't do that every time we have a disagreement," I said, trying to sound stern but failing spectacularly. He was wearing a slippery smile that would have irritated me if I hadn't been completely enamored with him, and it reminded me of another question I had been wanting to ask for a while. "What made you change your mind, by the way? About me?"

"What do you mean?"

"I thought you hated me for, like, a significant amount of time."

"I never hated you. You're just cute when you're mad," he said with a shrug. I gaped at him, shocked by his bullheadedness, and he pointed a finger at my face. "That's it, that's the look I'm always aiming for."

"Wow, I totally hate you right now."

"You don't," he said, dismissing my lie with a wave of his hand. "You have a big fat crush on me. You kissed me in the moonlight. You can't say shit."

I pushed his hand away from my face, but he captured it in his as he threw back his head and laughed, unguarded and ridiculous and annoyingly attractive. This, I thought, was exactly why I had held off on admitting my feelings for Jaime for so long. I had always known that once I did, there would be no going back.

Then, just as I stepped away and started pulling my shirt over my head, a twig snapped out in the clearing. Both our heads whipped toward the sound, but Jaime was standing closer to the hole in the wall. When he looked down, the smile dropped from his face.

"Man, what a dump," said an unfamiliar gruff voice. "This place is falling apart. How is it worth the trouble to tear it down? Look, the roof is already caving in on its own."

Jaime ducked out of sight in a flash, grabbing my hand and tugging me to the far end of the small room. My heart pounded as we huddled together where the roof sloped closest to the floor, kicking up dust in the process.

"It's the cops," Jaime said in a strained whisper as another voice rang out in the clearing below.

"If it means we never have to file another report about this place, then good fucking riddance. Come tomorrow, none of this will be our problem anymore."

I looked sharply at Jaime. Tomorrow? We were supposed to have four more days.

"Should we go inside and take a look around?" the first officer asked. "Might be some historical stuff in there, you never know."

Jaime's hand tightened around mine. The second officer paused, and I held my breath.

"They don't pay me enough to give a shit. Let's just take the pictures for the demo crew and get out of here."

My pulse hammered in my ears as they circled the property, and it didn't slow until the footsteps receded into the forest.

"Please tell me I heard them wrong," I said quietly. That was what seemed to unfreeze Jaime, and he rose to his feet so fast it made me jump.

"It can't be tomorrow," he said numbly. "We need more time. I'm not ready."

"Jaime—"

"No, we have to call Taylor."

Jaime was already halfway down the access ladder when I rose to my feet, but as I did, the floorboard below me buckled under my weight. I managed to catch myself before I fell back, but it popped out of place again. Below it, the corner of a wooden box caught the dim morning light. It took a little work to pry open the box's rusty hinges, but when I did, my heart stopped.

"Jaime?" I shouted, my hands hovering over the open lid. "You're going to want to get back up here."

When Taylor finally showed up at the house, Jaime and I were huddled together over the dining room table. We had been in there long enough that the cool early-morning light had faded from silver to gold, but with the contents of the box spread out on the table, our mood was far from sunny.

"Hellooo," Taylor called from the entryway. "Anyone home?"

"That's a terrible joke and you know it," Jaime called back. "We're in the dining room."

"How was the birthday celebration?" Taylor said, rounding the corner of the hall. But before I could respond, she stopped in the doorway, her eyes flitting between me and Jaime. "Wait, you got together and you didn't tell me?"

I gawked at her. "There's no way your sixth sense works that well."

Jaime stifled a laugh, and Taylor shook her head. When I still didn't get it, she tapped a long finger to her neck and grinned knowingly. "Yeah, not quite."

I realized a second too late that I must have had a hickey or two or five from last night on display, and it took everything in me not to clap a hand over my neck. I turned to glare at Jaime, but he looked so proud of himself that I didn't have the heart for it. God, what a disaster. What a beautiful, stupid disaster we both were.

"Believe it or not, this might be the least interesting thing you see this morning," I replied. Taylor quirked a brow at me in response, but her expression shifted when I stepped aside to show what was littering the tabletop behind me. "We found this hidden in the attic."

Taylor inched closer, eyes raking across the contents of the box. It had been filled to the brim with family heirlooms, everything from a heart-shaped gold locket to diary entries and ribbon-tied locks of chestnut hair. There were photographs of two young parents and a baby girl. Jaime slid a photograph to Taylor showing a somber young woman in a high-collared dress.

"This is the person I've been seeing in the house and in my dreams, but it's not Josephine," he said. Taylor squinted at the photo, but she seemed lost.

"Then who is it?"

Jaime unfolded the brittle, yellowed poster, which he had saved for last. *Wanted for the July 3, 1896 murder of Josephine T. Harris*, it read in bold block letters. *Alice Bishop and accomplice Edwin Bishop. $5,000 reward.*

"I don't understand," Taylor whispered, voice sounding small for the first time since I'd met her.

"We couldn't figure out why your dad was so invested in this place, why he would have wiped it clean so we couldn't find out who lived here," Jaime said, watching Taylor as she let the poster flutter back onto the table. "Now I think we know why. He must not have checked the attic. It was a good hiding place."

Suddenly, Taylor moved around the room, making a beeline for the table settings that were still neatly laid out. It wasn't until she held up one of the cloth napkins that I understood what she was getting at.

"The monogram's not a 'B' for 'Blackwood,' it's for 'Bishop,'" she said, shaking her head. "We've been talking about the house like it was haunted by some stranger, but it was my own family.

This must have been why my mom was obsessed with Blackwood. God, I feel so stupid. How did I miss this?"

"It's not that you missed it. It was being kept from you," I said. "But, Taylor, you have to talk to your dad. We think the demolition got moved up. If he knows the full story, if he knows anything that could help us pull this spell off, you have to find out now."

"I will," she replied firmly, and I believed her. Her eyes shone with defiant unshed tears as she opened the locket, studying the photo of Alice and Edwin Bishop inside. "This has been a long time coming with me and my dad—over a century, by the looks of it. I'm going to follow it through to the end. No matter what happens, I'm finding out the truth, and we're getting you out. I promise."

CHAPTER 30
TAYLOR

WOLF'S HEAD SEEMED DIFFERENT by the time I made it back in the early afternoon. It felt grayer somehow, like the truth had sucked the color out of the life I knew before. I used to think the day I confronted my dad about all the things he was keeping from me would be one of the most satisfying days of my life. Now that I knew it was happening, I just wanted to get it over with.

When I got home, I climbed up to my dad's office. There was no point in tiptoeing around him anymore, and if Elias and I were going to have it out, I sure as hell was going to walk away with my mom's grimoire. It didn't take long for me to find it again, and I went to my bedroom next. Pulling out a duffel bag, I numbly began packing herbs, candles, and power-amplifying relics that might help with Jaime's spell. I heard Elias come to stand in my doorway just as I was finishing up, but I didn't turn around.

"Where were you all morning?" he demanded.

"Blackwood," I replied.

Elias didn't say anything, I could instantly feel a shift in the air. An eerie sense of calm washed over me as I took the Wanted poster out of my pocket and carefully unfolded it. Elias read the words silently. He didn't look angry, he looked defeated.

"I need you to explain everything," I said, "from the beginning."

Elias moved to take a seat in the green tufted chair in the corner of my room, and motioned for me to sit on my bed across from him. I didn't.

"There are things you don't know about your mother's side of the family, things we kept from you to try to protect you," he started. "You know your mom's family settled in New England in the early nineteenth century. They were herbalists, healers, and they opened an apothecary like ours in Burlington. But the Puritan culture here and their alternative practices didn't mix, and they faced a lot of harassment. They decided to move up north for a chance at a quieter life."

"So Blackwood was ours?"

"It was," Elias said with a sigh. "They took all the money from their business and built a home in an area so remote that nobody would ever bother them again."

"That doesn't sound like the end of the story," I said warily. Now, I did drop onto the edge of my bed. This might have been the longest conversation I'd had with my dad since the spring.

"It's not. Your great-great-grandmother Alice didn't plan to ever go back to healing. But there was a big smallpox outbreak in 1895, and Saint Juniper didn't have a doctor. She saw how everyone was suffering and decided to start taking patients again.

"Of course, it didn't take long for people in town to get paranoid. Rumors spread that a witch lived in the woods, and the harassment picked up again, only worse. People would hike out into the valley to throw rocks through the windows. Once they even tried to burn the house down. It ended up being a self-fulfilling prophecy: the more violent the townspeople became, the more she turned to real magic to protect her family. Everything came to a head in 1896, when a patient who was too far gone died on the property after Alice tried to use blood magic to revive her."

"Josephine, right?" I asked, and Elias nodded. There was a hurt in his expression I wasn't sure I would ever truly understand. In a way, I resented it. Maybe in another life, if I had known the truth from the beginning, I could feel the centuries-old pain that still plagued him and must have plagued my mom.

"Then what? There was an investigation, right?" I asked, but Elias shook his head.

"Josephine's story started spreading to other towns, and the people here didn't want it to reflect poorly on Saint Juniper," Elias said quietly. "A group of vigilantes broke into Blackwood and hanged Alice for Josephine's murder. Her husband, Edwin, barely escaped with his life, but he managed to take their baby girl and flee town."

I let the truth sit between us for a few beats, soaking it all in. Alice's locket, which I had taken with me from Blackwood, suddenly felt heavier around my neck. The story explained a lot about the way Alice acted as a ghost, bitter and territorial. But it didn't answer all the questions buzzing around my head.

"That was over a hundred years ago, though. You think I'm going to be burned at the stake for practicing witchcraft now?"

"I don't think you're listening—it was *only* a hundred years ago. This was a witch hunt that never made it into history books. They got away with it all with no repercussions. And these Bishops," he said, tapping the wanted poster, "do not look like you."

"It's not the eighteen hundreds anymore. Things aren't like that today," I murmured, taking the paper out of his hand.

Elias gave me another dark look. "You have no idea how wrong you are."

I remembered the way Theo's boss had looked at me, and her automatic assumption I was getting Theo into trouble. I pushed the thought away as I zipped my duffel bag closed and hefted it onto my shoulder.

"I don't understand why you hid this from me all this time, or why you always told me to stay away," I said. Elias trailed behind me as I moved out of my room and down the stairs.

"Because your mom was consumed by the same story for years. She wanted to honor Alice's memory by opening an apothecary in Wolf's Head, but that wasn't enough for her. When she visited Blackwood and realized Alice was haunting the property, she decided to start practicing blood magic to try to cleanse the property. But she didn't know how powerful it could be. It only made her obsession worse, and it wore her down."

I paused, reaching the bottom of the stairs. "When was this?"

"The spring," he said simply. The second the words left his mouth, I realized I didn't even need him to answer.

Do not cry, I thought desperately. *You can deal with this later.* "You could've told me."

"I couldn't, not when you were mourning," he said, then followed up quickly when he saw I was starting to turn away. "You did your best to try to hide it, but I could tell. I can always tell when something is going on with you, even if you don't believe me."

"If you know me so well," I said carefully, "then why couldn't you tell it hurt me how you never talked about her? Her death was an accident, right? She pushed herself too far, but it was an accident. Why are you acting like it was all her fault?"

Elias's dark eyes raked over my face. He didn't look mad, not anymore. Instead, the only emotion that was plain on his face was pity.

"She knew what she was doing, mija," he said quietly. "She left me, and she left you too."

In the moments after the words came out of his mouth, I could see the whole conversation from his perspective. I could clearly see the logic in his words and feel his anger as vividly as if it had been mine all along. But even though I understood, I had to push it out of my mind.

"She didn't choose to leave us," I said firmly.

"She always had a choice," he replied. "I hoped you would make a better choice than she did, but it's clear that you won't listen to me. That's why I called the sheriff and got them to move up the demolition."

My heart dropped into my stomach. "You *what?*"

"It was the only thing I could think of to stop you," he said, practically pleading. I had never seen him so desperate. "I know I've hurt you in more ways than one this past year, but I'm doing the best I can. Everything I've ever done has been to protect you. I don't want to lose you too."

"Well," I said, turning away from him, "you already got halfway there on your own. Why stop now?"

I left the Wanted poster and my keys to the shop on the counter, and Elias silently watched me go.

CHAPTER 31
THEO

IT WAS EARLY AFTERNOON by the time we heard Taylor making her way back through the woods, duffel bag in tow. We stood together around the dining room table, staring at the family relics strewn across the dark wood as Taylor recounted Alice's story.

"I think I get it now," Jaime said once Taylor had finished. "Why she was calling me out here, and why she wanted me to stay. She was rejected by the people of Saint Juniper just like I was as a kid. She probably didn't want me to be persecuted like she had been."

Taylor nodded, nudging one of Alice's photos on the table. "In a twisted sort of way, she probably thought forcing you to stay here would keep you safe. She just died in such a horrific way that any goodwill or kindness in her heart from when she was alive is long gone."

"That makes me a little sad, I guess," Jaime said. "She told me that we were the same. And in a way, I get it."

"But your stories don't have to end the same," I pointed out, weaving my fingers through his. "You can come back to Saint Juniper and everything will be fine. You'll be safe—we'll make sure of it."

Taylor nodded. "You're going to be free of her, of all this, sooner rather than later. We're going to have to perform the spell tonight."

Jaime's face went blank. "So the demolition did move up."

"My dad called the sheriff, but it can't be helped. I got every-thing we need from my place," Taylor said, pulling the duffel bag onto the table. "I got my mom's grimoire back, and any of these family heirlooms could work as the personal item we needed to exorcise Alice."

"What if I'm not ready yet?" Jaime asked, panic seeping into his voice.

"You *are* ready. Even if you're not, I've got your back. It's now or never," Taylor said firmly.

So even though it felt completely surreal, we started to set up for the spell. Jaime decided to practice controlling his powers in the final hours he had left, which left me to help Taylor with prep. Her notes seemed pretty extensive, but Taylor assured me that if we worked together we'd be able to kick it off before midnight.

Taylor started off by smoke-cleansing the property, calling it the first line of defense for hostile energy. We hung dried chamo-mile, angelica, and sage bundles in every doorframe, then sprin-kled salt and powdered yarrow across each windowsill. After that,

Taylor marked off the corners of every room with rosemary oil, the earthy scent of it filling the house. Each step was uniquely suited to dismantle Alice's grip and banish the century of ill will she had built up haunting Blackwood.

It was precise, well-executed work, and I had no doubt Taylor was as prepared as she possibly could be. But I could tell by the way her hands shook as she flipped through her mom's grimoire, comparing all her notes to the original material, that she was petrified. Between her nervousness and Jaime's self-isolation, I couldn't help but think I was missing something.

Eventually, Taylor got so drawn into her prep work that I decided to give her some space. I crept up the stairs to find Jaime in one of the second-story bedrooms. He was sitting on the bed, staring at the treetops through an open window. After the chaos of the last few hours, the silence felt almost sacrosanct. I lingered in the doorway, soaking up the sight of him for a few more moments. Feeling the weight of my stare on his back, he turned and nearly jumped out of his skin.

"Jesus Christ, stalker," he muttered.

He reached for my hand absentmindedly as I approached the bed, tangling his fingers in mine. "Try not to kill me before I get out of here, okay?"

"I'll try my best. Can I kiss you?"

"Yeah, you don't have to keep asking," he chided, but I could tell he was pleased as he tilted his chin toward me.

"I know," I said, feeling smug and content in equal parts. "I just like hearing you say yes."

I wondered, as he smiled against my lips and his hands ghosted under the hem of my shirt, how I had ever thought my feelings for him were platonic.

"Working hard?" I asked, settling next to him on the bed.

"And thinking, I guess," Jaime said. "About us, about school."

"Oh, right. You probably won't get your books in time, but I doubt the teachers will mind if you borrow mine until you have your own."

Jaime turned to me, his face much more serious than it had been moments before. "Listen, I meant to talk to you about this at some point, but I guess we're out of time. Have you actually thought this through?"

"I mean, yeah. It won't be that much of a hassle to share for a while."

"No, not the books," he said stonily. "You, me. At school."

Oh. I'd figured this conversation was bound to come up at some point. As far as I knew, Jaime didn't go out of his way to hide his relationships in public. From his foster parents, yes, but that was more of a necessity for self-preservation than an attempt to stay in the closet. Still, I wanted to hear what he had in mind.

"What about it?"

Jaime looked at me in a somber, resolved way that seemed a little out of place for the conversation we were having. Or it did until he opened his mouth.

"If this needs to end, I get it."

I balked at him. "I'm sorry, *what?*"

"I'm just saying, I get it if you don't want to do this," he said quickly, gesturing between us. "Like, be with a guy publicly."

"Why on earth would you say that?" I asked, equal parts amazed and concerned at how calm he was. Did he really think we wouldn't be together after this was all over?

"You said you hate how everyone in town knows your business. If we did go out, we wouldn't exactly blend in," he said, and there was a tightness around his eyes I couldn't quite place. "It's just, I dragged you into this whole mess. The last thing I want is to drag you out of the closet too."

And there it was. I reached out and took Jaime's hand in mine again, and I could feel the nervous anguish through his fingertips. I couldn't believe he was making himself sick worrying about this. Well, I could, but I didn't like it.

"You're right, keeping things private here isn't really an option. Everyone is going to know, so whether I like it or not, I'm either in the closet or out of it. That idea used to scare me so much it paralyzed me. Coming out to myself felt practically the same as coming out to everyone. But I came to terms with that when I came to terms with us." I squeezed his hand, and he squeezed back half-heartedly. "This is all a secret now, but I'm not going to keep *you* a secret."

Something broke in his facial expression that told me I had hit on exactly what he was already thinking. "You say that now, but—"

"No, listen." I rest my free hand on the side of his neck. "I didn't fall into this by accident. I want to be with you, all right? I choose you. And I'm going to keep choosing you, so get used to it."

"And what if this plan to break me out doesn't work? What then?" he asked quietly, the anxiety on his face tugging sharply at my heartstrings. I knew he lived in the what-ifs as much as I did, he just usually did a better job of hiding it. But like he said, we were out of time.

"That's not going to happen," I said firmly. He looked like he wanted to argue, but he didn't say anything else.

I let Jaime go, reclining against one of the bedposts. As he turned to look out the window again, I knew he was right. There was a chance this wouldn't work, and if I thought about it for more than a few seconds, I was overwhelmed with a sense of helplessness heavy enough to drown me. So I chose to put on a happy face for him, because really, it was the only thing I could do.

I thought about what it might be like if everything went right. I imagined him untethered from the house, older and happier and freer than he had ever been. I could see us graduating, heading to college. I could picture it all like it was already written in the stars, and I wanted it so badly it made my chest ache. I was determined to make it happen for us no matter what.

Something about that moment stuck with me long after the amber light faded from the room, long after summer rolled over into fall and curled into winter. It's impossible to know which memories will be lost forever to the nagging pull of time. Or maybe worse, painted over in retrospect by counterfeit emotions and twisted into some cheap copy, never to be recovered in their original form. But being with Jaime on that specific August afternoon felt like we were carving our initials into time, like we were made to be remembered.

Sensing my gaze, he tilted his head sleepily in my direction. The glow from the open window gilded his hair like a halo. He was a young god.

"What are you looking at?" he asked, dazzling.

"You," I said, dazzled.

His expression softened a fraction, the corner of his mouth quirked up in a nearly imperceptible half smile. He closed his eyes for a moment, dark lashes casting shadows on his cheeks just like the day we met. Then he turned away, face to the sun, and I wondered if I might have fallen in love without even noticing.

———

Before the sun set, Taylor and I drove to Maple City Diner to pick up dinner. Town square was decked out in lights and packed with booths for the Summer's End Festival, but we didn't have time to linger. The welcome scent of hot burgers and greasy french fries filled the car as we drove past the hedges that lined the narrow entry to the valley. They had a slight tinge of yellow, the earliest sign of fall starting to rear its head.

By the time we got back to Blackwood, the brown paper bags holding our food were about seventy percent grease and thirty percent bag. We crowded together onto the velvet couch in the library and dug in as soon as we could, opening the windows wide so we could soak up the last rays of late-summer sun before it dipped behind the mountains.

"So," Jaime said around a bite of burger, "this is kind of like the Last Supper, huh?"

Taylor and I exchanged uneasy looks. Mine was exasperated, hers was infinitely more tense.

"If you mean the last supper before you eat something with nutritional value again for the first time in two months, then yes," I corrected Jaime, which won a little smirk from him. "Anything more depressing than that isn't allowed."

"Agreed," Taylor piped up, popping a fry into her mouth. "No shop talk for the next thirty minutes."

"Does 'shop talk' cover all supernatural topics, or am I the only one that's off-limits?"

"Just you. All other cryptids are still on the table," Taylor replied, and they fell into their typical pattern of banter that I could hardly have kept up with even if I'd tried. The pit that had been in my stomach all day eased up just a little.

Someone must have started a bonfire over the ridge, and the familiar smell of burning wood lulled me into a stupor as Taylor and Jaime chatted away. Jaime leaned into me, his warmth shielding me from the cool evening air leaving goose bumps trailing up my arms. As I looked out over the treetops, it felt odd that the valley used to make me feel so nervous and unmoored. And with a start, I realized that some part of me was actually upset at the idea of leaving Saint Juniper soon.

I had always thought if it was possible to have some grand, epic adventure in life, Saint Juniper would not be the place it would happen. But maybe I'd spent so much time wishing I could leave that I never took the time to make the most of it. At least, I hadn't until I met Jaime.

Then, from one month to the next, it was like I'd blinked and this place had changed shape completely. Or maybe *I* was the one who had changed shape, and I'd finally outgrown it in the way I'd wanted since I was old enough to think for myself. I only wished I could have known it was happening before it was nearly over.

Taylor crowded into my space, her curls tickling my cheek as she broke me out of my daydream.

"Don't you think," she said, waving a fry at me, "that after all this, you can at least acknowledge that there's a small chance Champy is real?"

I looked between Jaime's waggish expression and Taylor's overly eager one. "Champy, like the lake monster? Absolutely not."

"Jaime, tell your boyfriend he's being irrational."

Jaime looked up at me with an excitement in his eyes that I couldn't place, and I belatedly realized that was the first time either of us had used the word "Boyfriend."

"You're being irrational," he said after a pause. "There's too much documented proof for it to just be a coincidence."

"I'll tell you what, I'll believe it when I see it. Sound good to you?"

Jaime considered me, then nodded with conviction. "Here's a compromise: I'm gonna get a tattoo of Champy on my ass so you'll be forced to look at him all the time. A Champ tramp stamp, if you will."

"I don't think you know what 'compromise' means," I said, fondly pushing Taylor's face away from mine as she snorted in my ear. "Also, you might be overestimating how often I look at your ass."

"Actually, I've estimated a perfectly reasonable amount. And no, I will not elaborate," he crowed. Taylor rocked away from me and started in on some new conspiracy theory analysis with

Jaime, both of their voices carrying out into the dusk. I was happy knowing that even if I couldn't help directly with the magic surrounding the house, I had somehow managed to bring them together. Maybe it was the best thing I could have done regardless.

As they kept chatting, I think I felt terribly, unstoppably young for the first time in my life. For once, I didn't feel the steady fall of sand in an hourglass just out of reach. It was just me and them and the lightness between us. I thought if I could choose to just exist in that moment forever, I would.

But then I looked between Taylor and Jaime, and I realized that this very well could be the last time the three of us would be together like this, loud and carefree and unafraid. Suddenly, the scene was colored over with a heartache that hadn't yet come to pass. I felt a sense of nostalgia for a moment that I was still in the middle of living, and there was a spot in my chest that was hollow and bursting at the seams at the same time.

I wondered why it always felt like my happiness could only grow so far until it got pruned back. All I wanted was a sense of belonging, of rightness, that couldn't be tempered or changed by a shifting tide. But I knew as soon as I hoped for it that it would all change anyway. And ultimately, I was horribly, painfully right.

CHAPTER 32
JAIME

AS THE SKY BLED from blue to black, I was pretty sure I was going to hurl at some point before the night was through.

Even though I had been making decent progress with controlling my powers, and I'd tried my hardest to get in the mindset that leaving was the right thing to do, I still wasn't completely confident that I'd be able to break free on my own.

I watched silently from the stairs as Taylor drew a large sigil in white chalk on the floor of the foyer. Theo hovered behind her, even more of a human bundle of nerves than he usually was. I stood by what I had said to Taylor, that I wanted to be free of Blackwood by the end of the day no matter what happened. And I stood by my decision not to mention any of this to Theo. As long as we managed to pull it off, it wouldn't matter either way.

"Almost ready?" Theo asked as Taylor finished up the sigil.

"Only thing left is to cast a circle around the property. It'll help me set my intentions for the spell and banish negative energy," she replied evenly. "Just give me a few minutes and then we can start."

My stomach lurched. We had been talking about this nonstop for days, but now that it was actually about to happen, none of it felt real. I looked helplessly to Theo, and he instantly picked up on my hesitation.

"Will you give us a sec?" he asked Taylor, and she nodded, barely looking up from her work.

Theo followed me dutifully, not asking where we were going or what I was thinking. We had barely made it up one flight of stairs when I started feeling off. By the second-story landing, his fingers intertwined in mine felt like a goodbye. And by the time we climbed up the ladder into the attic, there was a pit in my stomach that felt like it was there to stay.

I stared at the hole in the ceiling, at the picnic blanket from Theo's birthday the night before. It seemed like our celebration had happened centuries ago, pitifully out of reach, and I was in a museum looking at relics of my own life. *Boy stuck in house, oil on canvas.* I wasn't sure why I felt so torn about leaving. This place wasn't mine to be homesick over in the first place.

"Jaime?" Theo placed a hand on my arm, and I could see in his eyes that he was as lost as I was.

I didn't know what to say, so I pulled him into me instead. He slipped his arms around my shoulders as I buried my face against his chest, two puzzle pieces clicking into place.

Holding him was more than just a physical comfort, it was proving to myself that I could still feel at home with Theo no matter how strange everything around me was becoming. I let out a sigh that was a mix of contentment and sorrow, and he pulled me even closer. I wanted to just stand there like that forever, to melt into him and fuse into one person and never be afraid again.

"What are you looking forward to most about getting out?" Theo asked softly after a few minutes, lips against my hair.

"You," I said without really thinking. "Getting to go on a real date. Hanging out in places that aren't riddled with termite damage. That kind of thing."

He let out a soft laugh, his breath against my neck sending a pleasant shiver down my spine. "Very sweet. Also kind of gross. Aren't you excited to stop taking truck stop showers?"

"Running water will also be a major plus," I said, and I could feel Theo smile even though I couldn't see it. We stood in comfortable silence for a bit longer, me feeling the rise and fall of his chest against mine and him stroking his hands up and down my back in the way he knew I loved.

I regretted breaking the silence before I did, but there were too many things I had to say before it was too late. "You kind of changed my life, you know?"

Theo tried to pull back to get a better look at my face, but I held him tight so he couldn't move too far. He was my life raft, and I couldn't afford to let him go just yet.

"You're choosing now to get sentimental?" I could tell he was trying to keep things lighthearted, but there was real emotion in his eyes that told me this was as painful for him as it was for me.

"Yeah, I am. Just let me say this, okay? I felt like nobody before this all happened. I was just scraping along, and I wasn't even doing a very good job of that—"

"Don't treat this like a goodbye," he said suddenly, and I worried he was so busy being anxious he wasn't hearing what I was saying. "Jaime, I'm serious. It'll kill me if you do."

But the truth was there was no guarantee the spell would work. I could be stuck there indefinitely, or I could get hurt, or god knows what. If there was even a tiny chance things could go wrong, then I wasn't going to miss the opportunity to say everything I needed to.

"It's not, I swear," I lied, then pushed ahead. "I spent too much time being an asshole to you, and now there's so much I haven't said. Like, I thought you were beautiful the second I saw you standing outside the greenhouse. I wanted to kiss you back then, even when you were being a pain in my ass."

"For the record, I think I wanted to kiss you back then too. *Especially* when you were being a pain in my ass," he said with a sad little smile. I planted a kiss at the corner of his mouth just to feel it move into something that wasn't so miserable, and it did.

"You changed me too, you know," he said. "You have no idea how much. I don't think I knew who I was before you, honestly. I was on autopilot, just going through the motions, but I wasn't really living. I was, like, this shell of a person. And even if I still don't fully know who I am, I do know I feel more like myself with you."

I tried to imagine Theo as a shell of anything and quickly found it impossible. Living, breathing miracle Theo Miller was the opposite of nothing. Theo, who would tuck my hair behind my ear before he kissed me and watched me and waited for me, held so much light inside him that he made me feel the opposite of nothing every single day I knew him.

But I couldn't say any of that to his face without bursting into tears. The only thing I could manage to say without choking up was "You're very welcome."

"You're an ass," he laughed, but I could hear something in his voice that was just on the verge of breaking, so I couldn't even fully enjoy it. I reached up to put my hand on his cheek, and he leaned into my touch.

Even then, with him looking so crushed, I still wanted to kiss the freckles on his eyelids. My bucket list of things I wanted to do with Theo would never end. I could never have enough of him. But while I had him in my arms, I was going to make the most of it.

So I did kiss the freckles on his eyelids. I pressed another kiss into his temple, then another on the opposite cheek, and another on the tip of his nose. With every kiss, I silently thanked him for saving my life, for being exactly who I needed all this time, for letting me fall in love with him even though I hadn't had the chance to say it out loud yet. I tried to memorize the feeling of his skin against mine, and every second was sanctified.

When I pulled away, Theo took a painfully shaky breath. "Tell me things aren't going to change."

So he could sense it too, the feeling that everything was going to end, or maybe that it had ended already.

"Nothing is going to change," I lied again. "Things will be different, but things will be good."

I could tell he didn't believe me. The look on his face was shredding whatever resolve I had been building up for days. His mouth was twisted with a sort of sadness I couldn't bear. It reminded me a little of the way he'd looked at me when he first found me in the woods, back when we were strangers. I pulled him to me one last time, and our kiss felt exactly like the goodbye we refused to say out loud.

When I let him go, he had that curious look on his face again, the one I had caught him making at me on and off for weeks. I wondered if I had ever looked at him that way. I wondered if I was looking at him that way now.

"What, are you falling for me or something?" I asked softly, half joking and half so terribly in love that it almost hurt to breathe.

"I fell for you a long time ago," Theo said simply.

He reached up to place a hand over mine, turning it over to plant the softest kiss on my palm. Everything in me screamed not to go back downstairs, because I could clearly see what I hadn't wanted to admit to myself all this time. In the middle of the woods, I had managed to create the life I had always wanted. And now that it was time to leave, I didn't want to let it go. But then Theo tugged on my hand, and I couldn't not follow him. I'd follow him to the ends of the earth if I had to.

"Let's go down," he said. "Taylor is waiting."

CHAPTER 33
TAYLOR

JAIME AND THEO SEEMED changed when they came back downstairs. I had been prepared to make a joke about what had kept them for so long, but my mouth snapped shut the second I saw their somber faces.

We had done everything in our power to prepare for this moment, but there was no denying that we had been rushed into this. From the tension surrounding the boys, it was obvious they understood we were taking a risk trying to break Jaime free that night. But I was the only one who *truly* knew how much was on the line, how volatile and powerful this spell could be.

Alice's locket hung heavy around my neck as I lit a handful of pillar candles, lining them up one by one on the porch. If I had any lingering reservations about using blood magic, about not telling them how dangerous it could be, the time to voice them had already passed. I had to believe that it was all going to turn out all right, because we were out of time and out of options. But seeing the boys huddled together in the doorframe, Theo whispering something in Jaime's ear, it was hard not to feel choked by the pressure.

Once the candles were lit, I brought Jaime's old T-shirt and a handful of peridot gemstones to the front lawn, arranging them in a semicircle around where I would stand to cast the spell. Finally, I picked up my mom's grimoire from where it was waiting, nestled in the grass. My hands shook as I smoothed out the pages, trying not to think about how my mom would have felt if she could have seen me then. The shaking only got worse when Theo walked over to stand with me. If he had wished Jaime good luck one last time, I had missed it.

"If it doesn't work, we can just stop, right?" he asked, quiet enough that Jaime wouldn't overhear from where he was waiting at the front door.

"Yeah, we're gonna be fine," I replied with confidence I didn't really have, then turned to Jaime. "Are you ready?"

"Ready as I'll ever be," he said, his tone lacking its usual bravado and bite. We locked eyes, and I knew instantly that he was just as terrified as I was.

But there was no avoiding it anymore. Jaime shut his eyes and sucked in a breath, centering himself just like I had taught him. I waited for a beat, then started to recite the words from the grimoire.

I felt the giddy nervousness that always came with doing spellwork, but after a minute, the words flowed easier, and I slipped into an almost meditative state as I continued to chant.

Theo's jumpy energy beside me faded into the background, and the sounds of the forest dampened in my ears. I wasn't sure how much time was passing, but the atmosphere seemed to darken all around us.

I had waded deep into the intoxicating warmth of the spell when the first drops of rain started to fall. The storm didn't roll in from the mountains, rumbling down from the foggy peaks like storms normally did this time of year. It formed right above us, clouds pulling together in horrible harmony from nothing at all. It was the kind of storm that only a Bishop could summon.

"I can feel it," I heard Jaime say from miles away. "I think it's working."

He was right, because I could feel the spell working too. That addicting, invincible feeling I'd gotten when I tried Forget Me Not in my bedroom flooded back to me, and I could sense the grip Jaime had on the house as clearly as if he were holding on with his own two hands.

And slowly but surely, the grip loosened. Jaime's eyes were closed, his brow shiny from exertion as he inched forward. I saw Theo take a step toward the house out of the corner of my eye, a valiant knight painted silver with swathes of unnatural electric light. He might have called out to Jaime, but I couldn't make out what he said over the sound of the blood pumping through his veins.

I could hear every pint of it clear as day, roaring like rapids in my ears. It wasn't just him, though. I could hear the thrumming heartbeat of a bobcat over the ridge, could smell the coppery bite of blood dripping off a barn owl's talons in a nearby tree. I could sense every living thing within a ten-mile radius, taunting me with their vitality. Their blood was power, and I wanted it all.

A rumble of thunder snarled at us from above, wicked and commanding in all the ways I wished I could be. I didn't feel like I was there anymore, at least not as Taylor. I was the wind that whistled through the leaves, the roots of every pine tree, the animal bones buried dozens of feet beneath the grassy knoll.

"No matter how hard you try, he's never going to break free," a voice said, cutting through my bloodlust like a knife. It was a woman with skin as pale as the clouds that roiled behind her. The hair that whipped around her face was the same shade of chestnut as mine, but hers was streaked with silver. I recognized her from the photograph in the locket around my neck. "He's terrified of leaving, I can feel it. But he doesn't have to go. He can stay here with me forever."

"I'm going to get him out!" I shouted over the din of the storm, but Alice just laughed.

"It's too late. You're losing yourself to the spell." I wanted to deny it, but my craving for blood was overwhelming. It was a pull that started and ended in the basest part of my soul, and I didn't feel strong enough to say no to it. "You're drunk on power, because you're just like us."

"Like who?"

"Me and your mother," she said. "I'm just sorry you had to find out this way."

And that, to my absolute horror, was the moment I blacked out.

CHAPTER 34
THEO

FROM THE GUTS OF the storm, lightning splintered across the night sky in flashes of searing white light. Wind whipped in jagged patterns through the trees, and the metallic charge that buzzed around my shoulders left the hairs on the back of my neck standing on end.

I was never the type of person who was afraid of storms—a good storm always made me feel small and powerless in a satisfying way, a healthy way. Humans needed that sometimes, I thought. But this storm was something else entirely, because it wasn't just happening overhead, it was touching every part of the valley.

At first, there was just a solitary young buck, antlers still velvet, peering curiously through the underbrush. Then it was a raccoon on a low branch, eyes flashing in the lightning's silvery glare. The trees all around us bowed under the weight of birds collecting at the edges of the meadow, quietly watching the spell unfold.

"Theo, what's happening?" Jaime shouted, though I could barely hear him over the sound of the forest crashing into itself. He had one foot across the threshold of the front door, hands straining against the barrier. I would have been relieved if the storm didn't feel so violent and out of control.

A sudden motion at the edge of the clearing caught my attention, a mass falling to the ground like a stone. It happened again, only this time I saw it was a raven flapping its wings helplessly, once, twice, then falling dead to the ground.

"Taylor, I think something's wrong," I yelled frantically over the sounds of the storm, but when I turned to her, I wasn't sure if she could hear me.

Her eyelids had fluttered closed, and she was hunched forward over the grimoire at an unnatural angle. The words were coming out of her mouth faster, and where she had sounded almost timid before, now she was frighteningly assertive.

The storm growled at us directly overhead, a final warning before all hell broke loose.

I tensed up a split second before a bolt of lightning struck a tree on the far side of the meadow. An earth-shattering boom resonated deep in my bones and echoed across the surrounding mountains, and the flash of light that came with it was nothing short of blinding.

The tree shattered instantly, that was the only way I could describe it. One moment it was there, the next it had disappeared. The strike sent splinters flying, and the only thing that saved me from getting skewered was how far away I was standing from the horrible scene. I made a move toward Taylor, anything to make her notice the chaos around us.

"Don't stop her," Jaime shouted, and I froze with my hand inches from her shoulder. Everything sounded oddly dampened, and I wondered if the lightning strike had damaged my hearing. "We have to keep going."

"It's too dangerous. You're going to hurt yourselves! This is insane!" I called back, voice cracking as I realized just how helpless I was. But Jaime wasn't listening. His eyes were screwed shut, and it looked like he was trying hard not to pass out.

"This is my only chance!" he yelled back.

As the hairs on my arms rose again, a sharp, metallic smell filled my nose so fast it made me want to gag. My eardrums felt like they were about to burst, and I barely had time to brace myself before another flash and a deafening roar wiped out my senses.

My vision came back in shards of light. Jaime was almost through the doorway, but there were sparks cascading from the roof. My eyes caught on one of the iron banisters at the roof that looked as if it had just been pulled from a forge, white-hot and twisted at an odd angle.

An ember's glow in one of the upstairs windows cut through the darkness of the storm with horrifying vividness. The beginning of a fire in the attic, where we had been just minutes earlier, sputtered and then raged into existence. Dragging my eyes down to Jaime, the fractured picture in front of me finally snapped into place. I didn't know which would come to a head first, the fire or the spell. But if Jaime didn't break free from the house soon, he would be trapped there to die.

CHAPTER 35
JAIME

THE LIGHT WAS STRANGE and ragged as it shifted across Theo's hair, illuminating patches like amber held up to the sun. I thought, just for a second, his hair almost looked like a flame against the blackened trees churning and whipping behind him in the wind. But then I saw the reflection of real flames raging in his eyes, and the acrid smoke filled my lungs, and it all made sense. The house was on fire, and I was about to be on fire with it.

"Just give up," Alice said, appearing at the edge of the door. I had been expecting her. "Stay here with me and all the pain will stop."

"Shut up. Just *shut up*," I ground out, pushing against the barrier and gaining another inch. I was almost there. Almost free. "I'm leaving whether you like it or not."

"Even if leaving means your friends will die?"

My eyes snapped up to look at the clearing, and *shit*, Theo was making a beeline for Taylor again. She had fallen to her knees, grimoire still clutched in her hands, and I watched in horror as he reached out to grab her shoulder. But Taylor didn't wake from her trance. Instead, Theo was the one who suddenly recoiled.

He was staring at his hands with his eyes wide in horror, and in the dim light of the storm it took me a second to understand why. There was blood gushing from his palms like a tap had suddenly been flipped on. He wiped his hands frantically on his jeans, but the blood welled up again. Just like it was with the animals at the outskirts of the clearing, Taylor's spell was beginning to leech blood from Theo.

"You can't save them," Alice taunted. "Die here and be free from this torment."

Fury bubbled in my chest, as scalding and powerful as the fire at my back. I surged forward, my torso breaching the threshold.

"I'm not going to let it end like this," I growled, screwing my eyes shut and pushing with every ounce of conviction I could muster. "They're the reason I'm breaking out of here. They've given everything for me, and I'm not going to let that go to waste."

With my eyes closed and my body straining against the barrier, I pictured my life on the other side. Not the one I'd been dreading, but the life Theo and Taylor had promised me. One where Theo and I could be together in whatever way felt safe. One where Taylor and I could keep each other grounded. I pictured the life I wanted when I'd first found out I was coming back to Saint Juniper, and for a brief, shining moment, it didn't seem like a pipe dream after all.

And finally, *finally*, I broke free. My back leg pulled through the barrier, and for the first time in nearly two months, I was on the other side of the door.

But when I turned to look at Alice, the smile on her face hadn't dropped. It just spread wider as I wheeled away from her to look out onto the clearing.

The storm wasn't stopping. It circled us like a wild animal, grazing against the bloodred siding of the flaming house and sharpening its claws along the stoop's rain-dappled floorboards. In a panic, I ran to my friends, grabbing Theo's hands and pressing hard against his palms to try to stop the bleeding. Taylor kept on chanting, dead to the world.

"You can stop. It's over!" I shouted to her over the howling wind. But the animals at the edge of the clearing continued to drop to the ground, and the blood kept welling up in Theo's hands, surging between my fingers. I knew the spell, or some mutated version of it, was still in motion because I felt the power of it flowing through my veins. Taylor was sucking the life from Theo and the animals and giving it to me instead.

"She's too far gone," Alice called from the house. Her hair whipped around her face, reddish waves dancing with the flames behind her. "The blood is too addictive—she doesn't even know what she's doing. She won't stop until she's leeched all the life from the valley, or until she's dead. Whichever comes first."

My chest went horribly hollow. I didn't think Alice was lying, not anymore. Theo's fingers twitched weakly against mine, and when I turned back, it seemed like he could barely keep his eyes open. He was going to die, and it was all my fault.

"You have to get away from us," I begged, squeezing his hands even harder. "Go now and you might be able to make it."

"I'm not going to leave you," he said simply, tears and rainwater streaking his face.

That was when everything clicked into place. Of course Theo wasn't going to leave me—he never was, from the instant we met. But the blood kept gushing from his hands, and I could feel another bolt of lightning charging overhead. We were running out of time, all three of us. And if the only way to stop the spell completely and save Theo and Taylor was to take myself out of the equation, then that was exactly what I had to do.

Acceptance hit me with brutal, razor-sharp clarity. I gave Theo's hands one last squeeze, then let him go. By the look on his face, he knew exactly what I was about to do.

"Jaime, *don't*," he sobbed, clutching his hands to his chest.

"I love you, Theo. I'm sorry."

I ran back to the house, too quick for him to stop me when he was so feeble. Alice watched with barely restrained glee, sure she had won, but I didn't go back into Blackwood. I stopped on the porch steps, tilting my head back to look at the horrible clouds swirling above me. The lightning was cracking and spitting as it left the atmosphere, and when I lifted my hand to the sky, I knew it would hit its target.

In the millisecond before I was struck, I remembered how Theo looked when he slept, his face impossibly peaceful and unguarded. I remembered the way Taylor couldn't keep her eyes open when she laughed, how she threw her head back and held on to me like she would fall over if she didn't. I remembered every first day of school in every different town I had lived in. Every time I had gone to bed hungry. Every time I had wished I wasn't alive, and swore at myself for it. If this was my life flashing before my eyes, I probably should have lived a little bit more.

I wanted so badly to feel something, anything, before it was time to go. It felt wrong to die without crying one last time. It felt wrong to die without laughing one last time. It felt wrong to die without feeling Theo's hands on my skin one last time. But I was going to do it anyway. After all, if I could die for the people who made me feel after a lifetime of nothingness, then maybe dying wasn't so bad.

I wasn't wrong. Like falling in love, the funny thing about dying was that I didn't realize it was happening until it was too late. In the moment between the thunderbolt striking my hand and the moment that came after, I wondered if maybe I would live. Because after everything was said and done, I didn't really want to go.

But then my heart stuttered, and from one breath to the next, I went from digging in my heels to letting go completely. I saw myself from above, a bird's-eye view that could have been real or my imagination. My body felt distant, like I was looking at the scene through a reflection on a lake. When I stumbled down the porch steps, there were scorch marks where my feet had been rooted to the ground. And then I fell, soulless and horrible and limp like a rag doll.

CHAPTER 36
TAYLOR

WHEN I CAME BACK into my body, I couldn't make sense of the scene in front of me. Everything was moving in slow motion, even the flames that engulfed the house. Theo's body was thrown over Jaime on the front lawn, but something about the picture of them didn't add up. Smoke radiated off Jaime, and tears were streaming down Theo's face. He was pressing blood-soaked hands to Jaime's shirt, and the only cohesive thought that popped into my mind was *what the fuck happened?*

"I knew you wouldn't be able to control yourself," Alice said. My eyes snapped up to where she was framed in the doorway, exactly where Jaime had been before I blacked out. "Now look—all this suffering was for nothing."

"No, that can't be true," I said numbly, but Alice just shook her head, eyes glinting in the firelight.

"I told the boy he'd die out there, and I was right. I've always been right about this place," she said, a wicked smile spreading across her face like an open wound. "Even if this house burns to the ground, my spirit will live on. Saint Juniper's Folly is mine, and everyone will learn to fear it."

My breath caught in my throat. I had heard of spirits whose power kept growing if left unchallenged. But I couldn't let Alice become one of them. I couldn't let her lurk here for another century, waiting to ruin the life of the next lonely person who wandered into her domain. I had to end this now, and fast. I thought about the bloodstains on the rug in the library, and in one swift move, I tore Alice's locket off my neck and turned back to the grimoire.

"Didn't you learn your lesson?" she asked, but I ignored her, eyes racing across the rain-soaked pages. "Your friend doesn't have much blood left."

"That's fine. I won't need it," I said, and plunged the sharp edge of the locket into my palm.

Alice shrank away as I started chanting again, this time focusing on the blood flowing from my hand. Every time Theo's heartbeat called out to me with its addictive, incessant rhythm, I drove the metal deeper into my flesh.

"You don't have it in you. Your mother didn't either," Alice said, but the smile had slipped off her face, and she took an unsteady step back. "A century of pain is hard to undo."

She was right, but as the words of the spell flew out of my mouth at double time, I realized that was why I was going to succeed. I understood Alice's pain more than my mom had ever been able to. I'd been ostracized for my powers in my own way, and with the boys crumpled together on the lawn, there was a chance I might lose everything, just like Alice had. But I wouldn't end up like her, not when there was still a chance Jaime and Theo could still pull through.

I clenched my fist one last time, and with the rivulet of blood snaking down my arm, I delivered the final lines of the spell. The fury that had twisted Alice's expression all night shifted, and I recognized the heartbreak and shame in her eyes as clearly as if it were my own.

"Blackwood was meant to be a safe haven, but all it's ever been is a death sentence," she said.

"I know," I replied, dropping the bloody locket onto the grimoire. "It's time to let it go."

As the flames inside the house started to lick up her dress, Alice's face finally relaxed. For a moment, I could see my mom's features reflected in hers as clear as day.

"Oh, my dear child. Perhaps you are the best of us after all," Alice whispered, and then she was gone.

The second reality snapped back into full motion, I scrambled to my feet and stumbled over to Jaime and Theo. The fire was radiating enough heat that I could feel it from a dozen feet away.

"Theo? Is he—?" I didn't even know how to finish the sentence.

"He was struck by lightning," he said, voice shaking with violent panic. "We need to get out of here."

Later, I would barely remember carrying Jaime's body over the carcasses at the edge of the meadow, or sliding into the driver's seat of Theo's car as he loaded Jaime in the back with him. It was a miracle I got us to the hospital at all, speeding through the pelting rain, blood-slicked hands struggling to grip the steering wheel. The drive through town was a nauseating blur of lights and sounds from the Summer's End Festival, music and laughter mixing with Theo's sobs from the back seat. The only thing he said over and over was "Please come back, please don't leave me." I thought I would never get the sound of him gasping those words out of my head for as long as I lived.

A swarm of nurses took Jaime away the second we carried him into the emergency room. Theo and I were split up in a flurry of activity too, rushed off to get our hands patched. Theo needed a blood transfusion, and we both were told we might have some permanent hearing loss from standing so close to the lightning strike, but neither of us could focus on any of it.

There was a six-hour window where we didn't know anything about Jaime's condition, and the hospital felt like a prison. We only learned later that he'd gone into cardiac arrest, that his heart had completely stopped and they had actually brought him back from the dead. He seized a few times through the night and was barely stable when they finally gave us an update.

Theo was deep in shock for the first twenty-four hours or so we were there. He stared past everyone, even when they spoke to him directly. I figured that he couldn't look at me in particular because of what I had done, and I knew I deserved it.

It wasn't until Jaime was transferred out of the ICU that Theo became more aware of his surroundings. And when we did talk, I sat at the edge of his hospital bed and finally told him about the blood magic and about the promise I'd made to Jaime to get him out no matter what.

"I should have been honest with you about the spell, about how dangerous it was going to be," I said, forcing the words out despite the lump in my throat. "You trusted me, and I put all our lives at risk."

"You could have told me." He didn't say it in an accusatory way, just like he was thinking out loud.

"I know that now. I wanted to help so badly, and I felt like I didn't have any other option."

I didn't expect him to forgive me, or even say anything else. So when he pulled me into a hug, it was all I could do not to burst out crying.

"Maybe we didn't," he whispered into my hair. "Maybe we did the best we could."

"I'm so sorry," I said, pulling him closer. "I'll be sorry for the rest of my life. I don't know how I can possibly make this up to you and Jaime, but I swear I will."

Eventually, Theo filled me in on what had happened while I was blacked out. I was surprised how much I had missed while I was under the haze of the spell, especially when he told me about the moment Jaime got struck.

"He looked right at me and lifted his hand to the sky, and that's when it happened. He knew what he was doing. He saved us by ending the spell."

Theo looked down at his hands. They were clean and stitched up, but I could imagine the blood on them as clearly as if the nurses had never washed it off.

"I'm not surprised he would do that for us," I said quietly.

"You know what I told him, when I whispered in his ear before the spell started? I told him to be brave." Theo looked me in the eye then, and I could see the pain he was trying so hard to hold in. "I wish I hadn't."

And then the sheriff's department came. They wanted to separate us, but with the story of Alice's unjust death fresh in our minds, Theo insisted that they talk to us together or not at all. When they questioned us, we both said it had been a freak accident, that we'd cut our hands trying to break into the house and the storm had caught us by surprise. There was no reason for them not to believe us, but I was still so scared I could barely speak in complete sentences. The few times I fumbled over my side of the story, Theo stepped in to help. It was a simple act of solidarity that nearly brought me to tears.

But even after all that, I still had to tell the only person on earth who would be more disappointed in me than I was in myself. I pulled up Elias's contact info and stared at it until my screen dimmed, then went black. I sighed, unlocking my phone and clicking into my contact again, but a voice from across the waiting room stopped me.

"I hope you don't mind, but I had a feeling you might need us."

I looked up to see Anna a few feet away, with Elias close behind her. His eyes were wild, but the second they landed on me, he crossed the room in four long strides and swept me into a bone-crushing hug. It knocked the wind out of me, half from the force of it and half from surprise.

"Dios santo, you almost gave me a heart attack," he said, stepping back so he could give me a once-over. "Are you okay?"

"I—I'm fine," I stammered, "but my friend might not be."

The three of us sat in the far corner of the waiting room as I explained what had happened at Blackwood, quiet enough that the passing nurses couldn't hear. They sat silently through the whole story, all the way up to the very end. But when I told Elias that I had succeeded where my mom had failed and helped Alice cross over to the other side, he turned his face away.

"I'm sorry. You must be so disappointed in me," I said, struggling to fight back the tears that threatened to spill onto my cheeks. "I should have listened to you. Both of you."

Anna reached out to take my undamaged hand in hers. "I'm just glad you're okay. That's all I care about."

"The only person I'm disappointed in is myself. The whole drive here, I asked myself over and over what I did wrong," Elias said haltingly. It wasn't until he turned his face to me that I realized he was holding back tears too. "I've been so scared of losing you, but I tried too hard to keep you in line and ended up pushing you into trouble instead. I failed you."

And for the second time since I had been at the hospital, I realized just how wrong I was. Because despite the grief that pushed us apart, despite all of our differences and misunderstandings, my dad had never stopped caring about me.

"You didn't fail me, Dad," I whispered, but he shook his head.

"I wasn't equipped to help you explore your powers. I'm still not, so I need to help you find people who will train you properly," he said, then nodded to Anna. "And stop keeping you from ones who already understand you. It's the least I can do, mija."

I wasn't sure how to express the gratitude I felt for them in that moment, or my sorrow that the final chapter of my mom's life was finally closed. But they didn't press me on it. Elias just put an arm around me, and Anna held my hand tight, and I cried until I didn't have any more tears to shed.

CHAPTER 37
THEO

I SPENT MOST OF my time at the hospital watching Jaime. I guess in a funny way, not much had changed. I watched him as he slept, tracking the slow rise and fall of his chest and counting the seconds between to make sure he was still breathing. I would wake up in his room in the middle of the night and only feel okay when I could make out his profile in the soft glow of the monitors by his bedside.

I had actually never been to a hospital like that, never watched over someone while they were sick or dying. Everything about it was like the twilight zone, backward and confusing in the same way airports were when people were drinking beer at four a.m. and falling asleep on the floor. Doctors and nurses came in and out of Jaime's room at odd hours, checking his vitals and taking notes.

They had put Jaime into a medically induced coma so he could recover from the bulk of his injuries in peace. I was grateful he didn't have to be in pain, but a coma seemed incredibly grave and final. They assured me that they could wake him up at any time, but it felt too permanent for comfort.

It felt unreal, even days after the accident, that I had almost lost him. I guess technically, I had. They told me that his heart had stopped, but they'd brought him back. There were already some permanent reminders of the accident that would mark that horrible night forever.

When Jaime had been struck by the lightning, the hoop he wore in his left ear had soldered to his skin. It was the least of their priorities when he was coding on his way into the ICU, so they had simply cut it out and stitched his ear back up as fast as they could. One of the doctors had apologized for the hack job, but knowing Jaime, he would probably be psyched at how tough it made him look.

Then there was the gruesome scar across his upper body. It was common in lightning strike victims for blood vessels to burst from the electrical discharge and heat of the strike. A pattern of shiny pink scar tissue branched from his right palm to his shoulder and across his chest like the limbs of a tree, tracing the path the electricity traveled to his heart.

On a more cosmetic level, his nurses had cut off the parts of his hair that were singed during the strike. Seeing him with shorter hair and a in hospital gown instead of black jeans and a holey T-shirt was odd too. Selfishly, I hated it. Not because he wasn't handsome—he always was. It was because he looked nothing like himself, and I needed a little semblance of familiarity.

It was a bit overwhelming how much we couldn't know until they woke him from his coma. There was a chance the lightning had ruptured his eardrums and left him with permanent hearing loss. There was a chance he would have severe memory loss. There was a chance he would have chronic pain for the rest of his life.

That was the first thing Michelle asked when she came to visit him in the hospital. When she saw the scar peeking out from above the neckline of his hospital gown, she recoiled.

"Is he going to be okay?"

"We don't know," I said stonily, "but you're going to take care of him even if he's not."

It wasn't a question, it was an order. She just stared at me wide-eyed and nodded. I couldn't imagine the face I was making to warrant that expression, but I was too exhausted to care.

My parents had rushed to the hospital in the hours after the accident too. My mom couldn't stop crying, and my dad just seemed uncomfortable with the whole ordeal.

"Is this what you were doing all those nights you were away from home?" my dad asked once my mom had finally calmed down. "You were out in the woods with your friends?"

I nodded numbly. I told them what I'd told the police, that it was an accident. Just three kids caught in a storm, in the wrong place at the wrong time. If they thought my refusal to leave Jaime's side was strange, they didn't mention it. I had no energy to explain, and they didn't force me to, so I saved it for another day or week or month or year.

They weren't the only ones who were curious about what had happened. Some journalist in Burlington got wind of what happened, and before we knew it, hospital staff had to shoo journalists out of the waiting room day and night. Even without comment from me or Taylor, they still ran the story. It got picked up by a paper in Concord, then by a news station in Buffalo, and the bizarre tale of the boy who was struck by lightning, died, and then came back to life became the most popular story in New England that week.

After that, my phone was buzzing nonstop with messages from people in my class I hadn't talked to all summer wanting to hear a firsthand account. Taylor had to physically stop me from throwing my phone in the garbage in the hospital cafeteria. She was the only one who was keeping me sane and helping me hold it together. She didn't look at me funny when I brushed his hair off his forehead or adjusted his blankets for the fourteenth time in one hour.

And she was the only person I could talk to about the things that had happened that night, the types of things we could only think about once the night nurse had checked on Jaime and we had a few hours to ourselves before dawn. I told her that when the lightning struck him, I'd heard someone screaming and hadn't realized until seconds later that it was me. I told her about how Jaime had smelled like burned hair and burned skin, and on the worst nights, that smell still clung me in my nightmares. I told her that on the drive to the hospital, I'd realized I'd never had the chance to tell him I loved him back.

In a way, telling the worst parts of the story in whatever iteration I could helped me to see that Jaime had to survive. Living a life without Jaime, or going back to my life before him, was impossible. And even in my darkest hours in that hospital, I think I knew he was going to pull through.

When the doctors finally woke him a week after the accident, he was extremely groggy. They had warned me that he might not remember anything, that he might not even be able to speak for a few hours. I sat with Taylor, and together we waited. And waited and waited.

When he finally started to stir, his eyes were unfocused. I hadn't realized how much I missed the color of them until they landed on me. I held my breath, but just as I was starting to think he didn't recognize me at all, his whole face lit up. All the despair I had pushed down, the tears shed on sleepless nights, and the times I had wished I could switch places with him melted away.

"I thought you were a goner," I said, reaching out to take his hand in mine. *Don't cry, don't cry, don't cry*, I told myself. I almost managed not to. "You scared the shit out of me."

Jaime turned his face to me like a flower turning toward the sun.

"Sorry," he said, squeezing my hand weakly. "Not dead yet."

CHAPTER 38
JAIME

THEO AND TAYLOR WERE surprised to hear I didn't remember much from the night of the spell. There was a chance it was temporary memory loss from the accident, but we had no way of knowing unless the memories eventually came back.

Hearing everything that happened to me secondhand was bizarre and disorienting. I had a hard time wrapping my head around the thought that my heart had stopped and I'd been in a coma for over a week. At the very least, the burns on my arm and chunk taken out of my ear were painful enough to make that disaster of a night feel real.

I don't know what I would have done if Theo hadn't been there when I woke up. He waited patiently at the edge of the room as the doctors checked my eyesight, my hearing, and my vitals. Once they cleared me to have other visitors, he forcibly corralled Taylor back into the room. She stood at the foot of my bed, shaking like a leaf.

I knew I probably looked like a half-dead mess, but my heart sank at the thought she was afraid to look at me. But the second she started talking, I realized my ragged appearance was the last thing on her mind. Guilt was eating her up inside. She barely got a word of her apology out before she burst into tears.

It took a while for Taylor to explain everything that had happened during the spell. She told me she never should have done it in the first place, that the whole thing was a horrible mistake. I listened to it all in silence and let her apologize, only stopping her when she asked if I could ever forgive her.

"Well, I kind of wish you hadn't killed me," I said, "but at the end of the day, I'm not mad about what you did. I mean, it worked, didn't it?"

That just made her cry harder. When I reached out to her, she took my hand in hers and squeezed so hard I thought she might break a bone. We sat like that for a long time, hand in hand, until the doctors shepherded her back to the waiting room so they could conduct more tests on me in private.

I had a long road to recovery, though none of my doctors knew exactly what it would look like. I had appointments scheduled in advance with my cardiologist for the next year, just to be safe. In typical Theo fashion, he sat in on every single consultation and took notes. He promised the lead doctor on my case that he would make sure I came to my checkups.

"Sooo," I said to Theo in a rare lull when nobody else was in the room, "you sure you want to sign up to be in my life for the next year?"

"No being a smartass, doctor's orders," Theo quipped, but he smiled at me like it was the most brilliant thing I had ever said.

It was still surreal to me that I would be able to do what I wanted and go where I pleased, let alone that Theo would be by my side for it all. Even my DCF worker, who was none too pleased that I'd almost died in Michelle's care, bought the lie that my accident really was just an accident. After everything was said and done, I even managed to get a few brownie points with Michelle for not ratting her out. So I was free—I was broken, bruised, and burned, but I was free.

After I had been discharged, and after I could walk more than twenty feet without getting winded, Taylor, Theo, and I decided to go to the house one last time. The police had already been to the property to take photos, but they were too busy fending off questions from reporters to remove all the debris quite yet. I wanted to see the wreckage to make sure the house was really destroyed, and Taylor was anxious to recover her mom's grimoire, which she had left behind in the rush to get me to the hospital, before the authorities cleared away the rubble for good.

The fall foliage was just starting to take over as we drove into the belly of Saint Juniper's Folly, a vivid mix of yellows and oranges that made everything feel alien compared to what I was used to seeing in the valley. Theo and Taylor offered to wait in the car while I got my closure, saying they understood if I wanted to process it all on my own. But whatever I needed to do, no matter how gut-wrenching it might be, I wanted them by my side. The way I saw it, the house was as much theirs as it was mine.

It was odd approaching the clearing for only the second time in my life and not seeing the house looming there like I expected. The grass at the edge of the forest had miraculously remained untouched by the fire, but the earth closer to where the house had stood was completely scorched.

The bulk of the mansion had been burned to the ground, and what little of the structure was still standing was charred black as night. The porch was completely gone, and the greenhouse was mostly just a mass of splintered glass and twisted metal. Books from the library were strewn across the rubble, their blackened pages flapping gently in the early autumn breeze.

Looking at the remains of the house made me feel indescribably hollow. I hadn't realized how upsetting it would be to see it all ruined.

The three of us stood there, dazed, unsure of what to do or say.

"It looks so . . . small," Theo murmured, saying what we all must have been thinking. "It feels like everything happened eons ago. How is that possible?"

"Honestly," I said, "if you told me this was all some elaborate fever dream, I think I'd believe you."

Taylor snorted, linking her arm through mine as we looked over the ruins of the place her ancestors had once called home.

"You know, if there was ever proof that our lives were never meant to be normal, I think this is it."

I looked down at her, and I could see in her eyes that she really meant what she said. Taylor and I were forever changed by what happened, but whatever we decided to do next with our powers, I knew it would be fueled by a better, more honest version of ourselves.

"That's okay," I said, "I don't think I want things to be normal anyway."

She grinned up at me, eyes squinting against the sunshine. "Neither do I."

Taylor went off to find her the grimoire in the wreckage while Theo and I stayed behind, standing where the front lawn used to be. He slipped his hand into mind, the fresh scar on his palm fitting against the burn on mine. I realized with a start that Theo must have been standing in that exact same spot when he watched me get struck by lightning.

I would sacrifice myself again for Theo and Taylor in a heartbeat, but I should have known that we were all made to be survivors. If we'd managed to endure everything we had over the last two months in this one tiny clearing, we could do anything.

As if he read my mind, Theo asked, "How did we have all this when it was just us and a little old house in the woods?"

"I don't know," I replied truthfully. We stood in comfortable silence for a moment, taking it all in. The valley sounded so different from the last time we'd been there, and it was comforting to hear the leaves rustling and birds chirping as they always had.

I squeezed his hand, and he squeezed back. Then, just because I wanted to hear him laugh, I said, "I don't know how we managed not to kill each other."

Theo did laugh, loud and unfettered in the way I loved most, the sound of it filling the little grove with light. He pressed a quick kiss to the corner of my jaw. "Never say never."

Ash from the rubble took to the wind, and the wind chased us all the way back to the car. Theo and Taylor chatted away about the school year starting, Theo asking Taylor every question under the sun about her last-minute decision to cancel her deferral and start her freshman year of college the following week. Taylor held the grimoire, which she'd recovered from the rubble, tight in her arms, telling him about the witch her dad had found near campus so she could study witchcraft while she got her degree. Theo hatched road trip plans, and I vowed to call Taylor at least once a week for the Spanish lessons she'd promised me.

As we reached the main road, a gust of wind sent dried leaves skittering across the pavement. Climbing into the passenger's seat of Theo's car, I wasn't afraid to think about what was coming next. Theo and I would start our senior year in a handful of days, and Taylor would move into the dorms a week after that. We were all about to embark on our new beginnings, and though the future was more uncertain than ever, I couldn't wait for it.

As we drove through the winding tunnel of trees leading out of Saint Juniper's Folly, the one thing I knew for sure was that the forest wouldn't remember us. It was just like Theo had said a few weeks before, or maybe lifetimes ago. Decades would pass, and the scorched earth we left behind would eventually heal. Every mark we left in the valley would be washed away by rain, dampened by leaves, and blanketed by snow. But it didn't matter if the forest wouldn't remember us, because the three of us would remember instead. We would carry it with us no matter where we went, and that was all I needed.

ACKNOWLEDGMENTS

IT FEELS NEAR IMPOSSIBLE to express the immense gratitude I have for everyone who helped me get *Saint Juniper's Folly* onto shelves, but I'm definitely going to try.

First a huge thank-you to my agent, Mary C. Moore, for taking a chance on me and seeing the potential in this book when I worried nobody would. I'm so glad I have someone like you in my corner to keep me grounded and sane.

And to my editor, Ashley Hearn, who understood exactly what I wanted to do with this story from the very beginning. Your incredible insight and unfaltering enthusiasm have been a bright spot throughout this entire process. Thank you for loving my messy kids and helping me shape this book into something I'm truly proud of.

Thank you to everyone at Peachtree who touched this book and made it better along the way: Colleen Fellingham, Zoie

Konneker, Sara, Bree, Terry, Michelle, and the entire marketing team at Peachtree. And a massive thank-you to Lily Steele and Bri Neumann, who took the cover I'd been daydreaming about for ages and made it even more beautiful than I'd imagined.

More shout-outs are in order for my friends, who witnessed me speed-run the full gamut of human emotion in the last three years, and everyone else who inspired me along the way.

To Jenna, every piece of good news I've gotten in my writing career has been made sweeter knowing I'm able to celebrate with you. Thank you for the eight-hour FaceTime calls, for the in-depth reviews of movies I'll never watch, and for listening patiently every time I need to work through my writer's block. I'm so glad we passed each other on the street that day in June. I couldn't come up with a more perfect plot twist if I tried.

To Chai, an extraordinary human being with a brilliant mind and even more remarkable spirit. Our conversations on identity are permanently etched into my heart, and your perspective on life has shaped me, and this book, in ways I cannot begin to fathom. Thank you for seeing me for who I am. I guess the mortifying ordeal of being known isn't so bad when I'm experiencing it with you.

Thank you to Gibby, who was Jaime, Theo, and Taylor's first die-hard fan. You believed in me and this story when I needed it most, and I'll always cherish the unwavering kindness and support you've offered me over the years.

To Carlee, for cheering me on throughout this entire wild ride and never once telling me to stop being delusional. Thank you for beta reading this on the fly and sharing your industry knowledge with me when I had no idea what I was doing. And thank you for permanently changing my brain chemistry by introducing me to Jean Kirschtein. I'd be so much more normal right now if it weren't for you.

To Jordana, for introducing me to witchcraft and manifesting my beloved cat into existence. Meeting you made me believe in magic again in more ways than one. To Jamie, for lending me your name and your ear when I first started drafting this book. To Kendal and Emily, for being incredible cheerleaders and friends through it all.

Thank you to Maggie Stiefvater, without whom this book would never have been written. I walked into your writing seminar in 2019 feeling stuck and frustrated with another manuscript, and walked out knowing I wanted to go all in with this gay little haunted house book that had been simmering on the back burner for months.

Thank you to Matt, Ben, and Noel of *Stuff They Don't Want You to Know*, who supplemented so much of my supernatural research for this book and have kept me company on every commute and long-haul flight for years. To Lord Huron, because my writing playlists would be nothing without you. To Hex, who stared at me unblinkingly the entire time I wrote and edited this book.

Finally, thank you to the friends I've made through Twitter who helped me realize in 2017 that becoming a published author wasn't that far-fetched of a dream after all. If you're a writer and hoping for a sign to do the same, maybe this is it.

Born and raised by the Great Lakes, Alex Crespo writes about queer love, magic, and all the ways they intersect. When not writing, you can find him making art or daydreaming about Mothman. He currently lives in Chicago with an endless anime watchlist and his black cat Hex. *Saint Juniper's Folly* is his debut novel.

Find him on Instagram, Twitter, and TikTok
@byalexcrespo.